As Darker Grow The Shadows

A Novel of the French Résistance
Mj Roë

Copyright © 2014 Authored By Mj Roë
All rights reserved.

ISBN: 1500245410
ISBN 13: 9781500245412
Library of Congress Control Number: 2014911343
CreateSpace Independent Publishing Platform
North Charleston, South Carolina

As Darker Grow the Shadows is a work of fiction. Names, characters, places, and incidents are either products of the author's imagination or used fictitiously. Where some historical figures appear, actual events, locales, or persons are fully fictional in nature. In all other cases, any resemblance to persons living or dead is entirely coincidental.

Visit the author's website at www.roezes.com.

Cover and map by Brian Rollason, "The Pixel Chemist"

In Loving Memory of My Father
Charles A. Backman, Jr.
A Veteran of World War II

ALSO BY MJ ROË

The Seven Turns of the Snail's Shell
The Blue Amulet

London
UNITED KINGDOM
BELGIUM
Rhine
GRAND
REICH
THE CHANNEL
LUX
Rouen
GERMAN
NORMANDY
PARIS
ALSACE
annexed by
Germany
Strasbourg
LORRAINE
BRITTANY
OCCUPATION
Seine
ZONE
1940 - 44
Bourges
SWITZERLAND
ATLANTIC
VICHY
Lyon
ITALY
Dordogne
under Italian
occupation
after
Nov 11, 1942
OCEAN
FREE ZONE
until Nov, 11 1942
Avignon
PROVENCE
Nice
Toulouse
Marseilles
Toulon
CORSICA
MEDITERRANEAN
SEA
SPAIN
Ajaccio

As Darker Grow the Shadows

Ami, entends-tu le vol noir des corbeaux sur nos plaines?
Ami, entends-tu les cris sourds du pays qu'on enchaîne?

Ohé partisans, ouvriers et paysans, c'est l'alarme!
Ce soir l'ennemi connaîtra le prix du sang et des larmes.
—*Chant des Partisans*

Friend, do you hear the crows' dark flight over our plains?
Friend, do you hear the muffled cries of the country being shackled?

Ahoy! Resistants, workers, and farmers, the alarm has sounded!
Tonight the enemy shall know the price of blood and tears.
—Hymn to the Résistance

Prologue

Corsica
1924

The sun shone brightly in the clear, sea-blue sky as Jean-Pierre Dante Loupré kissed his wife, Tesa, and small son, Ferdinand, *au revoir*. He was headed to the capital, Ajaccio, by way of the interior. It would mean a long walk through the thick undergrowth known as the *maquis*. He had his machete with him and a pistol, should he need it, as the route he planned to take was dangerous. Wild boars were the least of his worries. He feared the bandits most of all.

"Don't worry," he told his pregnant wife, patting her belly. "I'll be back well before the little one arrives."

"But the robbers," she lamented, as she always did. "I worry, Jean-Pierre. I don't like to see you go now."

"I have to, *chérie,* you know that. We need the money with the baby coming soon. I promise I'll make it to Ajaccio and back in one piece." He kissed her again. "*C'est promis.*"

Part One

The good steed flew o'er river and o'er plain,
Till far away, —no need of spur or rein.
The child, half rapture, half solicitude,
Looks back anon, in fear to be pursued;
Shakes lest some raging brother of his sire
Leap from those rocks that o'er the path aspire.

—*Victor Hugo*

Chapter One

Fifteen Years Later

The early morning air was still. The birds chirped in the trees above, and the thyme-rosemary scent of the maquis, the rich vegetation that covered the entire island, was strong. The boy heard the clopping of the horse's hooves first. Then, he waited, hidden in the dense underbrush, watching as a lone horseman slowly climbed the serpentine path to the top of the steep terrain. He barely breathed as the horse and rider came closer. Just within his view, the mare stopped, then reared its head and snorted. A massive fallen tree trunk lay across the path. As the man pondered the situation, the boy raised his rifle. Hearing a rustle in the underbrush, the man looked up. Their eyes met. A loud pop echoed across the hills, and birds flew out of the trees. The frightened horse reared its front legs, flinging the man violently from his saddle. The boy waited, his ice-cold black eyes watching from his hiding place. The steed ran away.

After a few minutes, the boy stood and walked over to where the man lay motionless on the ground. Burning with hatred, he saw that the man's head had been dashed against a large boulder. The eyes were open and lifeless. The boy knelt down, listened for breathing, felt for a pulse. Assured that the man was dead, he rose and made his way down the steep hillside to the village below.

Chapter Two

The concrete-and-stone house stood at the edge of the village. Perched on the steep hillside at an altitude of over seven hundred meters above sea level, the medieval village had not grown in decades. In fact, it had diminished in population. At this hour of the morning, the streets were thankfully deserted.

The boy moved quietly. Though he often went out hunting wild boar early in the morning, on this day he didn't want to be discovered by his half brother André. He stowed his rifle in its usual spot in the barn, then opened the heavy door to the house and slipped in as quietly as he could.

"Is that you, Diamanté?" his ever-alert mother called from the kitchen. "Your breakfast is ready."

"I'm not hungry, *Maman*."

He went immediately to his small garret room on the upper floor. Sparsely decorated, it had been his boyhood refuge from the household violence. When his stepfather beat his mother, which happened often, he clamped a pillow tightly over his ears and cried.

He sat down on the lumpy single bed and stared at the half-packed tattered valise next to him. Then, he got up, went over to the small wooden chest, and pulled out the bottom drawer, dumping its contents into the suitcase.

His mother stood in the doorway watching him. Her middle son was a handsome boy, rail thin, dark piercing eyes, a head of curly black hair. She sighed. "*Enfin,* I wish you wouldn't leave." He heard a small sob. "What will I do, without you and Ferdinand?"

"It will be all right now, *Maman.* Don't worry."

He closed the valise and went to her. "It will be all right," he repeated, looking her directly in the eyes. "*Je t'assure.*"

She hugged him tightly. "Embrace your brother for me."

He left her standing there, in the hallway outside his bedroom, sobbing.

Maman will be all right now, Diamanté Loupré thought as he flung open the front door and walked away from the house. *The abuse is over.*

Chapter Three

Marseilles, France
The Last Week of August 1939

From the ferry, Diamanté spotted his brother standing on the landing, smiling and slowly waving a cap high in the air above his head. Diamanté had not seen him for several months, and he had missed him. Ferdinand was just two years older than he, and they had been inseparable growing up.

When the boat docked, the Loupré brothers ran to each other and embraced.

"I received your letter," Ferdinand said with a big smile. "I'm happy to see you."

"I couldn't stand it any longer." Diamanté spat. "After you left, it got worse."

"André?"

Diamanté nodded and lowered his eyes as he recalled the misery their half brother had inflicted on him after Ferdinand left home. "He's pure evil. I hate him."

"What about *Maman*? She must have been angry at you for leaving."

"She was upset. She cried." Diamanté hesitated, then shrugged his shoulders. "She'll be all right, now."

Ferdinand furrowed his brows and gave his younger brother a strange look.

"She'll be free to leave." Diamanté looked down at the ground and kicked a rock. "Maybe she will return to Speloncato, where she was born."

Ferdinand scratched his head, pondering what his brother hadn't said. It was not the Corsican way to ask questions, so he didn't. He just shrugged, then put his arm around Diamanté's shoulders. "Come on. I'll show you where we live."

The streets of the old port were damp from a recent rain. The smell of fresh fish in the harbor mingled with the heavy aroma of spices, cumin especially, and grilled lamb coming from an Algerian restaurant on the corner. They crossed the main thoroughfare, la Canebière, and followed the small curvy and windy streets that made up the surrounding neighborhood.

"*Le voilà*," Ferdinand said, pointing to a run-down apartment building. He opened a weather-beaten wooden door. "*En effet*, this is home."

Ferdinand's apartment was a one-room flat on the third floor. There was barely enough space for the bed, a table and two chairs, a small cook stove, and a chest of drawers.

"The communal WC is down the hall at the end of the corridor," he said. "You've got to get up early to avoid having to wait in line."

Diamanté threw his valise on the bed, then sat down beside it.

Ferdinand pointed to the chest. "I cleaned out the lower drawer for you." He pulled out one of the chairs from the table, turned it around, then straddled his legs over the seat. He rested his forearms on the chair back, clasped his hands, and leaned forward. "Do you have any money?"

"Some. From *Maman*. She gave me a franc occasionally when she could, when *he* wasn't watching. He would have beat her if he'd known." Diamanté's stomach growled, reminding him that he hadn't had anything to eat all day. "I managed to pay for the ferry and there's a little left."

Ferdinand nodded his head in understanding. "I think I've got you a job where I work. You'll have to lie about your age. Tell them you're eighteen. They'll believe it if I vouch for you. It'll be hard labor, but they need workers just now with the war coming. The pay is, well, not too good, but I'm saving a little so I can move to Paris and start a business someday."

Diamanté looked at his brother with curiosity. "What kind of business?"

Ferdinand's soft brown eyes lit up. "I'm going to buy a boat," he said resolutely.

Diamanté seemed confused. "In Paris?"

"*Mais oui*. A tourist boat. On the Seine."

Diamanté clicked his tongue and smiled.

"And then I'm going to find a girl and marry her."

"And what if the war comes?"

"I'll probably sign up," Ferdinand said with a sigh. "*Vive la France!*" He stood up and rubbed his belly. "You hungry?"

Diamanté nodded enthusiastically.

"*Eh bien, alors*, let's go get something to eat. I know a cheap place on the quay that's good." Ferdinand slapped his brother on the shoulder. "Let's have a beer, too, *mon frère*. We celebrate tonight. We're together again. Just like old times, *hein?*" He patted his shirt pocket. "And, I'm paying."

Chapter Four

On Monday morning, Diamanté and Ferdinand rose before dawn, packed their lunches—torn pieces of dry baguette and a generous slice of cheese—then headed for the factory where Ferdinand worked.

"Now, be sure to act like a grown-up," Ferdinand instructed his younger brother as they walked. "How old are you again?"

"Eighteen," Diamanté answered.

"And what year were you born?"

"Twenty-one." Diamanté looked at him. "But what if they don't believe me?"

"I'll vouch for you. Now, stand up straight."

Diamanté pulled his head back and straightened his shoulders. He was a slight boy, but he looked older than his fifteen years.

"That's better. Now practice lowering your voice."

"*Eh bien*," Diamanté grunted.

"*Non, non, non.* You sound like a goat."

Diamanté cleared his throat. "*Eh bien*," he tried again, this time with a rasp.

"Better. Keep practicing."

Diamanté put his head down and counted his steps as they walked, mumbling in his new low raspy voice, "*Un deux trois quatre cinq six…*"

He had nearly counted two thousand steps when Ferdinand put up his hand in warning. "*Ça suffit.* Don't say anything more. We're just about there."

Diamanté nodded, calculating in his head that they had gone about 1.5 kilometers.

The metallurgical plant was just on the outskirts of Marseilles, a dark, corrugated iron monstrosity on the waterfront. They entered the main gate, and Ferdinand pointed out the foreman's office.

"Over there," he said. "Let *me* do the talking."

The foreman, a muscular individual with the ruddy complexion of an alcoholic, was leaning over his desk smoking a cigarette and studying a blueprint spread out in front of him. At Ferdinand's light knock he glanced up and motioned to them to enter.

Ferdinand greeted the man, whom he called Monsieur Moreau, and introduced Diamanté.

Monsieur Moreau shook both the boys' hands.

"My brother here has just arrived from Corsica," Ferdinand explained. "He is a hard worker." He cocked his head sideways and added, "And he needs a job."

The foreman took a drag on his cigarette. As he eyed Diamanté, he blew a long stream of smoke into the air. "*Il a quel âge, ton frère?*"

Ferdinand answered, "*Dix-huit ans.*"

Monsieur Moreau pointed his finger at Diamanté. "*Et vous? Répondez! Vous êtes né en quelle année, exactement?*"

The voice resounded like thunder in Diamanté's ears. Clearing his throat and standing as straight as he could with his head high, he responded in a low, raspy voice.

"*Vingt et un, monsieur.*"

Moreau's beady eyes studied him, then narrowed. He nodded his head in Ferdinand's direction. "*Alors*, how old is your brother here?"

Diamanté tried to think quickly. It was clearly a trick question. "My brother has two years on me," he said finally, wagging an open-fingered right hand from side to side, "more or less." *At least*, he thought, *that wasn't a lie.*

After what seemed like an eternity, Monsieur Moreau spoke. "*Bon bref.* We need workers. You can begin today?"

Diamanté nodded.

"*Eh bien*, Ferdinand will show you around. We'll start you packing crates on the dock. You'll get paid, like the others, once a month. In cash." Then his eyes bore into Diamanté's. "If you work hard, you move up. Understand? If you don't..." He sliced his index finger across his neck.

Diamanté and Ferdinand turned and walked out of the office. Ferdinand slapped his brother on the shoulder.

"OK, we're in. Just don't screw up. *Compris?*"

Diamanté nodded.

"*Bon.*"

Diamanté noted that all the structures in the vast compound were similar in architecture: bricks, stones, vaults, and archways. They passed a large tank that permeated the air with an offensive odor. A sign on it read *DANGER ACID SULFURIQUE Port de lunettes et gants obligatoires.*

"We all enter and exit through the main gate," Ferdinand was saying, "and everyone is required to wear a *casque* at all times."

"A helmet?"

Ferdinand nodded. "It's a new invention. To protect our heads. Looks a lot like what the soldiers wore in the war, but it's not as heavy."

"What's it made of?"

"Aluminum. We have to wear goggles and gloves, too, when we're around the chemicals. They're pretty dangerous. We'll get you all the protective stuff you will need in there." He pointed to the largest of the buildings. A huge blast furnace stood high in the air, and the sign above the door read *Métallurgie*.

Inside the gigantic structure, the deafening sound of metal being pounded ricocheted off the high post-and-beam vaulted ceiling above. The racket was so intense that Diamanté covered his ears with his hands. As he stared at the vast industrial floor, a feeling of trepidation slowly crept through him. Everywhere signs warned of danger. Acrid smells made his nostrils hurt and his eyes sting.

Ferdinand motioned to follow him down a long aisle. They passed a group of masked welders, their shadows only visible through the smoke-filled air as glowing bright orange sparks spewed from their torches. The floor was dirty and strewn with metal shavings. Soot-covered workers in filthy coveralls barely looked up at them as they passed.

The supply shed was in the rear. From a pile, Ferdinand picked an assortment of protective items. Then he led Diamanté to a row of metal lockers. Diamanté chose an empty one next to his brother's and carefully placed his lunch sack on the shelf inside.

"OK," Ferdinand said, handing Diamanté his helmet. "Put on your *casque*. We're going out to the loading dock. The head man out there is known as Louis *le Grand*." He laughed. "You'll understand why when you see him." He shrugged thoughtfully. "He's a pretty good guy. He won't give you any difficulty, if you do your job and stay out of trouble."

Diamanté nodded. "*Où sont les pissoirs?*" he asked.

Ferdinand frowned. "We're only allowed during break." He looked at the huge clock hanging from the vault in the center of the manufacturing hall. "It'll be OK. I'll show you. Break time is in a few minutes anyway." He shook a threatening finger at his brother. "But next time you have to piss, you hold it. *Compris?*"

Chapter Five

The factory whistle sounded. Ferdinand and Diamanté joined the throng of workers as they headed to the courtyard for their break. Ferdinand waved to a young man who appeared to be about the same age as he. The man smiled in recognition and saluted.

"*C'est* Bernard," Ferdinand said. "He's my friend. He works with me in the aircraft plant. Come on. I'll introduce you."

Bernard was a short, gaunt young man with an unruly crop of black hair and a prominent nose. His black eyes, framed in wire-rimmed glasses, looked Diamanté up and down.

"Ferdinand has been telling us about you," he said as he extended his hand. "*Bienvenu à* Marseilles." He turned to Ferdinand. "So he made it past Moreau, *hein?*"

Ferdinand's eyes sparkled. "*Mais oui!*" He slapped Diamanté on the shoulder. "And I'm proud of him, too."

Bernard lit a cigarette, then offered one to Ferdinand who took it, using Bernard's to light his own.

Diamanté put his hands in his pockets and stared at the other workers standing in groups smoking and talking in low voices. Their clothing was covered with soot and some had rings around their eyes from the goggles they wore.

"You smoke?" Bernard asked him.

Diamanté shook his head.

Bernard held out his packet of Gauloises. "Here. Try one. Everyone smokes."

Diamanté tentatively plucked a cigarette from the pack and put it in his mouth. Ferdinand held his up to light it. Diamanté didn't know what to do.

Ferdinand smiled. "Inhale," he instructed.

Diamanté did as told. His lungs filled quickly with a pungent smoke that made him explode in a fit of coughing. Ferdinand pounded his back, and Bernard laughed.

"Take in a little less air next time," Bernard said. "You'll get used to it." He turned to speak directly to Ferdinand. "War is coming. I'm certain of it now. The nonaggression pact? Between the Nazis and the Russians? For those of us in the party, it's a new dilemma. What are we supposed to do? It's a mockery!"

Ferdinand nodded his head in agreement.

Bernard spat a piece of tobacco from his mouth and continued. "The question is whether France will be prepared."

Two loud whistles signaled the end of the short break. The workers dashed their cigarettes in unison, donned their helmets, and filed slowly back to their stations.

Ferdinand led Diamanté toward the dock. "Bernard is constantly talking about the possibility of war," he said. "I think he's obsessed about it because he's hearing all kinds of rumors from his relatives in Poland. Ah, here we are."

They had reached the loading platform. A tall, heavy-boned man with a beard stood at the end shouting orders. "That's Louis *le G*rand," Ferdinand said. "Go now. Introduce yourself to your boss. I've got to get to the aircraft building." He pointed in the direction of a newer-looking structure at the far end of the complex. "See you at lunch. Meet me back at the lockers." He slapped Diamanté on the shoulder and gave him a little push. "Go on. He won't bite." He gave his brother a smile. "Just do as he says, and they won't send you to the army."

Diamanté watched him walk away. He looked over at Louis *le Grand* and took in a deep breath. He was on his own now.

***

"How'd you get to work in the aircraft division?" Diamanté asked his brother that night as he lay on the bed. Every muscle in his body hurt from his first day on the loading dock.

"Hard work," Ferdinand replied. He handed Diamanté a bowl of soup left over from the day before. "When I first started, I was like you. I hurt like hell for two weeks. Then, I adjusted. It's long hours, heavy work. You don't get many weekends off. Everyone just expects you to go along with it. And, if you don't, they transfer you into the army. So I watched for an opportunity. One day, the foreman in the aircraft section asked me if I wanted to be a riveter." He held up his arms as if he were holding a rivet gun and made a machine-gun like sound. *Tac! Tac! Tac! Tac!* "I took the job just like that. If the war comes as soon as Bernard thinks it will, well, *bon bref,* France will need airplanes."

"Why don't they just put everyone in the entire plant to making airplanes then?" Diamanté reasoned.

"Everything else is needed, too. The railway, for example. We make the train engines and the rails." Ferdinand fetched a bottle from the cupboard. "You want some wine? It will help the sore muscles."

Diamanté nodded. He tore off a crust of baguette and dunked it in his soup. "All this war talk," he said. "There wasn't any of it in Castagglione."

Ferdinand nodded and sighed. "I'm not surprised. It's a small village. For most of them, the war, the Great War, is over." He shook his head. "Bernard says the Germans are just regrouping."

"What do you think? Are they?"

"I don't know."

"Is Bernard a *communiste?*"

Ferdinand looked at Diamanté. "*Oui.* What would you say if I told you I am also a member the party?" He took a sip of wine. "*Le Parti Communiste Français. C'est nous.* It's our future."

"I frankly don't know anything about the PCF."

Ferdinand smiled. "You should come with us to a meeting. Bernard, he's militant; he likes to stir up things. *Moi,* I just go along."

Diamanté took a sip of wine. Ferdinand had changed since they had last seen each other. Physically the hard work at the factory had given him strong arms and a muscular torso. His face had filled out, his jaw was more square, and his neck had thickened. The once-skinny legs he'd often complained about being ashamed of were sturdy and well developed now. At nearly eighteen, Ferdinand had become a man. But there was something else. His brother had a new self-assurance. His walk had the cocky masculine swagger of self-confidence, and he held his head high. Growing up, Diamanté had always considered his brother his hero. Now he admired him more than ever.

Chapter Six

On the loading dock, the bullying began almost immediately.
"Do you think he's old enough to be out of diapers?" a man, who called himself Sully, asked the other workers. He was short and stocky with a square face and bulging eyes.

Diamanté ignored him and concentrated on lifting a stack of heavy crates. It was only his second day on the job, and his sore muscles made the task more difficult.

"Where is your *maman, hein, mon petit?*" Sully continued, his bushy black eyebrows dancing up and down under his helmet.

The other workers put the backs of their hands to their mouths and made sucking noises.

"Didn't you hear me, you little worm?" the man persisted, delighted that he had an audience. "Put her *bébé* to work early, did she, *ta maman*? So she can get it on with her lovers during the day?" He puckered his lips and made loud kissing sounds.

Laughter erupted.

When the group didn't let up, Big Louis yelled at them. "*Beh*…let the new man alone." He winked at Diamanté. "Don't pay any attention." He clucked his tongue. "It's just *le bizutage*. The initiation. They like to pester the new arrivals."

But the harassment continued over the next few days, and it made Diamanté painfully aware of his youthful appearance. He practiced speaking in his new low raspy voice constantly, even when he was in the apartment with only Ferdinand. He didn't drink any liquid all day so that he wouldn't have to use the *pissoirs* and accidentally expose his adolescence. He wore his jacket buttoned high so the lack of hair on his chest wouldn't be noticed. During breaks and lunchtimes, he made haste to meet Ferdinand and Bernard, doing his best to smoke a Gauloise without coughing. Always he kept a vigilant eye out for Sully.

The wily group of dock workers succeeded more than once in sabotaging Diamanté's work, too, accidentally knocking over heavy crates that he had just finished stacking or deliberately moving the crates to the back so it would take longer for him to load them onto flatbeds.

That's more than just hazing, Diamanté thought to himself as he considered the situation while walking home one evening. He knew he had to ignore the escalating insults and humiliation, but inwardly he seethed with anger. *I wonder what those bullies would think if they knew what I am capable of*.

Ferdinand, who had become increasingly preoccupied with current events, didn't seem to notice his brother's predicament, and Diamanté didn't talk to him about it.

At breaks and lunch, Bernard ranted almost continuously that the PCF was being compromised. It would give the government an excuse to close down the Communist newspapers, he said, remove party senators and deputies from their seats, dissolve hundreds of Communist-led locals, and arrest militants.

"We have to be careful," he warned.

The sudden arrival of military police in the factory made them all nervous. Rumors ran rampant, especially among the aircraft workers. Supervisors pressured the workers to increase production, and they watched them constantly. Any sign of trouble would mean immediate dismissal and assignment to a military unit. Morale was low, and an atmosphere of distrust, fear, and suspicion pervaded.

In the courtyard at lunchtime one day in early September, no one spoke of much else but the news of the Nazi invasion of Poland that had occurred on the first, followed, two days later, by France's declaration of war against Germany.

"The *Boches* slaughtered thousands of civilians," Bernard fumed. "Rumors are half of them were Polish Jews. They forced them into the synagogues and burned them alive." Bernard, who was Jewish, choked back emotion and lamented that he had missing relatives.

The discussion drew others in, and a small group formed around them. Several wondered aloud if and when the Germans would try to take France.

"If they do come, the Maginot will hold. I'm certain of it," said a tall man with a long face speaking of the concrete fortifications that ran from Switzerland to the Luxembourg and Belgian borders.

An older man with a bulbous nose spoke up. "I think you are right. It's unbreachable. The Germans won't get Alsace-Lorraine."

Some shook their heads; others nodded in agreement.

Another man who was missing an arm that everyone understood had been lost during the Great War at Verdun took a drag on his Gauloise and spat out a piece of tobacco. He nodded authoritatively and declared in a deep voice, "The Maginot will provide all the protection necessary."

Bernard shook his head and threw up his arms in frustration. "I think it's wrong to assume that. *Mon Dieu*," he fumed, his black eyes angry. "It's defensive thinking. France can't just sit and wait."

The factory whistle sounded twice, and the workers broke up.

Chapter Seven

In the third week of September, Ferdinand and Diamanté arrived home from work one evening to find a letter slipped under the apartment door. It was postmarked Corsica.

Ferdinand picked it up and carefully opened the tissue-thin paper envelope. "It's from *Maman*," he said. "She writes to me once a month." He shrugged his shoulders nonchalantly as he removed the contents and unfolded the pages. "It's mostly always news of the village. Not much of interest." He sat down on the chair and began reading silently.

Seconds later, his eyebrows rose in surprise. He glanced briefly at Diamanté, then continued reading.

Uneasy, Diamanté sat down on the bed, leaned forward, put his elbows on his knees, and nervously clasped his hands.

When Ferdinand had finished, he sighed and handed the pages over without comment.

Diamanté took the letter. Written in his mother's fine cursive, most of it in their native language *Corsu*, she began by relaying the news that Larenzu Narbon, their stepfather, was dead.

> By pure coincidence, it happened the day of Diamanté's departure. Larenzu left early that morning for his usual ride. When his horse came home without him, and he didn't show up, André set out to search. He found him dead in the maquis, his head dashed against a huge boulder. At first, André thought the steed had thrown his father, but then he saw the bullet hole. He had been shot between the eyes. We buried him here in Castagglione. May his soul rest in peace, the bastard. Je m'en fiche. He was an abusive husband.

Diamanté suppressed a smile. He could hear his mother's low, resolute voice saying, "I don't give a damn. *Je m'en fiche.*"

> André took his father's death very hard. He was convinced that the Louprés had killed Larenzu, insisting it was the return of the vendetta. I tried to convince him it was merely robbers. Larenzu was, after all, a rich man. Mais non! André insisted it was revenge. As with his father, the Louprés were always to blame for everything bad that happened. When a house burned, or a horse died, it was suspected to be, bien sûr, a vicious act of retaliation by the Loupré family, whether it could be proven or not.

His mother went on to explain that there would be no investigation of the murder by the local police.

> The private war between the two families has not been mentioned. It is the unwritten law of Corsica. If the vendetta was the cause, it is not a police affair. Officially, his death has

been ruled accidental; a hunter out early most likely mistook him for a wild boar. Fin de l'histoire.

In the end, only the maquis knows. As the old Corsican proverb says, it has no eyes, but it sees all. A machja, ochji un ha ma ochji teni.

Remember always that the Narbons will be suspicious that one of you killed Larenzu, and they will hold you responsible. Ora vivu ora mortu. *At birth, your fate was written. Your* maman *prays for your souls.*

Diamanté paused reading and scratched his head. He had been born just after his father was killed on his way home to Castagglione. His mother had told him his stepfather had had him murdered. She was sending him a subtle message that she knew he had avenged his father's death that morning in the maquis.

André has departed just this week for the start of the fall term at that fancy boarding school near Paris his father sent him to last year. Basta, *I say. Enough. I don't expect to hear from him anytime soon. He has always been a difficult boy, your half brother. He is my own flesh and blood, but we have never been close, and I regret that I couldn't prevent the cruelties you suffered at his hands while you were growing up.*

For my part, I have left Castagglione and returned to Speloncato. Do you remember the house on the edge of the village I used to point out to you? The one where I was born, with the lone pine tree? It has been uninhabited for years, so I cleaned it out and moved in. Now I am content. I can go to church, do what I please.

The last few pages contained news of happy reunions she had had with her family and friends since returning to Speloncato. Diamanté finished reading and looked up.

Ferdinand was watching him. He put up his hand. "I don't ask."

Diamanté shook his head. "She will be all right, but we can't return to Corsica, you and I…not for a very long time."

Chapter Eight

At the beginning of the last week of September, Diamanté and Ferdinand left work to walk home at the end of the day. The clouds hung heavy in the sky, and it was starting to rain.

Diamanté pulled the collar of his jacket around his neck. "Louis *le Grand* told me today I'm to be transferred from the loading dock."

"*Ah bon?*" Ferdinand seemed concerned. "Where to?"

"The metallurgical building. Louis took me to Monsieur Moreau's office at the end of the shift today. They told me I'm to report tomorrow."

"Wear your old clothes," advised Ferdinand.

They turned the corner and picked up their pace. The rain was coming down harder, and rivulets of water ran down the cobblestone street. They hurried to open the door of their apartment building and entered.

"Is it because of Sully that you're being transferred?" Ferdinand asked as he towel dried his hair. "The word got around. Everyone knows what he's been doing to you."

Diamanté sighed. "I never fought him." He straightened his shoulders and his eyes narrowed. "But more than once, I wanted to. I could have beat him, you know."

"Even if you won the battle, you'd lose."

Diamanté shook his head. "I couldn't risk it."

"*Eh bien,* there won't be any bullies to worry about in metallurgy. There's too much noise."

"Did *you* ever work there?"

Ferdinand nodded. "Prepare yourself. It's grueling."

***

The following morning, Diamanté reported to the gigantic main plant. He was given a face mask and heavy gloves. The foreman, a burly individual whom everyone called *le Chef*, assigned him to follow a man named Delouche for the next few days.

"Delouche will show you how to tap the blast furnace by burning out a plug at the bottom," *le Chef* told him, "every three to five hours."

By the end of his first week on the new job, Diamanté had learned what Ferdinand meant when he said the work in metallurgy was grueling. He sweat profusely from the heat of the molten metal, and his nostrils stung from the fumes. What hair he had on his arms became singed, and his clothing was dotted with small black spots where sparks had landed. In spite of the difficulty, he was glad to be away from Sully and the gang of bullies on the loading dock.

On the last day of September, after the final whistle, the workers lined up in the rain to receive their monthly pay. As they walked home, Ferdinand complained about how measly the wages were for all the hard labor, but Diamanté felt like he had earned a fortune. While Ferdinand heated broth and cut thick slices of bread for their evening meal, Diamanté sat at the small wooden table in their apartment and counted and recounted his francs. Then he handed all but one coin over to Ferdinand.

"To help with the rent and food," he said. "I don't need much for myself."

Ferdinand took it. "We'll eat better now," he said with a smile. "Maybe even add a bit of meat and some vegetables to our broth." Then he ruffed up his younger brother's hair and added cheerfully, "Hey! It's Saturday night. What say we go down to the bar on the quay for a beer later? To celebrate your first payday."

Diamanté flipped his five-franc coin in the air and caught it. "You know what I'm going to do with this?"

Ferdinand shook his head.

"I'm going to buy myself a beret."

"*Ah bon?*" Ferdinand slapped him on the shoulder. "Well, *mon frère*, I think a beret will make you look very handsome… and older."

***

In the locker room the following Monday, Diamanté carefully removed his new black beret and placed it on the shelf alongside his lunch.

Ferdinand bid him *bonne journée*. "You'll have to walk home alone tonight," he said in Corsican as he closed his locker. "Bernard and I have a PCF meeting." He waved and headed out the door.

Diamanté was just about to follow his brother when a voice came from somewhere behind him in the back of the locker room. "*Di chi paese site?*"

Surprised at hearing his native *Corsu*, Diamanté turned around. He saw a young man standing at the other end of the long bench that ran down the center of the room. He was small but sturdy, with a head full of curly, jet-black hair, an aquiline nose, thin lips, and large bright eyes.

The stranger came forward and extended his hand. "Name's Trigère," he said. "Maurice Trigère. But call me *le Tigre*." He made a ferocious face, growled like a tiger, and held his hands as if showing off two sets of claws. "You're new here, aren't you—in metallurgy, I mean." He pointed his thumb to himself. "*Moi aussi*. I've been assigned to the other job nobody wants. Tapping off the slag." He smiled. "*Di chi paese site?*" he asked again in *Corsu*. "Which village are you from?"

"*Haute-Corse*," Diamanté said, extending his hand. "Castagglione." He introduced himself just as the factory whistle sounded.

"*Corse-du-Sud*. Casalabriva," Maurice said proudly. "I'll see you at the break, *hein?*"

Diamanté smiled and nodded in agreement.

From that day on, Maurice Trigère joined Diamanté, Ferdinand, and Bernard during breaks and lunchtimes. Ferdinand and Bernard were mostly preoccupied with discussions about the war and their activities in the PCF. Diamanté and Maurice, on the other hand, found that they had other interests in common. Both had been born in a small Corsican village and, like Diamanté, Maurice liked to hunt in the maquis. They never discussed their ages, but Diamanté suspected that Maurice, like he, had also lied to get a job.

The two became best friends.

Chapter Nine

A chance opportunity in early November freed Diamanté and Maurice from the factory for an entire weekend. On a Friday afternoon, they were called to Monsieur Moreau's office and informed that the blast furnace was to be shut down, or blown out, as the foreman called it. A temporary situation, he explained, just long enough to allow for cleaning and repairs. Starting on Monday morning, they would be asked to do other jobs around the factory. In the meantime, they would be given Saturday off.

"Do you want to go hunting tomorrow?" Maurice asked Diamanté as they walked through the port on their way home. Maurice, as it turned out, lived with his mother and a younger sibling just a few blocks from Ferdinand and Diamanté's apartment.

Diamanté nodded. "*D'accord*," he said enthusiastically. "But I don't have a rifle."

"I've got one we can share. Bring your lunch and meet me on la Canebière early. We'll take the tramway to the end of the line." Maurice smiled. "From there, we go on foot. I've found a very good hunting spot."

***

Ferdinand arrived home at the apartment late that night. He and Bernard had attended a PCF meeting.

Diamanté was listening to the radio set when he entered. The broadcast told of France's plans to evacuate the city of Strasbourg on the Rhine and went on to debate whether the United States would continue to remain neutral.

"I heard the blast furnace has been shut down," Ferdinand said as he took off his coat.

Diamanté nodded. "They gave me tomorrow off. Then I'll get temporary assignments for a while."

Ferdinand whistled. "A day off. You are in luck. What are you going to do?"

"Maurice and I are going hunting. What do you suppose they hunt here?"

Ferdinand thought for a moment. "I don't know. Wild boar maybe. Just like in Corsica. Do you have a gun?"

"Of course not."

"I have one you can use. Bernard got it for me." He grinned. "It's one of those new Walther PPs the PCF managed to get its hands on."

Diamanté raised his eyebrows.

"I know." Ferdinand shrugged his shoulders. "You don't go hunting with a pistol. It's the only weapon I've got."

Diamanté smoothed his hand over the intimidating German-made handgun. It was the first time he'd held a firearm since he left Corsica. He had vowed he would never shoot a rifle again, but this wasn't a rifle. His eyes brightened. "*Superbe*," he said with a chuckle. "There won't be any buckshot in the meat. I'll just shoot the heads off."

Chapter Ten

The next morning, Diamanté packed his lunch and Ferdinand's pistol inside a cloth sack.

Ferdinand watched him. "I know you're a good shot," he said approvingly. "Bring home some meat. We'll have a feast." He handed Diamanté a coin. "Here. You'll need this for the tram."

Diamanté thanked his brother. He closed the apartment door and skipped down the staircase in high spirits. It seemed to him it had been months since he'd gone out hunting, but in reality it had only been a few weeks since he had arrived in Marseilles. The early winter weather was dull and drizzly, but for him it was springtime. He was getting the chance to spend the day outdoors. With his sack swung over his shoulder, he headed toward the port.

Maurice waited for him on la Canebière.

"*Salut, mon ami*," he greeted him.

The two walked to the nearby tram station. They purchased their tickets, boarded an open compartment, and sat face-to-face on wooden benches. There was an outer platform separated by glass windows where passengers could stand, but no one was out there today because of the weather.

"What do you hunt here?" Diamanté asked.

"We're in luck. The season is open. There will be partridge, small game, pigeons, pheasants, thrush. Stag possibly."

"*Pas de sangliers?* No wild boar?" Diamanté asked.

"Oh. *Mais, bien sûr.* Just like on Corsica, but they're elusive, and smart." Maurice tapped his temple. "I don't expect we'll see one today. *Pour moi*, my favorite is the wild rabbit. There are hundreds of them everywhere. And they're good to eat." He grinned. "*Chez nous, c'est une tradition familiale.* It's a family tradition, *le lapin de garenne*. My mother makes a wonderful rabbit stew."

Before long, the tram reached the end of the line, and they descended.

"*Bon.* We climb that hill, then on the other side, we'll start looking for our dinner," Maurice explained, pointing to the steep, wooded terrain off in the distance. He made a gesture of handing over his rifle. "Here. You go first. We'll take turns."

Diamanté looked at the rifle and shook his head. He pulled Ferdinand's pistol from his sack. "My brother gave me this," he said.

"*Ah bon?* A Walther?" Maurice considered him for a moment. "That's an impressive weapon. What kind of shot are you?"

Diamanté shrugged. "Passable."

***

That evening, Diamanté returned to the apartment with a heavy sack flung over his shoulder. The day's bounty had consisted of five pheasants, three wild rabbits, and a partridge.

"*Eh bien, mon frère*," Ferdinand declared when he saw the size of the take. "We'll be feasting all month on these."

Diamanté handed him the Walther. "It's a good pistol," he said. "I got more game than Maurice did with his rifle."

"It's yours. Keep it," Ferdinand said with a smile. "You've earned it."

Chapter Eleven

Diamanté worked late that evening cleaning his wild game in the alleyway behind the apartment building. He was forced to act quickly under the dim light of a single bulb, a *minuterie* that hung over the doorway. Meant only to be on as long as it took tenants to dump trash into the garbage bin, it switched off every sixty seconds.

To begin, he strung a line and hung the rabbits by their hind legs. Then, with his knife he cut a ring just above the foot joints. With an expert hand, he gently peeled the furry skin the entire length of the body, being careful not to tear the meat around the tail area. It took him only a few minutes to finish skinning all three rabbits. Next, he plucked and eviscerated the fowl and wrapped all the meat in paper to be stored in the small icebox in the apartment.

The next morning, he awoke early and slipped out of bed quietly so as not to awaken Ferdinand. Rain pounded heavily on the windowpane as he went over to inspect the contents of the pantry cupboard. The shelves were mostly bare, but he found what he was looking for.

Ferdinand turned over under the covers and opened his eyes. "What are you doing up?" He blinked, yawning. "It's Sunday. We can sleep in."

"I'm going to make us a rabbit stew," Diamanté declared.

"Since when do *you* know how to cook?"

"After you left, *Maman* let me help her in the kitchen."

"*Ah bon?* You should have told me sooner. I'm a terrible cook."

Diamanté nodded his head in agreement as he laid an onion and jar of coarse ground mustard on the work counter. "We don't have any fresh herbs," he complained.

Ferdinand yawned again. "Madame Boulon, the concierge, grows some in the window of her *loge* on the ground floor. Go ask her. She should be up by now. She always attends early mass at Sainte Marie Majeure."

Diamanté grabbed one of the paper-wrapped rabbits from the icebox and ran down the stairs. He was just about to knock on the door of Madame Boulon's *loge* when she opened it.

"Oh, *mon Dieu*, you startled me!" she cried, patting her chest. The petite woman with a brown scarf partially covering her white hair came forward. "I was just leaving for mass." She studied him with her black eyes. Her brow furrowed. "You're Ferdinand's brother, aren't you? What's your name?"

"Diamanté."

She smiled, then let out a sigh. "That was my late husband's name. He was a good man." She waved the back of a bony hand dismissively in the air. "Too bad he drank himself to death."

"I was hunting yesterday," Diamanté said shyly as he presented the package to her. "I thought you might like a rabbit to cook. It's been cleaned. I got three of them. We can't eat them all."

"*Oh là là!* Three? You must be a fine hunter."

"Plus five pheasants and a partridge."

Madame Boulon's eyes widened. She accepted the gift and went into her small apartment. "Come in for a minute," she said, pulling off her scarf and removing her coat. "I don't have to leave immediately. I'm always too early for mass anyway. Would you like a cup of tea, *mon cher*? The water is still hot."

Diamanté nodded.

Madame Boulon motioned to him to sit on an antique, brocade-upholstered loveseat. The apartment was quaint, and spotless. A mahogany hutch filled with antique crystal and china sat against the far wall, and a wrought-iron chandelier hung from the high ceiling above.

Madame disappeared through an arched doorway. After a few moments, she returned carrying a silver tray with two china cups and a teapot. She sat down across from Diamanté, placed the tray on the table between them, and poured the tea.

"Now, tell me, *mon cher*. How did you become such a good hunter?"

Diamanté took a sip of the tea and told her briefly about his home in Castagglione and hunting for wild boar in the maquis.

"And what brought you two brothers to Marseilles, *alors?*" she asked.

"Work. There's not much to offer in Castagglione."

She nodded in understanding.

"Can I ask you?" Diamanté hesitated. He glanced at the apartment's atrium window filled with potted plants. "Could you spare a few clippings of your herbs? I'm going to make *le lapin de garenne* today, and we don't have any."

"*Mais, bien sûr,*" she said. "What do you need?"

Diamanté thought for a moment. "A sprig of rosemary, two or three sprigs of thyme, maybe a bay laurel leaf…"

"And I think you will need sage, too," she contributed. "It always adds a lot to *le lapin*." She got up and grabbed a small garden tool. "*Voyons,*" she mumbled to herself, "Let's see," as she began to snip away.

Diamanté finished his cup of tea as Madame handed him the fresh cuttings. "*Voilà!* This should be sufficient for your stew," she said. "*Maintenant*, I've really got to depart for mass, *mon cher*."

He thanked her and, clutching his fistful of herbs, bounded up the stairs, two steps at a time.

Two hours later, when Diamanté had finished cutting the meat into stew-sized pieces, there was a knock on the apartment door.

"You expecting someone?" Ferdinand asked as he got up to answer.

Madame Boulon stood in the hallway. "*Bonjour, mon cher,*" she said, holding up a cup of cream and a handful of mushrooms. "I thought…"

Diamanté came to the door wiping his hands with a towel.

Madame Boulon smiled at him. "I thought," she repeated, eyeing the two scrawny boys in front of her, "some cream and mushrooms would make your stew much better. You look like you could use some nourishment."

They thanked Madame profusely.

"There's one more thing," she said to Diamanté. "If you want, I have a few extra clay pots that aren't being used. You could start your own herb garden on your windowsill. They're easy to grow. I'll help you."

"I would like that very much," Diamanté said, nodding his head. "*Merci, Madame.*"

After Madame Boulon left, Diamanté went to work on his stew. He sautéed the meat and onions in olive oil, then deglazed the pan with the cream, mustard, and a bit of wine, added the rosemary, thyme, sage, and bay laurel leaf, and tossed in the mushrooms cut into small pieces.

While Diamanté worked, Ferdinand sat at the table concentrating on a letter he was writing.

"Who's that to?" Diamanté asked him.

"*Maman.*" Ferdinand looked up. "I'm telling her about the wild game you brought home and what a good chef you are. I think from now on you should do the cooking."

"I like to cook," Diamanté said. "I'm going to open a restaurant someday."

Ferdinand raised his eyebrows in surprise. "Since *when* did you decide that?"

"Since today. I can't work in a metallurgical factory all my life."

"I think that is a fine goal, *mon frère*. I'll have my tourist boat, and you'll have your restaurant." A few minutes later, as he folded the letter carefully and placed it in an envelope, Ferdinand looked up at Diamanté. "*Eh bien,* I've an idea," he said. "Christmas is coming. It's on Monday this year. We'll have two days off. Why don't we take the train to Paris?"

Diamanté's black eyes lit up. "Can we afford it?"

Ferdinand nodded. "*Oui*, but we'll have to be sensible."

All afternoon, as the stew simmered slowly on the stove, and the rain fell in buckets outside, the apartment filled with a mouth-watering aroma, and Diamanté and Ferdinand dreamed of spending Christmas 1939 in Paris.

Chapter Twelve

A full moon hung low over the port and lit up the street as Ferdinand and Bernard followed Diamanté and Maurice through the factory gate after work.

"How are your temporary assignments going?" Ferdinand asked Diamanté and Maurice.

"For me, it wasn't too bad today," Maurice said, looking over his shoulder at Diamanté. "I had office duty. Monsieur Moreau put me to filing his mountain of blueprints."

"You were the lucky one." Diamanté laughed. "*Zut alors.* I had to clean *les latrines.*"

"*Merde!*" Bernard sympathized, holding his nose.

"*Exactement.*" Diamanté spit on the cobblestones.

Ferdinand lit a cigarette and inhaled deeply. "Have you heard when the blast furnace will be back in operation?"

"It's supposed to be next week," Diamanté answered. "In comparison to the latrines, it will be a relief."

"Bernard and I are going to a PCF meeting this evening," Ferdinand said. "Do you two want to tag along with us? It's just off la Canebière on the rue de Rome."

Diamanté and Maurice looked at each other. "*Pourquoi pas?* Why not?" they said in unison.

***

The four entered a noisy, smoke-filled bar just a block from the Vieux Port. It was the kind of seedy place on the waterfront that fishermen and sailors off the boats were drawn to and locals frequented nightly to drink pastis and play billiards. An occasional fistfight or two was not unexpected.

Bernard pointed to a large, crowded room at the back of the bar.

They took the remaining four open seats in the last row.

Diamanté spotted Delouche and a number of the other workers from the factory.

The meeting began almost immediately, and the discussion centered on what everyone was calling *le drôle de guerre*, the "phony war."

"*Incroyable!*" a tall man with a booming voice yelled to the others. "France declared war on Germany and then *phfft!*" With his hand, he made the motion of tossing something invisible into the air. "There is no war!"

Another man, whose beret sat flat on his pumpkin-shaped head, tapped his temple with his index finger and winked. "They are smart, *les Boches*. They want to make us sweat." His ruddy face was studded with barnacle-like warts.

A sea of black berets bobbed up and down in agreement.

Delouche reported that he had heard from his brother in Alsace on the German border. "The city of Strasbourg is a dead city," he lamented, throwing up his arms in exasperation, "but still nothing happens, and *ce putain* de Roosevelt."

He spat. "Declaring neutrality." He spat again. "France won't be getting any help from the Americans."

"It's only a matter of time. The Nazis will come," Pumpkin Head commented. "We've got to be prepared."

The last remark was Bernard's cue to enter the discussion. "What we need is more weapons," he said, standing up. "*Écoute*, we need automatic weapons, hand grenades, plastic explosives. I know where we can get them."

The group turned in their chairs and craned their necks to get a better look at the speaker. Diamanté, seated next to Bernard, felt scrutinizing eyes.

"But we need money," Bernard went on, looking around the room. "Who's in? We need to find some people to back us financially."

A distinguished-looking, white-haired gentleman in a business suit raised his hand. "I have a cousin in banking. He may be acquainted with some rich sympathizers."

"It's worth asking," Bernard encouraged. "But be careful."

A lengthy discussion followed about the Russian Communist Party and how to deal with it now that it had made a nonaggression pact with the Nazis. Everyone agreed. The French Communist Party was not going to become a propeace party.

"If the Germans come, we will resist!" someone yelled. At that, the participants stood up and shouted in unison, "*France! Toujours France!*"

"*La Résistance*," Diamanté said with youthful enthusiasm later as he and Maurice walked home from the meeting. "I like the sound of it."

"Think we should join up? The PCF, I mean," Maurice asked.

Diamanté shrugged. "*Beh. Sais pas.* But I'm going to attend meetings from now on."

"I think my *maman* will not like it if I join," Maurice said. "She is against war."

"If war comes," Diamanté said, cocking his head sideways, "we have to defend France."

Chapter Thirteen

On Monday morning, Diamanté and Maurice arrived early at the factory and reported as usual to Monsieur Moreau's office to receive their assignments. A man they didn't recognize instructed them to go wait with the others in the courtyard.

"What's going on?" Diamanté asked the worker next to him.

The fellow scratched his head and shrugged. "*Beh*, I don't know."

A short time later, a stern-looking fellow with a mustache, bushy eyebrows, and a receding hairline arrived. He stood before the group and held up his hands to get their attention. "Monsieur Moreau," he began, "has fallen ill. My name is Louvois. In Monsieur Moreau's absence, you will receive instructions from me." He studied their faces, then cleared his throat. "A large shipment is going out today," he continued. "All of you are needed on the loading dock. Report immediately to the foreman."

Diamanté braced himself. "Watch out for the *type* named Sully," he warned Maurice. "He's mean."

Maurice made his ferocious tiger face and growled. "*Moi, je suis le Tigre,*" he reminded Diamanté, then he smiled and slapped his friend on the back. "Come on. Don't worry. I won't let him bother me."

"*Quand même,*" Diamanté said nervously. "Be careful, *mon ami.*"

As predicted, Sully was relentless. Now both Diamanté and Maurice became his targets. By the end of the day, Maurice had had enough. In the courtyard, as they waited in line at the exit gate, he grabbed Sully's collar and put his nose to the man's face.

"You want to fight?" he challenged.

Sully laughed aloud. "With you?" He spat. "You're a baby."

That was all Maurice needed. He pulled a fist and punched the man hard in the face.

Momentarily stunned, the bully drew back, blood spurting from his nose, then he threw his own punch that knocked Maurice to the ground.

Sully's cronies from the loading dock cheered their comrade on.

The cut above Maurice's eyebrow bled profusely. Diamanté helped him stand. "Come on," he whispered. "Let's get the hell out of here."

Maurice pulled away. Fire in his eyes, he lunged at Sully with all his strength and began beating him with both fists.

When Sully put his arms up to protect his face, Maurice slugged him hard in the stomach. Both individuals, splattered with blood, dropped to the ground, punching and kicking violently at each other. The crowd shouted obscenities.

Diamanté panicked. He knew things could get bad for Maurice if the foreman became aware of what was happening.

"*Viens,* Maurice," he begged, trying to pull Maurice off Sully. "It's not worth it. Come on, *mon ami.*"

But it was too late. Monsieur Louvois flew out of the office followed by Louis *le Grand.* The crowd parted.

From behind, Ferdinand grabbed Diamanté with both arms and pulled him back. The look in his brother's eyes told Diamanté he had better obey.

Meanwhile, Louis *le Grand* broke up the free-for-all. Both fighters, bloody and covered with dirt, struggled to stand.

"You know the rules," Monsieur Louvois hollered. "No fighting." He put his hands on his hips and looked at them. "Louis, take them to the office," he ordered. Then he glared at the crowd. "So, what are you all gawking at, *hein?* It's quitting time, *non?* Go! *Allez-y!* Go home to your families. *Bande de'idiots.*" Mumbling to himself, he turned and stomped away.

"Come on," Ferdinand said to Diamanté. "Let's get out of here."

"But Maurice..." Diamanté protested. "I have to explain."

"He is responsible for his own actions," Bernard said, shaking his head in disgust. "He was the one who started the fight."

"*L'enculé...*" Diamanté spat. "*Zut!* The asshole bullied him, us, all day," he muttered as Ferdinand pulled him toward the exit.

"Sully's a tyrant. He terrorizes everyone. You should have warned Maurice."

Diamanté frowned. "I did."

***

The next day, Maurice didn't meet Diamanté on la Canebière to walk to work. Diamanté was assigned to report to the aircraft factory. At breaks and lunch, he stayed clear of the courtyard. When the end-of-the-day whistle sounded, Maurice was nowhere to be found.

"Something's happened to him," he told Ferdinand as they walked home together. "I need to find out what."

"Do you know where he lives?"

Diamanté nodded. "Not far from us. On rue Breteuil. He lives with his mother and his little sister. They moved here from Corsica after his father was killed at Verdun."

Ferdinand looked at him sympathetically. "*Eh bien*, in that case, I'll go with you."

***

Ferdinand and Diamanté quietly knocked at the door of the small apartment. A petit woman opened it cautiously. She had Maurice's aquiline nose and large bright eyes. Behind her a small girl with olive skin and black curly hair peered curiously at them.

"Who are you?" the woman asked.

Diamanté removed his beret and bowed slightly. "*Madame* Trigère?"

She nodded.

"I am Diamanté, Maurice's friend from the factory. This is my brother, Ferdinand. Is Maurice here?"

"*Entrez*," she whispered as she pulled them quickly into the apartment and closed the door. "He's in the back." She pointed toward a small kitchenette. "Through there."

Maurice was seated on a cot in a pantry-like space with a low ceiling. His face was swollen, and both eyes were black and blue. Diamanté sat down on the cot beside him.

"I was worried," he said.

Maurice gulped. "I lost my job. They said I was a troublemaker."

Diamanté looked down at his hands.

"I know. You warned me," Maurice continued. "I just… *zut!*" He kicked the end of the cot in anger.

"What will you do now?" Diamanté asked.

"The army. I'm to report in a week."

Nearby in the kitchenette, Maurice's mother let out a sob.

"She's upset…because of the war coming." Maurice lifted his head and smiled. "But I'm strong, *mon ami*, like a tiger." He waved his fist in the air. "*Le tigre, c'est moi.*"

***

That night Diamanté couldn't sleep. In the darkness, he groped for the Walther PP he had stowed under the bed. *Someday,* he vowed, *I will get even with Sully.*

Chapter Fourteen

Three Days before Christmas

Ferdinand sat at the table in the apartment counting their money. "I purchased our tickets for Paris today," he said, looking up. "We only have enough francs for one night in a hotel." He shrugged and smiled.

At the counter, Diamanté slathered crusty baguettes with homemade aioli and added generous slices of cheese and some dried herbs. "I'm making us sandwiches to eat on the train," he said. "And we can take along those oranges Madame Boulon gave us."

Diamanté had taken over the cooking in the apartment since the *lapin de garenne*. The evening's soup, a fish stew, was thick and studded with white beans Madame Boulon had brought him from her trip to the *marché*. The concierge insisted the brothers needed to be better nourished, and Diamanté willingly accepted her help. On the windowsill of the apartment sat clay pots growing rosemary, thyme, marjoram, sage, and even the diminutive sprout of a bay laurel tree. With ingredients supplied by Madame Boulon, he had been able to recreate the cuisine of his native Corsica in their small kitchen in Marseilles.

"*Maman* always talked about Paris," Ferdinand lamented. "I wish she could be going with us."

"We should get her a souvenir."

Ferdinand laughed. "With our budget, it'll have to be a pebble from the street."

Just then there was a quick tap on the door.

"*Entrez*, Madame Boulon," Ferdinand called without getting up. By now, they recognized the concierge's familiar knock.

The petit woman hastened into the room struggling to carry a large box wrapped in brown paper.

"Ah, *mes chers*," she chirped, her face barely visible over the top of the package. "This arrived for you today. I think it's from your *maman*."

Ferdinand lifted the burden from her arms, set it on the table in front of him, and began slitting open the top with a kitchen knife.

"*Ensuite*," Madame Boulon continued, fumbling in the pocket of her apron. "I've *une adresse* for you. Ah, *la voilà*." She handed a piece of paper to Ferdinand. "My nephew, Marcel, and his wife, Françoise, live in Paris. They manage a small hotel on rue Saint-Jacques in the fifth arrondissement. I've sent them a telegram, and they are expecting you." She put up her hand to stop their questions. "It will be *gratuit*. Marcel will not accept any payment. He is a generous man, and it is Noël after all. You'll be his guests for both nights. Just go and enjoy yourselves." She winked at Diamanté. "My nephew is also an excellent chef. He will like it if you offer to help him with the preparations for *le réveillon de Noël*."

Ferdinand and Diamanté were speechless at such generosity.

Finally Diamanté asked, "You aren't going to Paris, then, *Madame*, to see them?"

"*Enfin, non. Malheureusement*, my work here as concierge, you know. I must stay and make sure the building is tended to."

The boys nodded in understanding.

"*Mais*," she wagged an index finger, "I always reserve August for my *vacances*. Then I go to Paris and stay with Marcel and Françoise for the entire month."

The boys nodded again.

"What will you do, then, for Noël?" Diamanté asked her.

"Oh, *bien sur*, I'm going to midnight mass at Sainte Marie Majeure, then, as always, I'll be making the *réveillon* supper for the tenants." Embracing them, she air-kissed their cheeks. "*Joyeux Noël, mes chers enfants, et bon voyage.*"

"*Merci, Madame, et Joyeux Noël*," they said in unison as she opened the apartment door to leave.

"Now, let's see what *Maman* has sent," Ferdinand said, eagerly opening the box.

The two peered inside. To Diamanté, the contents smelled familiarly of home. Their mother's lavender perfume. The familiar herbal scent of the maquis.

Ferdinand lifted a package wrapped in the plain paper of a *charcuterie*. He untied the string and carefully unfolded the paper to reveal a jar of smoked and cured pork, a tin of dried herbs, and a chestnut cake.

Diamanté found a bottle of rosé. "A Fiumicicoli," he said, "from Sartène. And look! My favorite, Brocciu." He held up a carton of soft cheese made from ewe's milk.

There were four more gifts wrapped and tied with ribbon. Two were marked "F" and two "D."

"*Maman* has outdone herself this year," Ferdinand said as they eagerly tore open the largest of the packages.

Each received a warm woolen sweater. Ferdinand's was gray, Diamanté's a chestnut brown.

"Just in time for Paris!" Ferdinand exclaimed as he held the garment in front of him.

Diamanté found a black journal in his second package. Confused, he opened it. Inside the front cover his mother had written a message.

> Chi va pianu va sanu E chi va sanu va luntanu.
> *He who goes slowly, goes surely; and he who goes surely, goes far.*
> *Tell your story, my son, and have no regrets. From your loving* maman.

He lifted the journal to his nose and sniffed the new leather binding.

Ferdinand watched him thumb through the blank pages. "What will you write in it?" he asked.

Diamanté raised his eyebrows. "The past, maybe. I don't know. The future…" His eyes brightened, and he smiled with youthful anticipation. "My future."

Ferdinand unwrapped a gold pocket watch. He turned it over. His father's name, Jean-Pierre Loupré, was engraved on the back. He sighed. "We didn't send *her* anything."

"Now that we have a hotel to stay in," Diamanté observed, "*merci beaucoup*, Madame Boulon, we'll have some extra francs to spend in Paris. We can get *Maman* a souvenir after all."

***

The next day, Friday, seemed to creep along at a snail's pace. For Diamanté, it was the longest he had ever spent at the factory. When the final whistle sounded, he hurried to the locker room to meet up with Ferdinand. The two washed the grime from their hands and faces, changed into clean trousers, and put on the new warm sweaters their mother had sent.

Bernard watched them. "I envy you," he said. "Paris."

"What will you do with your two days off?" Ferdinand asked.

Bernard shrugged his shoulders, then leaned in close and put his hand up to shield his mouth. "We've got a shipment of rifles coming in," he whispered conspiratorially. "A big one." Straightening up, he said in a normal voice. "What time does your train depart, *mes amis?*"

"Midnight," Ferdinand answered.

"*Ah bon.*" Bernard nodded his head in the direction of the exit gate. "*Venez, alors.* I'll walk with you to the Square Narvik. We've plenty of time to celebrate with a beer before your departure."

***

Just before midnight, Ferdinand and Diamanté bid Bernard *au revoir* and climbed the great staircase of the Gare Marseille-Saint-Charles. The station smelled of cigarette smoke and urine. When they reached the departure platform, the steam engine for Paris was waiting, its cars already loading.

Diamanté looked around in awe as they entered the elegant carriage. The walls were made of lacquered fine-grained wood, and there were brass handles and fittings on the doors and windows. He and Ferdinand peered through the glass into an individual compartment where there were only two other passengers. A young couple smiled and gestured for them to enter. Ferdinand stowed their valise on the overhead rack, and they took seats facing each other next to the window.

It wasn't long before they heard a whistle, a hiss of steam, then a jolt and the sound of the wheels on the rails. Soon red and green lights passed by the window, then telegraph wires, a bridge over a canal, and finally the carriage was in almost total darkness. The young couple nestled into each other's arms. Diamanté pulled his beret over his eyes, but he was too excited to sleep. He was going to Paris.

Chapter Fifteen

Paris
Saturday, 23 December 1939

Diamanté pulled his collar around his ears and shivered. It was bitterly cold and drizzling as he and Ferdinand walked out of the Gare de Lyon in the twelfth arrondissement.

"Did you sleep at all on the train?" Ferdinand asked.

Diamanté blew warm breath into his cupped bare hands then rubbed them together. He shook his head.

They paused at a newspaper stall to read the banner headline of the daily edition of *le Monde Illustré*. "Coldest Weather in Decades Hits France!" Then a full-page photo of an armored tank in the snow and below it: "Finland Counterattacks!" Diamanté thought about his friend Maurice who had departed for the army two weeks before. Where was he now, Diamanté wondered.

Ferdinand pulled the piece of paper Madame Boulon had given him from his pocket. "Can you tell us how to get to this address?" he asked the attendant behind the counter.

A gloved finger pointed to nearby stairs that descended below the street. "Take the *métro*." The vapor of his breath rose above his thick woolen scarf in the crisp morning air. "Get off at Maubert Mutualité. Boulevard Saint-Germain leads to rue Saint-Jacques." He handed them a map. "Have you been to Paris before?"

They shook their heads in unison.

"It's easy." The vendor removed one glove. "There are twenty arrondissements, arranged in a circular direction." He made a clockwise motion with his index finger. "Like a snail's shell. You are here, in the twelfth." He pointed to a location on the map. "Your hotel is over in the fifth." He moved his finger further to the left. "If you want to see the Eiffel Tower, it's in the seventh. *La voilà*. Just take the *métro* wherever you want to go." He put his glove back on and saluted. "*Joyeux Noël*."

They thanked him, descended the stairs, and bought tickets at the *guichet*. The smell of sewer gas assaulted their senses as they waited on the platform.

"What do you think Madame Boulon's nephew will be like?" Diamanté asked.

Ferdinand removed his beret and scratched his head. "*Sais pas*. She said he was a good chef."

Diamanté looked over at his brother and smiled.

Just then, the subterranean train roared monster-like from its dark tunnel. After it had screeched to a stop in a cloud of soot, an elderly woman in front of them flipped a door latch and entered the nearest car. Diamanté and Ferdinand quickly followed her and took seats by a window. The doors slammed shut, and the car lurched forward as the monster took off again.

At the Maubert Mutualité stop, they realized they had to get off. The boulevard Saint-Germain was all but deserted. The few people out were bundled in heavy coats and scarves, their faces barely visible. Despite the cold, Ferdinand and Diamanté stopped to admire a window filled with pastries and confections for the holiday season. Whimsical figures depicting a cheerful family scene, complete with Christmas tree and Father Christmas, appeared in the storefront display next to the patisserie, and bows of evergreen were strung over the entrance to the café on the corner.

At rue Saint-Jacques, they turned right and passed a Gothic church. Diamanté consulted the map. "It's called St.-Séverin," he said. "Why do you suppose they have sandbags stacked against the sides?"

Ferdinand shrugged. "Probably for reinforcement. They're getting ready for war, for bombs," he said. "Look up there." The church's windows had been completely taped over.

The Hôtel Saint-Jacques was just a short walk in the direction of the Seine. They found it in the middle of the next block, flanked by an Alsatian bistro on one side and a pharmacy on the other. A sign in the hotel window advertised "*Confort Moderne.*"

"What do you suppose that means, 'modern comfort'?" Diamanté asked.

"Probably an electric lightbulb in each room," Ferdinand answered with a chuckle.

The hotel was quaint, and there was no one in the tiny lobby when they entered. Ferdinand pressed the button on the bell at the front desk.

A thin man appeared. "*Bonjour, Messieurs.* Can I help you?" he said as he squinted at them through reading classes.

Ferdinand removed his beret. "*Je m'appelle* Ferdinand Loupré," he said hesitantly. "*Et voici mon frère*, Diamanté. *Nous sommes…*"

The man's brown eyes lit up in recognition. "*On vous attends*," he said, removing his glasses and extending his hand eagerly. "*Bienvenu à Paris, mes amis.* Marcel Forestier. *Tante* Amélie wired us to expect you today."

Ferdinand and Diamanté shook his hand.

"Come with me," Marcel said. "I want you to meet my family."

They followed him down a long hall and up a stairway. He was a slight man of about forty, erect in stature, with a quick, energetic walk. He opened the door to an apartment on the first floor. Cooking smells mixed with the scent of fresh evergreen filled their nostrils.

"We've just brought in our Christmas tree," Marcel said. He pointed to the tall pine topped by an angel figurine sitting in the corner of the room. On the floor next to the tree sat a large cardboard box filled with straw ornaments.

"Françoise," Marcel called. "Come meet our guests."

An attractive woman in a red dress, high heels, and burgundy-colored shawl came through an arched doorway. Her black hair was pulled back into a chignon, and her gold earrings sparkled as she took the boys' hands.

"*Enchantée*," she said in a soft voice. "Delighted to meet you. Please, remove your jackets and have a seat."

Diamanté and Ferdinand did as told and sat side by side on a brocaded sofa, their hands folded in front of them. The salon was elegant and inviting. A glass cabinet with crystal, assorted china, and figurines sat in the corner. The wood fire crackling in the fireplace warmed the room.

"Are you hungry?" Marcel asked.

They nodded in unison.

"We've just arrived at the *gare*," Ferdinand said. "We took the overnight train."

"*Oh là là!* You must be starving, *alors*," Marcel said. "I'll be just a minute." He disappeared through the arched doorway.

"Tell me," Françoise said. "How do you know *Tante* Amélie?"

"She's our concierge," Ferdinand replied. "She takes good care of us."

Françoise smiled. "*Tante* Amélie is a wonderful person. We don't get to see her as often as we'd like."

Two children raced into the room.

Françoise motioned to them. "*Viens, mes chers*. I want you to meet our visitors."

The children, a boy of about five and a girl of about seven, presented themselves in front of Ferdinand and Diamanté.

"*Je m'appelle* Pauline," the girl said politely. She was wearing a pink dress with a sash tied around her waist.

The boy, shorter than his sister, round-faced, with a dimple in his chin, bowed to them with his arms behind his back. "*Et moi*, François."

Marcel entered the room and placed a tray on the table next to the sofa. On it were two steaming bowls of hot chocolate and a basket of croissants. "A *chocolat chaud* will warm you," he said. "I can't remember a Christmas when it's been this cold."

Ferdinand and Diamanté eagerly accepted.

A petite young woman with light brown hair and sparkling clear blue eyes entered and stood shyly in the doorway with her hands behind her back.

Noticing Ferdinand and Diamanté staring at her, Marcel motioned with his hand. "*Venha*, Elise," he encouraged. "Come. Meet our guests."

She nodded and came dutifully to stand behind the children. A gold and lavender scarf was tied artfully at her neck, and she wore a light-blue dress that matched the color of her eyes.

"*Je vous présente* our Portuguese nanny, Elise Carbua," Marcel said. "She only arrived in Paris two months ago, but she speaks very good French already."

Diamanté quickly put down his croissant, wiped his mouth with his napkin, cleared his throat, and extended his hand to her. "*Enchanté*," he said awkwardly.

Ferdinand grinned and held out his hand eagerly. "*Enchanté, Mademoiselle*," he said.

Elise accepted their hands and gave them each a quick smile. Then she returned to stand by the arched doorway.

"Did you bring *le Père Noël* with you from Marseilles?" François asked them.

Their mother laughed. "The children are so anxious. They can't wait to put their shoes out for Father Christmas to fill tomorrow night."

"I want a miniature train set," François said.

His father nodded in agreement.

"*Pour moi, une poupée*, a baby doll," Pauline chimed in.

Marcel rose from his chair. "*Eh bien*. I'll show you to your room now. You probably want to rest a bit." He led them back down the hallway and into a tiny *ascenseur*. The three of them crushed together in the metal-cage lift, and Marcel closed the gate. "Your room is on the second floor, overlooking the street," he explained as they slowly ascended. The elevator jolted to a stop, and the gates opened onto a narrow, windowless hallway with red-patterned carpet and five brown-painted doors on either side. Marcel opened the first door on the right, number 30. The room was a small chamber, wallpapered in blue and white stripes with a border along the ceiling of gold fleurs-de-lis. There were two single beds, each with a thick, white, down-filled duvet. An armoire sat against one wall, a mirror over a table with a wash basin next to it against another.

Ferdinand placed their valise at the end of one bed and went to look out at the balcony through the French window. "It's snowing!" he exclaimed.

"Rare for Paris," Marcel said, "but with this weather, it's not a surprise." He touched the radiator next to the wall. "You should be warm enough. We put in *le chauffage central* just last year but so much coal to heat the entire building is expensive, so we only turn it on when necessary." He laughed.

"Beware, it is noisy. You will hear grunts and groans and other odd sounds during the night."

"*Confort moderne*," Ferdinand whispered to Diamanté. "Plus an electric light, too."

"The water closet and bath are at the end of the hall," Marcel continued. "There are towels and cakes of soap in the armoire in the hallway. Help yourself." As he turned to leave, he handed Ferdinand a key attached to an enormous metal tag and added, "We're going to decorate the pine tonight… before dinner. If you would like to help, come down to the apartment around *dix-neuf heures*. Dinner will be at eight. You're invited to dine with us."

They nodded and thanked him for his hospitality.

After Marcel had closed the door, Ferdinand lay back on the bed and put his hands behind his head. He stared at the ceiling for a few minutes, then heaved a sigh. "Did you see that girl, Elise?" He blew air through his lips.

Diamanté smiled from the other bed. "Petite, delicate hands, eyes blue as…" He searched for the right word. "Eyes blue as periwinkle flowers," he said finally. "How old do you think she is?"

Ferdinand chuckled. "Too old for you. I'd guess about seventeen, give or take a few months."

Diamanté rolled over and propped his head on his hand. "*N'oublie pas.* I'm going to be sixteen on January first."

Ferdinand laughed. "*Eh bien, mon petit frère*, the challenge is on."

The brothers fell asleep, both of them thinking about the Portuguese girl they had just met with the periwinkle-blue eyes.

***

Two hours later, they were awakened by a loud pounding on the door. Ferdinand got up to answer.

The children, Pauline and François, stood outside in the hallway. They were bundled in heavy coats, woolen scarves, mittens, boots, and knitted hats.

"Elise is taking us to *la tour* Eiffel to play in the snow before it gets dark," Pauline explained. She and François bounced up and down with excitement. "Do you want to come with us? We're going to stop for hot chocolate on the way back."

Ferdinand and Diamanté nodded their heads enthusiastically.

"*Bon!* Elise says to meet us in the lobby in five minutes."

With that, the children turned and ran down the hallway.

***

The colossal iron framework of the Eiffel Tower, its pinnacle shrouded in fog, stood directly in front of them as they surfaced from the *métro* at the Champ de Mars.

Diamanté stood with his hands in his pockets staring at the iron symbol of Paris in the falling snow. "It's bigger than I expected," he said to Ferdinand, "and far more sturdy than in the photos." The wide expanse of the park below the tower was covered in a blanket of white, and the trees lining the landscape were frosted.

Pauline and François dashed eagerly ahead. There were very few cars in the streets, and the entire scene was serene and quiet except for the crunch of their footsteps as they walked on the snow.

Elise fumbled in her pockets. "I think you need these," she said, shyly handing Ferdinand and Diamanté each a pair of gloves. "They are from Marcel. He noticed you didn't have any."

"*Magnifique!*" Ferdinand exclaimed as he put his on. Then he stooped to gather a handful of the white fluffy crystals.

Pauline ran up and threw a snowball at him, dusting his shoulder in the powder.

Elise giggled. "You have to throw back to her," she encouraged, making a pitching motion.

Diamanté gathered a clump of the cold stuff and tossed it in Ferdinand's direction, but it fell apart before it hit its target.

"*Oh là!*" Elise exclaimed, packing her own snowball tightly in her gloved hands. "I show you how to do it. You have to really hit him. Like this." She flung it hard against Ferdinand's chest, then tossed her head back and laughed as the snow bomb exploded.

The children, Diamanté, and Elise pummeled Ferdinand gleefully until, covered in snow from beret to pant leg, he raised his arms in surrender.

"*Oh là*," Elise said, a look of concern on her face. "You shiver." Ferdinand was much taller than she, and she had to raise up on her toes to help him brush the snow from his jacket collar. Then she removed the gray woolen scarf from around her own shoulders and wrapped it tightly around his neck. "There," she said, smiling into his brown eyes. "You will be warmer now, I think."

Ferdinand looked down at her and grinned. "I'm already warm," he said.

Pauline tugged on Diamanté's jacket sleeve. "Come on," she said, jumping up and down. "Let's build a snowman next."

Chapter Sixteen

The next morning, Diamanté and Ferdinand rose early.

"I spoke with Marcel last night," Diamanté said as he buttoned his trousers. "He agreed to let me help him with the preparations for *le réveillon* today."

Ferdinand pulled his sweater over his head and combed his hair. "*Ah bon! C'est super!*" He studied himself in the mirror, turning his head from side to side to view his face from different angles. Then he spun around. "Do I look OK?"

Diamanté had noticed that his brother had spent an extra amount of time shaving. He raised an eyebrow. "What makes me think *you* have plans also?"

Ferdinand smiled and nodded. "Elise has the day off. She's going to give me a tour of the city."

"*Tiens!*"

"*Oui*. She asked if I had visited Paris before, and I said no." Ferdinand shrugged and raised his arms. "So she offered to show me around. How could I refuse?" He grinned.

Diamanté chuckled.

***

"We start, I think, with the Île de la Cité," Elise said in halting, Portuguese-accented French as she and Ferdinand left the hotel an hour later. They walked up the rue Saint-Jacques toward the Seine. "You have to see la Cathédrale de Notre-Dame first." She made a moue. "But it's so sad. They removed all the windows in September."

She hooked her arm shyly in his.

Ferdinand was pleased at the gesture, silently hoping it indicated more than just being afraid of slipping on the ice.

"The government handed out gas masks, too," she continued. "Everyone is supposed to carry them around, but nobody does." She paused, then cocked her head to the side. "But I prefer not to talk about the war today, I think."

He nodded in agreement.

"From the cathédrale," she continued, "we cross to the right bank. It is a long walk up the Champs-Elysées to the Arc de Triomphe, but I like it very much." She lifted her face to look up at him. Her vivid blue eyes sparkled.

"You won't be too cold?" he asked.

She laughed. "If I am, we just walk faster."

Ferdinand noticed that her nose wrinkled and seemed to draw up into her forehead when she smiled.

They reached the river. Under the gray sky, the dark water looked frigid.

"*Oh là*. Look!" Elise exclaimed, pointing a gloved hand toward one of several wooden boxes mounted on the wall alongside the river. "There's a bookstall open. What a surprise in this weather, too. The poor man, he must be so cold."

They greeted the *bouquiniste*, a crusty old character with a long gray beard who stomped his feet in an attempt to keep himself warm.

Ferdinand browsed through the bins of *bouquins*, their paper yellow with age. His eyes landed on a small volume bound in faded gold silk titled simply *Poèmes Victor Hugo*. "My *maman* in Corsica loves poetry," he said, thumbing carefully through the brittle pages.

Elise looked at him curiously. "You are from Corsica?"

He nodded. "Originally, but we live in Marseilles now, my brother and I. How much for this?" he asked the vendor.

The man smiled, took the book from him, and peered inside the front cover. His bare fingers protruded through ragged holes in his gloves. "How much you offer, *Monsieur?*" he said in a raspy voice.

Ferdinand studied him, then narrowed his eyes. "I'll give you two francs."

The man made a face and shook his head. "Ah, *beh non*! Look at it, *Monsieur*." He held the book open for Ferdinand to see. "It is in good condition. Six francs, *au moins*. I have rent to pay."

Ferdinand hesitated. He didn't have much extra money to spend. "*Quatre*, and we have a deal."

The man smiled.

Ferdinand paid him four francs and wished him *Joyeux Noël*.

"Will it be for your *maman?*" Elise asked as they walked away.

"*Oui*, a souvenir from Paris."

"I think she will like it."

They crossed the Petit Pont to the Île de la Cité. Immediately to their right, across the square, stood the immense Cathedral of Notre-Dame.

"It looks beautiful, just the same, even with all those sandbags stacked against it," Ferdinand said.

Elise sighed. "Do you want to go in?" she asked. "I'd like to light a candle for my family in Portugal."

Ferdinand nodded.

They entered the high-vaulted central nave and walked down the main aisle. In front of them was the massive transept, the choir stalls on either side, and the altar at the far end. A faint aroma of burning incense filled the air.

Elise saw Ferdinand staring at gaping holes on each side of the transept. "That's where the rose windows used to be," she said with a sigh. "They've taken most of the statues away, too, but not yet Notre-Dame de Paris." She led him to a fourteenth-century sculpture of the virgin and child. In front of it stood a prayer-candle rack with rows of votives flickering in the dark, drafty cold of the windowless cathedral.

Ferdinand watched her as she knelt, dropped a coin in a wooden box, lit a candle, then made the sign of the cross and closed her eyes in prayer. Feeling awkward, he knelt beside her, lit a candle, and tried to decide what he should pray for. He glanced sideways at Elise on the kneeler next to him, her soft brown eyelashes fluttering over closed eyes. She had high cheekbones and wore no makeup that he could see, but her pointy nose was faintly reddened from the chill, and her lips, moving in silent prayer, seemed to him the color of pink roses. His eyes fell to the delicate hands clasped in front of her, and he imagined the bare breasts, the slim waist, the female wonders to be discovered beneath all that heavy winter clothing. He clenched his jaw as a youthful frisson of desire ran through his body. Slightly embarrassed by the sudden physical manifestation of his inner thoughts, he rose quickly and headed for the cathedral's entrance.

Outside, Elise caught up with him and pulled on his sleeve. "Are you upset?"

"*Non non*," he muttered, taking his packet of Gauloises from his coat pocket. "I...I just needed a cigarette."

She made a face. "I don't much like the smell of them."

He stuffed the packet back into his pocket.

She smiled up at him and slid her arm under his elbow. "Next, we cross the Pont Notre Dame to the right bank. Paris will be especially beautiful today, I think. After the snow."

He was listening intently to her voice, the image of the delicate flame twinkling in the votive still strong in his mind, when a group of boys in military prep school uniforms came toward them, joking and hassling each other. One face stood out. Ferdinand narrowed his eyes. Not wanting to be seen by his half brother, André, he lowered his head and pulled up his collar.

"You walk very fast," Elise said, struggling to keep up with him. "Are you cold?"

He kept a watchful eye on the group until they had passed.

"I think they make you nervous, those boys," she said.

"Just one of them."

"From Corsica?"

He nodded and stared into the distance.

She gave him a quizzical look, but he seemed to be lost in his thoughts.

Chapter Seventeen

In the Forestier kitchen at the Hôtel Saint-Jacques, Marcel and Diamanté set out the utensils, pots, and pans they would need for the preparation of the traditional Christmas Eve feast.

"First, I'm going to ready the duck and chestnuts for roasting," Marcel said as he tied the strings of an apron around his waist. He looked over his wire-rimmed glasses at Diamanté. "Do you know how to shuck oysters?"

Diamanté nodded that he did.

Marcel handed him a towel, then plucked an oyster from the pile in the sink and held it up. "OK, show me," he said.

Diamanté smiled. He wrapped his left hand in the towel, then cradled the oyster in the center. After studying it for a moment, he picked up the oyster knife, inserted it into the sliver of space between the shells, and gave it a twist. "*Et voilà!*" he said with a shy smile as the top and bottom shells separated.

"*Très bien!*" Marcel exclaimed later as he watched Diamanté chop the mushrooms for the oyster stuffing. "You seem to be a natural in the kitchen."

"I like to cook," Diamanté said. "I'm going to own a restaurant some day. A Corsican one."

"*Ah bon?*" Marcel exclaimed. "I'll have to introduce you to the owner of the Alsatian bistro next door. He's a friend of mine. We grew up together."

"You're from Alsace?"

Marcel nodded. "*Oui.* My younger brother Claude lives there, or did." He shook his head. "Now that Strasbourg has been evacuated and there is fear that Hitler will try to take Alsace back, he has fled the city with his wife and new baby." He checked the antique clock on the kitchen wall. "They are planning to arrive this afternoon. Then they will stay with us for a while."

Diamanté looked at him. "Do you believe the *Boches* will take France?"

"They will try, but the army is strong. The Maginot will hold. Everyone thought at first that would happen right away after France declared war in September. Françoise and I even sent the children to stay with her parents in the country. When nothing happened for two months, we brought them back."

"There are groups in Marseilles who are preparing, *quand même*."

Marcel looked at Diamanté, intrigued. "*Ah bon?* You mean..." He hesitated. "To resist?"

Diamanté nodded.

"There are some here also who are thinking the same. I have a friend who is already planning to produce a clandestine newspaper..."

At that moment François burst into the kitchen.

"*Oh alors, zut,*" Marcel exclaimed in frustration. "What is it, *petit?*"

"Pauline won't let me…"

Marcel put up his hand. "Go tell your *maman* all about it. I'm busy, François, with *la fête.*"

The boy hung his head and stomped out of the room.

Marcel went back to his chopping board.

Next, Pauline came skipping into the kitchen and plucked a piece of cheese from the counter. "What are we having for dessert, *Papy?*" she asked.

"You know already, *mon petit chou,*" her father replied, trying not to show his frustration at yet another interruption. "You saw me making the *bûche de Noël* yesterday. Remember? With the chocolate frosting and raspberry filling." He went over to the kitchen door and pleaded with his wife. "*Chérie, s'il te plaît. Pfttt! C'est insupportable.*" He flapped his hands in the air.

"Pauline, *viens, chérie. Laisse ton père travailler.*" The summons came from Madame Forestier.

"*D'accord, Maman,*" Pauline said reluctantly as she snatched another piece of cheese and skipped out of the room.

Diamanté raised his eyebrows and chuckled.

Marcel clucked his tongue and went back to work.

***

They gathered for the Christmas Eve feast after midnight in the wood-paneled dining room of the Forestier apartment. Following tradition, the table was set with white linens, fine crystal goblets, silver, and china. A silver candelabra with lit candles twinkled in the center, flanked by festive bows of evergreen. Among the pine branches were nestled tiny figurines from the nativity scene, the virgin and child in the center, surrounded by an assortment of angels, shepherds, and barn animals.

Marcel sat at the head of the long table, Françoise at the foot, and Diamanté and Ferdinand to her right, across from Elise and the two children. Marcel's brother, Claude, and his wife, Marianne, filled in the other two places.

"Good of you to let us stay awhile," Claude was saying to Marcel. "Can we help you out in any way?"

"*Eh bien*, there is something you can do," Marcel said. "Françoise wants to take Elise and the children to the country, to her parents' house near Brignancourt, for Christmas Day dinner tomorrow. I'd like to go with them, but even though there are few guests now, I can't leave the hotel unattended since I gave my assistant the day off. It wouldn't mean a lot of work. Just go to the lobby when someone rings the bell."

"Go on with your family. It's no problem. I'll cover the desk," Claude said, nodding his head decisively.

Watching them, Diamanté thought the Forestier brothers looked just alike. Claude appeared to be in his forties, with brown eyes, a wide face, and, like his brother, slight and energetic in his demeanor. His Alsatian accent was much more pronounced than Marcel's, however, and he seemed more stern.

Marcel poured champagne, then lifted his crystal flute into the air. "A toast," he said. "To peace."

They all raised their glasses and enthusiastically repeated, "*À la paix.*"

"So what have you two chefs been concocting for us all day?" Françoise asked.

"We start off with *foie gras*," Marcel said. "Then *huîtres farcies*, expertly shucked and stuffed by this young man." He gave a little nod in Diamanté's direction. "A natural in the kitchen he is, too."

Ferdinand winked at his brother.

"*Ensuite*," Marcel continued, "smoked salmon, and then *la pièce de résistance, le canard aux marrons*, the duck." He paused, then glanced in Claude's direction. "And of course, as always, we have the traditional *choucroute*, in honor of our Alsatian homeland."

The children clapped their hands in anticipation, and a collective "Ahhhhh..." emanated from the gathering as Marcel brought in the first course. "Now, *tout le monde*, it is time to eat. *Bon appétit!*"

Elise looked across the table at Ferdinand, then blushed when she saw he was staring at her.

Chapter Eighteen

On Christmas morning, Diamanté and Ferdinand were awakened by church bells and delighted children running through the hotel halls. Someone pounded on their door, and they heard a young voice announcing, "*Le Père Noel est arrivé! Venez descendre.*"

They quickly dressed and raced down the stairs. The decorated pine in the salon was lit with candles, and the family was gathered. A large tray of croissants sat on the table, and steaming bowls of thick hot chocolate were being passed around.

Ferdinand and Diamanté found new warm scarves in the shoes they had left by the fireplace.

Elise draped Ferdinand's around his neck and stood back to admire it. "You look very handsome, I think," she said, pointing above them. A sprig of mistletoe was hanging from the chandelier in the center of the room. She wrinkled her nose and smiled; her bright eyes sparkled. Then she kissed him, *les biz*-style, first on one cheek, then the other.

Diamanté chuckled at Ferdinand's blush.

***

Everyone gathered in the hotel lobby two hours later as Marcel, Françoise, Elise, and the children prepared to depart.

Marcel presented a thick volume to Diamanté. "I think you are ready for this, *mon ami*," he said warmly.

Diamanté's face brightened when he saw the title: *Le Guide Culinaire August Escoffier*.

"It is not for the amateur cook," Marcel said. "It is for the artist who wants to achieve cuisine that is unique and notable for its excellence. It will teach you everything you need to be a chef."

"I don't know how to thank you," Diamanté said as he flipped through pages.

"Keep your dream alive. You'll open your restaurant someday," Marcel said. He hugged Diamanté warmly and shook Ferdinand's hand. "Come back to Paris whenever you wish. You are always welcome to stay here."

They thanked him profusely for the hospitality he and Françoise had shown them.

"Next time," Diamanté said, "I will make you a Corsican feast."

"I'll look forward to that," Marcel said.

"Give our love to *Tante* Amélie," Françoise added. "Tell her we miss her."

Marcel went over to have a word with Claude who stood by the front desk.

Elise kissed both Ferdinand and Diamanté on each cheek. This time, it was Diamanté who felt himself blushing.

"What will you do today?" she asked them.

"I'm going to show my brother *tout* Paris," Ferdinand said. "Now that I've had a guided tour."

Elise giggled. "Write to me about it."

Ferdinand's face became serious. "*Oui*, I will." He cocked his head sideways. "That is, if you will write back."

Elise nodded eagerly.

"It's time to depart for Brignancourt," Marcel called from the open door. "We've a train to catch to *grand-mère*'s house." And out into the street they went waving and calling *Joyeux Noël* after them.

***

It was a clear, crisp day. The snow the day before had left the air clean and the sky crystal blue. Diamanté and Ferdinand put on their jackets and their new warm scarves and set out to see the City of Light with the few hours of Christmas Day they had left before their train departed for Marseilles.

They walked briskly up the avenue des Champs-Élysées from the Place de la Concorde. Mounds of snow under leafless chestnut trees lined the wide boulevard.

Ferdinand cleared his throat and frowned. "I saw André yesterday."

Diamanté stopped and turned to face him. "Did you say anything to him?"

Ferdinand shook his head. "He didn't even see me. He was with his Saint-Cyr buddies."

Diamanté heaved a sigh of relief.

Ferdinand nodded in agreement. "He likes to win. If he even saw Elise…" He didn't finish the sentence.

He didn't need to. Diamanté knew exactly what he meant. Their half brother was competitive and destructive, and capable of anything. The possibility of running into him in Paris hadn't even occurred to Diamanté, and it suddenly filled him with fear. If André thought Ferdinand was old Narbon's murderer, he would surely seek revenge.

Ferdinand knocked his shoulder playfully against him. "Hey, don't worry," he said. "I told you he didn't even see me. It's a beautiful day. It's Christmas, *mon frère*. We're on the Champs-Élysées. Next stop the Arc de Triomphe!"

***

A week later, on the first of January 1940, Diamanté celebrated his sixteenth birthday.

Chapter Nineteen

The first of several letters from Diamanté's friend Maurice began arriving in early January. Maurice wrote that he had been assigned to the Maginot Line. It had been a cold, snowy winter, but the front remained quiet.

> Spirits are low, so we try to keep ourselves busy. We play cards, read, watch the German troops through binoculars playing soccer on the other side of the border.

In a second letter, he reported rumors that the Jews in Poland had been forced to leave their homes.

Diamanté wrote back that things had changed at the factory. He was now working in the aircraft division as building warplanes had become a priority. He chuckled to himself as he added another piece of news that he knew Maurice would enjoy.

> I have not seen old Sully since just after you left for the army. He is in the hospital. Rumor has it he was set upon

> one night after work and beaten within an inch of his life on the wharf. They never caught who was responsible.

Diamanté went on to describe at length the PCF activities that were being put in place in case of an invasion.

> Bernard has a way to purchase rifles, and people with money are arranging to pay for them. We have more and more members every day. Women, too, have joined.

Maurice responded in the next letter that he had heard from his mother who had returned to her native Corsica. The Corsicans, she had told him, were formulating a resistance plan. They would call themselves after the maquis, where they would take refuge.

At the next meeting of the PCF, Diamanté reported on this piece of news. Others in the room, who were also Corsican, stood and shouted in unison, "*Nous sommes tous maquisards!*" We are all members of the Maquis!

***

In February, they were seated one evening at their usual spot in the bar by the wharf having a beer after work when Bernard announced suddenly that he was leaving for Paris the next day.

Ferdinand and Diamanté looked up in surprise.

"It's…there's a girl," Bernard explained. "I knew her in Poland. We were…" He blushed and searched for a word. "She was my *petite amie*, my girlfriend."

Ferdinand laughed and slapped him on the back. "And you never told me about her before this?"

"I was hoping to save enough money to bring her here," Bernard said. "But now I've had a letter from her. She escaped Poland, and she's in Paris. I don't know what has happened to her family." He paused, then continued. "Her name is Sara. Such a beauty she is. Soft brown hair, hazel eyes."

"What will you do? Bring her back to Marseilles?"

Bernard shook his head. "I don't know."

"What about the PCF?"

He furrowed his brows and looked at Ferdinand. "You will have to continue without me."

They said *au revoir* and wished him well.

Two months went by. Bernard didn't return to Marseilles, and they heard nothing from him.

***

A spring storm was passing through late one evening in April when Madame Boulon knocked at the door of the apartment.

"I've just had a telegram from Marcel," she said. She handed it to Diamanté. He took the paper and read aloud. "Invasion imminent—stop—Paris darkened—stop—family sent to country—stop." He looked up at Madame Boulon. She had tears in her eyes. Fierce thunder shook the windowpanes. Madame Boulon jumped, startled.

"Oh, *mon Dieu*," she said, shaking her head and wringing her hands.

***

In early May, the Loupré brothers were listening to music on the radio set one evening when the broadcast was interrupted with the urgent news that Hitler's army had breached the Meuse and plunged through the heavily wooded Ardennes. Ferdinand turned up the volume, and they heard the somber tone of the announcer's voice.

> *In the early hours of May tenth, German troops began to penetrate Holland, Belgium, and Luxembourg. The French army was alerted during the night of the aerial bombardment that the enemy had begun. Hitler's army has landed in different territories of Belgium and Holland and from there have begun an aerial attack on France, in the north and east. The attack continued throughout the day and French DCA (anti-aircraft defenses) have inflicted heavy losses on German aviation. Forty-four enemy airplanes were shot down over French territory. All governments involved have called on the allied countries for help.*

Diamanté whistled. "It's begun."

Part Two

Tomorrow, in the so-called unoccupied zone in France, every house will be decked with the Tricolour flag. In each town and village Frenchmen and women will march past an appointed spot. Everywhere "La Marseillaise" will ring out, rising from the hearts of the people and bringing tears to their eyes. What will be the meaning of these flags to their eyes? What will be the meaning of these flags, these processions, this "Marseillaise?"

First, they will show that France lives on, that she has not been submerged by the ocean of her tribulations, that she is still France despite invasion and tyranny.

Next, the flags, processions and the singing will show our country still remembers, that she has not forgotten her glory, her wounds or her humiliation, that she thinks of her children who are dying for her on all the battlefields of the world or at the hands of firing squads.

Finally, these flags, these processions, the "Marseillaise" will signify that France is making ready, that she secretly gathers strength for the day of wrath when the Allies are present on our side, and the traitors are swept aside and the entire nation will rise to drive out and punish the enemy.

The flags stand for pride, the processions for hope, "La Marseillaise" for fury. We still have pride, hope and fury. This will be made plain tomorrow.

>   —General Charles de Gaulle
>   Speech broadcast from London, England, Bastille Day eve, 1942

CHAPTER TWENTY

Occupied Paris
14 July 1942

Diamanté and Elise stood side by side on the brick-paved Quai Saint-Michel. The twin towers of the Cathedral of Notre-Dame rose high into the sky above them, and in the distance, over the rooftops, they could see the pinnacle of the Eiffel Tower. It was Bastille Day, and despite the presence of the invaders everywhere and the decree by the Vichy government that there be no national celebration, Parisians walking along the banks of the Seine could be heard humming "La Marseillaise."

"It is his dream," Elise said as they watched Ferdinand push a small barge-like wooden excursion boat from the landing below. The tricolor flew from its bow in direct defiance of the Germans who had forbidden the display of French flags in Paris.

Elise sighed. "*Oh là*, he's been building it for many months now in the back alley behind the hotel. He planned the launch deliberately for today." She looked up at Diamanté admiringly. At eighteen, he was taller and much more muscular than his brother. She smiled. "He thinks it will be a very good business someday, you know."

Diamanté nodded.

"He is pleased you are here to see the launch." Then she added, "Actually, so am I…pleased, that is, that you came."

Diamanté cocked his handsome head sideways and turned to her. "You are?"

She smiled and nodded.

Ferdinand jumped into the back of the boat and looked up at them with a wide grin on his face.

They waved and shouted encouragement, then watched with nervous anticipation as he started the engine and steered the craft into the middle of the river.

A few curious bystanders lingered, cheered briefly at the sight of the tricolor, then quickly moved on.

"I asked him how many people it will hold," Diamanté commented. "He said he planned to begin with small, private parties and expand as the business grew." He laughed, then whispered, "I wondered if he'd take the *Boches*."

"And how did he answer?"

He shook his head. "*Pas question*."

"Oh, *mon Dieu*, it's going in circles!" Elise exclaimed as she glanced back at the river. "I don't think it's supposed to do that."

The boat's engine sputtered and stopped. Ferdinand started it again, but almost immediately it quit.

"*Quelle catastrophe!*" Elise cried out. "It's definitely not supposed to do that. *Oh là*. Look. It's taking on water, too!"

They stared in dismay as Ferdinand leapt from the sinking boat and swam frantically toward them. Together they pulled him out of the water, catching a last glimpse of Ferdinand's dream excursion craft as it disappeared beneath the surface of the river.

"I guess we're out of business," Ferdinand declared with a shrug. Then he laughed.

Just at that moment, a patrol boat, its black, white, and red flag bearing the German naval insignia, rounded the bend in the river, speeding straight for them.

"*Merde*. Run like hell!" Ferdinand yelled. And they did.

They reached the safety of the hotel and broke into fits of laughter.

Elise patted Ferdinand's cheek. "Will you try again?" she asked.

"Probably," he replied. "I will wait until after the war is over until I do." He laughed. "But tonight, that German patrol boat might just explode by accident."

Diamanté chuckled. "Actually, *mon frère*, today might have been a good day to take the *Boches* for a little excursion on the river!"

Chapter Twenty-One

15 July 1942

It was to be Diamanté's last day in Paris before returning to Marseilles. He was working at the counter in the Forestier kitchen when Elise entered and climbed onto a stool across from him. She picked up the jar of dried herbs on the countertop and sniffed.

"What are you making?" she asked.

"A rabbit stew," he replied, smiling at her. "It's my specialty."

"How did you manage to get a rabbit here in Paris?" she asked. "With the rationing…"

"I brought it with me. I shot it near Marseilles." He stopped chopping onion and studied her face. "You get prettier every time I see you," he said.

She smiled, and her blue eyes sparkled. "*Oh là.* You probably say that to all the girls in Marseilles."

He glanced at her figure, then looked down. "Actually, I don't say it to anyone but you."

She jumped off the stool and went over to the sink.

His piercing black eyes followed her.

She glanced back at him. "You have the most interesting eyes," she said suddenly.

"How is that?"

She hesitated. "Like a wolf's." She seemed to be deciding something. "I think I will call you *Lobo* from now on. It means wolf in Portuguese." She smiled at him, then said playfully, "I think you are sly like a wolf, too."

He chuckled. "I like that very much."

She blushed and flirtatiously lowered her eyelashes. "So, *Lobo*, are you still living by yourself, then, working at the factory everyday in Marseilles? Don't you ever go out? Have any fun?"

He heaved a sigh, then put his kitchen knife on the counter, wiped his fingers on his apron, and went over to her. Looking her in the eyes, he wrapped his arms around her, drew her in close to him, and kissed her.

She threw her arms around his neck and kissed him tenderly, allowing her soft lips to linger against his.

Gently he kissed her shoulders, then her neck and behind her ears. "I thought you were Ferdinand's girl," he mumbled, nestling his nose in her long hair.

She shook her head. "He's too busy with his studies at the university and the partisans." She ran her fingers through his hair and looked directly into his eyes. "I adore him, but I'm not in love with him."

He brought her hands to his lips and kissed them tenderly, then turned them over and kissed the palms. "Elise," he said, gently rubbing her fingers, "there's something…"

Suddenly, there was heavy pounding on the door that led to the back stairs and courtyard below.

Elise jumped in alarm. "*Oh là*. Who can that be?"

Diamanté went to the door. As quickly as he unlatched the lock, a young man pushed his way into the kitchen, slammed the door shut, and looked out the window to see if he had been followed. Then he turned to them, wild-eyed. Diamanté saw the yellow star sewn on the pocket of his jacket.

"I...I thought Ferdinand would be here," he said nervously. "I need to see him. It is urgent."

"You don't remember me, do you, Bernard?" Diamanté asked, extending his hand.

Bernard stared at him. "Diamanté? Sorry, I...I didn't."

"Ferdinand is upstairs doing some repairs," Elise said. "Come quickly. I'll take you to him."

She led Bernard to the metal-cage elevator. "The fourth floor," she directed.

Bernard closed the gate and ascended.

Elise returned to the kitchen. "You were saying?" she said with a shy smile.

Diamanté went to her and enveloped her in his arms. He kissed her cheek. "I wanted to know if you would be my girl."

Elise nodded and pressed her forehead against his chin.

***

Bernard sat between Ferdinand and Diamanté on the sofa in the darkened salon of the Forestier apartment later that evening.

Marcel fanned himself in the blue brocaded Louis XIV–style chair across from them. "Damned curfew," he mumbled.

"It's too hot. *Ces putains de Boches* making us keep the windows closed and shuttered."

Ferdinand lit a half-smoked cigarette, inhaled a full breath, then exhaled. The smoke contributed to the already stuffy air in the room. "Bernard has come here to seek our help," he said suddenly.

Bernard leaned forward with his elbows on his knees and clasped his hands. "It is rumored there will soon be a mass arrest of Jews," he said.

"And not by the *Boches*," Ferdinand added.

"French?" Diamanté exclaimed.

"*Oui*," Bernard sighed and went on. "Alas, with the blessing of Pétain, too," he spat. "My girl, Sara…" He studied his hands. "Sara is very fearful for me. Today she begged me to get the hell out of Paris before it is too late."

Marcel was listening carefully, shaking his head. "I too have heard rumors to the effect," he said. "My sources tell me it could happen at any moment." He leaned forward. "You should depart immediately."

Bernard nodded.

"What about Sara?" Ferdinand asked.

Bernard shrugged. "She refuses to leave. She doesn't believe the women will be arrested."

"We can get you out of Paris tonight, but someone needs to escort you." Marcel looked at Diamanté. "Can you go with him?"

Ferdinand put up his hand in protest. "*Non. Absolument non.* I am the oldest, and Bernard is my friend. I'm going with him."

Marcel shook his head. "We need you here, *mon ami.* There's a big job planned for tomorrow night. Remember? Furthermore," he continued, "I think it is time for us to involve your brother in our plans. I have friends in Normandy I want him to make contact with. We are beginning to think about an escape line to the South."

Diamanté lit his own half-smoked cigarette and exhaled. "In Marseilles," he said, "we've already begun working on a network over the Pyrenees to Spain. If we combined the two, we'd have a formidable escape line."

Marcel nodded. "Just what we had in mind. We'll discuss details later."

Ferdinand took a final puff and twisted his cigarette into the base of the ashtray. "*D'accord. Bon,*" he said finally, "but I don't like it."

Marcel turned to Bernard. "Now then, here's the plan for getting you out of France." He cleared his throat. "The owner of the restaurant next door can arrange for a delivery truck to take you to the outskirts of Paris. I will alert you when it's ready to depart. That will be sometime just after midnight. The driver will leave you off in the village of Brignancourt where my wife's parents live. We'll load two bicycles. It will be only a few kilometers for you and Diamanté to ride to their farmhouse. My father-in-law, Doctor Lemonier, will then take you to Normandy. A friend of ours from Alsace is there. His name is Guy de Noailles. You'll stay the night, then he will see you on to Rouen in the next day or two." He eyed Bernard's jacket. "For your safety, I recommend you remove that immediately and burn it."

Bernard put his hand over the yellow star that Sara had carefully sewn on his pocket. He looked down then nodded his head. "In the beginning, we wore the stars with pride," he said.

Ferdinand put a hand on his shoulder. "*Courage, mon ami*," he said.

"My friends in Normandy have connections," Marcel continued. "You will be taken to England via a fishing boat, but," he put up an index finger, "I warn you. It will be dangerous. The channel is crawling with German boats now, and all of Normandy is being heavily patrolled."

"If I make it to England," Bernard said, "I assure you I will join de Gaulle."

Marcel poured them glasses of port and raised his into the air. "*Vive la France Combattante!*" he said in toast.

Chapter Twenty-Two

There was a light tap on Diamanté's door just after midnight. He had been wide awake, staring at the ceiling, for the past hour thinking about Elise. Earlier he had told her he would be leaving and that it had to do with Bernard. She had kissed him, worried aloud that he would be in danger, then whispered in his ear that she loved him.

He smiled now as he replayed her whisper.

"I am not afraid of death," he had assured her. "Not after you tell me that."

He heaved a sigh, then rose from the bed and quickly put on his jacket and beret. Outside in the hallway, Marcel and Bernard waited. Bernard seemed nervous. Diamanté nodded in his direction. Together they descended the stairway quietly so as not to arouse suspicion. Marcel led them into the alleyway behind the hotel. A delivery truck was parked at the rear of the restaurant next door. The back of the truck was open, stacked with crates of wine except for a space the driver had made for Diamanté and Bernard to load the bicycles. They threw in their backpacks, shook Marcel's hand, and climbed in.

The driver finished stacking more crates of wine two deep and six tall to create a barrier. Next, the door was lowered with as little noise as possible, and soon they heard the engine start and felt the truck moving. At first, it seemed to proceed slowly, but it gradually picked up speed as Diamanté imagined them moving through the dark Paris streets in the middle of the night. Occasionally his heart leapt when he heard a siren over the roar of the engine.

It was some time before Diamanté felt he could relax. In the darkness, he became aware of the moldy, musky smell of spilled wine.

Next to him, Bernard lay down on the rough floor and fell asleep.

***

Diamanté had dozed off and was suddenly awakened by the sound of men's voices. The truck had stopped. Marcel had warned him about the checkpoints. He sat up quickly.

Bernard was awake also. Diamanté put his finger to his lips and listened intently, but he couldn't understand what was being said. There seemed to be a lot of shouting, most of it in German.

Suddenly the tailgate of the truck clanged open. They could hear the voice of the driver explaining in French that he was merely making a delivery of wine to local restaurants. There seemed to be some discussion about the quality of the wine and whether it was any good. Diamanté smiled to himself. *Marcel was smart*, he thought. *The* Boches *are more interested in the booty than in any possibility of people being smuggled*.

There was more discussion, then a harsh grating sound as a crate was removed. Through a crack in the truck's side wall, Diamanté saw the shadow of a man in a round helmet inspecting the vehicle. He ducked as the beam of a flashlight roved the outside panel. Another crate was removed. More light flooded into the back of the box. *One more crate,* Diamanté thought, *and they'll spot the bicycles.*

The beam of another flashlight scoured the upper crates, then roamed down the sides. More discussion took place. A stick of some sort prodded through the slats. The heavy sound of boot steps surrounded the truck.

Diamanté slowly drew his Walther from his jacket pocket. Bernard's eyes were wide.

They waited, hardly taking a breath for fear of being discovered.

It seemed an eternity before they heard the clink of a glass, then another, and soon the Germans were laughing loudly. Finally, the driver bid the group *bonsoir*, the engine started, and they were on their way again. Some distance beyond the checkpoint, the driver pounded twice on the wall of the box. It was his signal that they had successfully passed the first hurdle.

Diamanté breathed a sigh of relief. He opened his pack, took out two cheese sandwiches he had made, and handed one to Bernard.

***

Dawn broke over the village of Brignancourt as the delivery truck pulled to a stop in an alleyway behind Le Café de la Côte. Diamanté heard the flick of a lever, and the back door swung open with a clang.

The driver, a cigarette dangling from the side of his mouth, put his hands on his hips and grinned. "All is clear, *mes amis*," he announced. He helped Diamanté and Bernard unload the bicycles. Then he shook their hands and wished them *bon courage*.

Diamanté surveyed the small sleeping village. The shutters on the houses were closed, and there wasn't a soul in sight. Marcel had warned him not to hang around too long. "Brignancourt has a population less than two hundred. Anyone who sees you will be immediately suspicious." He had drawn them a crude map. "Françoise's parents live near the Étang du Moulin de Vallières, a large marsh just on the outskirts of the village. Follow the dirt pathway around it. After you cross the wooden bridge, you will see, just ahead, their large two-story stone house and nearby a white outbuilding with a gray slate roof."

Diamanté mounted his bicycle and motioned to Bernard. "*Allons*, let's get out of here before someone wakes up."

Across the square, a lone dog, paws tucked under its chin, lay watching them from the steps of a stone church. Becoming suddenly curious, the mutt stood, lifted its nose in their direction, and sniffed the air. As they sped anxiously past, the mongrel emitted a low growl and bared its teeth. Diamanté fumbled nervously in his pocket and tossed out what was left of his cheese sandwich. The dog lumbered over to the peace offering, nosed it briefly, quietly downed it in one gulp, then, keeping a wary eye on them, returned to its place on the church's stone steps.

They left the village and peddled down the dirt pathway toward the marsh. In the distance, the tall tower of a cumulonimbus cloud rose high into the summer sky; a family of ducks bathed in the nearby pond. Diamanté breathed in the fresh morning air. The lush, sweet-scented landscape reminded him of the fragrant undergrowth in his native Corsica. He almost expected a goat or two to come bounding out at any moment.

The tranquil scene was suddenly interrupted by the roaring sound of an airplane overhead. Diamanté looked up. Behind him he saw Bernard turning quickly off the path and heading for the nearby woods. Diamanté followed him. They took cover in the underbrush and watched as the plane circled and swooped down low over the pond, then disappeared from sight.

Diamanté heard a distant rumble. Was it thunder or, he wondered, a burst of gunfire? He felt his scalp prickle. The woods seemed too still. Not a single bird chirped. Something, someone, moved in the shadows behind them.

A minute later, another plane flew over, its two swastikas clearly visible. It swept down, skimmed the pond, soared upward again. Then it too vanished below the tree line.

Diamanté looked at Bernard.

"*Fritz*," Bernard said. "Those were German fighters."

Diamanté's piercing eyes surveyed the sky. When all seemed quiet, he pointed to the bridge.

Bernard nodded in agreement.

They climbed back on their bicycles and pedaled as fast as they could.

There was no sign of life as they approached the old stone farmhouse. Diamanté put out his hand in hesitation. This could be a trap. They dismounted and slowly crept alongside the barn until they were directly across from the shuttered house. Just then, they heard the sound of another plane approaching.

"*Merde*," Diamanté said. "We'll be seen."

Bernard tried the door of the outbuilding. It was not locked. They pushed their bicycles inside, slammed the door shut, and waited, crouching in the darkness as the plane roared overhead.

A minute later, the door opened slightly, and the shadowy figure of a man wielding a pitchfork stood framed in the opening.

They were trapped. His heart pounding, Diamanté felt in his pocket for his Walther.

The figure stepped inside. Sunlight streamed into the barn. Diamanté could see him clearly. He was about fifty years of age, medium build, with sandy red hair, bushy eyebrows, and a busy mustache that was redder than his hair. He peered cautiously at them through small wire-rimmed glasses, then smiled and offered his hand in welcome.

"*Bienvenu*. Hubert Lemonier," he said. "My son-in-law got word to me that you would be arriving this morning."

Diamanté heaved a sigh of relief and shook his hand.

They hid the bicycles under bales of hay, then Lemonier led them to the house and into a large country kitchen. The room was bright and cheerful. Blue-and-white-printed curtains adorned the windows. A wood-burning stove stood in the corner, and a long table with chairs dominated the center of the space. Above the table hung a wrought iron chandelier.

The mouthwatering smell of food cooking reminded Diamanté how hungry he was.

Lemonier's wife was working at the counter. Above her hung an array of various-sized copper and bronze kettles.

"Ah, *mes amis*," she said warmly. She looked like an older version of her daughter, Marcel's elegant wife, Françoise. "We have been waiting for you. Come sit down. I've just finished making *omelettes aux asperges*."

They took seats at the table, and Madame placed plates of food in front of them.

Diamanté stared at the fluffy omelets filled with fresh stalks of green asparagus.

"Is there something you don't like?" Madame asked.

Diamanté smiled and picked up his fork and knife. "Oh, *non*, *absolument non,* Madame. It's just that we can't get eggs in Paris. Everything is rationed."

She raised her chin and cackled. "You know what we say here in the country? Catch the egg as the chicken lays it or the *Boches* will get it!" She placed steaming hot bowls of a light brownish liquid next to their plates. "It's *café crème* without the *café*." She shrugged. "We improvise on that part, but our cows still produce."

"Eat quickly, *mes amis*," her husband said, "and we'll be on our way."

Diamanté and Bernard hungrily devoured the food.

They had just climbed into Lemonier's old truck when another plane flew low over the farm.

"Bothersome pests," Lemonier grumbled, putting on his ragged straw hat. "Noisy. The *Boches* have built an aerodrome over by Moussy. It's camouflaged so it can't be seen from the air. Their flight pattern is directly over my house." He started the engine and added, his blue eyes twinkling, "We have plans for that airstrip, my friends and I."

Chapter Twenty-Three

Late that afternoon, they reached the next stop in their journey. Three kilometers from the village of Epinay, at the end of a single-track lane in the quiet Calvados countryside of Normandy, stood a huge two-story stone farmhouse with shuttered windows and a steep flat-tiled roof.

Doctor Lemonier pulled up to the front door and stopped the truck. "*Voilà. On arrive.*"

A large brown dog with pointed ears, an Alsatian breed, came from behind the old barn, barking and wagging its tail.

Diamanté surveyed the tranquil setting. Hens roamed across the lawn; birds chirped. An orchard of apple trees flanked the driveway. The scent of fragrant fruit infused the hot afternoon air.

They heard the creak of the farmhouse's heavy carved wooden front door. A young man stepped out and waved to them. He was about twenty-five, small, thin, dark-haired, with a handlebar mustache.

Doctor Lemonier climbed out of the truck and motioned for Diamanté and Bernard to do the same. The dog sniffed at their shoes, then followed them to the door.

The man smiled and shook Lemonier's hand. "Did anyone see you?" he asked. His black eyes sparkled under distinctly close-knit eyebrows.

"*Non. Non.* All went well," Lemonier replied. "But I must return immediately." He winked at Diamanté and Bernard. "Job to do tonight." He bid them *au revoir*, then hurried back to his truck and drove away.

"My name is Guy de Noailles," the young man said in a soft voice. "We are pleased to welcome you, my wife Marguerite and I."

Madame de Noailles, a pale, pretty woman, came from behind him. She took their hands warmly. "Please come in," she said. "Would you like something cold to drink? It's so hot today."

Diamanté and Ferdinand removed their berets and nodded.

As Monsieur de Noailles led them into the house, he saw them noticing his severe limp. "A war wound," he said briefly in explanation. "Happened in Italy."

He showed them into a large, comfortable *salon* with a high slanted, wood-beamed ceiling. The room was cool despite the heat outside. One wall was lined with bookcases filled with books. A painting leaning on the mantel above a hand-carved limestone fireplace depicted the great cathedral of Strasbourg with its single spire.

Madame placed a tray with glasses and a pitcher of lemonade on a small oval table in front of the sofa. The ancient grandfather clock in the corner chimed five times.

Guy de Noailles sat in the chair opposite, studying them as he twirled the ends of his black mustache between his thumb and index finger. "You will stay here tonight. Tomorrow we go to Rouen. It is not good to be in any one place too long these days. The *Boches* come around every so often…to *visit* us."

"To raid our food supply," Marguerite added, angrily clicking her tongue. "They take what they want. What we haven't hidden, that is. Then they go away."

Guy shrugged. "So far they don't give us any trouble. Alas, that could change at any moment. Others have not been so lucky."

A girl about the age of five or six entered the room.

"Ah, here is our daughter Nathalie," Guy said. "Come, *chérie*, greet our guests."

The girl curtsied. "*Bonjour, Messieurs,*" she said. Then she turned to her father. "Can I go play with Hannibal now?"

Guy laughed. "Hannibal is the big dog you met when you came into the yard," he explained. He gave his daughter a tender smile. "Go on, *ma petite*," he said. "But don't wander too far from the house."

She nodded and left.

"I don't want her to be afraid," he said. "But these are dangerous times."

***

Later that evening, they were seated at a wooden table in the large kitchen. Marguerite served them a savory potage accompanied by crusty homemade bread, then a creamy Brie, and finally a salad of fresh greens from her garden.

Nathalie wrinkled her nose at the salad in front of her. "What's for dessert, *Maman?*" she asked.

"Your favorite," her mother answered.

"*Tarte tatin?*"

"*Oui.*"

The girl clapped her hands.

"*Mais*," her mother wagged her index finger in the air, "you have to finish your salad first, *ma chérie*."

They had just taken their first bites of the warm upside-down apple cake when the quiet of the countryside was interrupted by the drone of airplanes. In the distance, they heard the *ack ack ack* of anti-aircraft guns.

Guy's eyes widened.

Marguerite and Nathalie scurried into the pantry.

Guy blew out the single candle on the table and went over to peer through a crack in the shutter.

"They're British," he said. "I can tell by the sound."

Diamanté joined him at the window. In the dark sky above a plane spiraled downward, its engine on fire.

"He's been hit," Guy said. They watched as the fighter soared up into the air, then banked its wings severely. Within seconds, they heard the sound of an explosion, and the sky lit up. In the flash of light, Diamanté saw a parachute hurtling toward the ground not far from the farm.

Guy had seen it, too. "It's the pilot," he said.

"We've got to do something," Diamanté said.

Guy looked at him and nodded. "If he's caught by the *Boches…*" He didn't say more. "*Merde.* I…I can't move very fast with this damned leg."

Diamanté didn't hesitate. "I'll go."

Bernard was standing behind them. "*Moi aussi*. I'll go with you."

Diamanté put his hand on Bernard's shoulder and shook his head. "*Non*," he said. "We can't risk it."

"There's a path from the back of the garden through the woods," Guy explained. "Follow it. If he came down where I think he did, you'll find him in a clearing not too far from here. The dog will go with you. He's trained for the hunt. You won't know he's there, but if you hear a soft, low growl, *faites attention*. He'll alert you to danger." He handed Diamanté a folding-blade hunting knife. "Take this. You're likely to need it."

Diamanté slipped the knife into his pocket and donned his beret. Then he opened the kitchen door and slid quietly out into the garden.

***

Diamanté moved slowly, one step at a time, trying to make as little noise as possible. Only a sliver of moon lit the dirt pathway. Frogs croaked; crickets chirped. A brittle twig cracked under his foot. He stopped and listened. Just behind him, he heard the dog's soft panting and in the distance short bursts of gunfire. The two, man and canine, inched forward in the darkness.

They had just reached the edge of the clearing when a flock of planes roared overhead. A few seconds later, a single aircraft flew low over them. Searchlights combed the air. Diamanté ducked into the brush.

Suddenly he heard a low growl. He turned to look at Hannibal. Ears raised, the Alsatian's head was pointed at the vague silhouette of a man hanging just above the ground directly ahead of them. A white parachute suspended him from the branches of an oak tree like a limp puppet.

Diamanté drew the hunting knife from his pocket, unfolded the blade, and reached up to cut the cords.

The man landed with a thud and moaned in pain.

Quickly pulling the parachute from the tree's branches, Diamanté rolled it into a ball and stuffed it under the thick brush. "*Pouvez-vous vous lever?*" he asked the flier in a low voice.

The man gasped for breath, barely coherent. "No speak French," he mumbled.

Diamanté pulled the flier to a seated position, then hoisted him onto his shoulders and ran.

They reached the farmhouse just as more planes flew low overhead.

Guy de Noailles was watching through a crack in the door. He opened it quickly, and Diamanté, out of breath, lowered the man to the floor of the kitchen.

Marguerite lit a candle.

The man's face was covered in blood. One arm dangled awkwardly at his side; a splinter of broken bone punctured the skin just below his elbow.

Diamanté lifted an eyelid. "He's alive," he said. "Barely."

"Let's get him upstairs," Guy said. "There's a room just above where we can hide him."

Bernard helped Diamanté, and following the limping Guy they carried the stranger up a set of narrow wooden steps that lead from the pantry to a small garret above the kitchen. They laid him on a bed. The man's eyes fluttered open briefly.

Marguerite brought a basin of water and towels. She worked quickly. First she took off the man's jacket and shirt. Then she examined his wounds. "The face is lacerated," she lamented, looking at her husband, "and his arm is obviously broken. It's a shame Doctor Lemonier left so soon."

Guy nodded his head. "I'll get word to him. He won't be able to come until tomorrow morning."

Marguerite felt the man's side.

The flier yelped in pain and passed out.

"Probably broken ribs," she said, shaking her head.

Guy fingered two thin rectangular-shaped metal tags hanging on a chain around the man's neck. The tags had been imprinted with raised letters; each contained the same information: a name, some numbers. One of the tags was dented. "This man is not British," Guy said, looking up. "His name is Stuart Ellis. *Un américain.*"

Chapter Twenty-Four

Sometime after midnight, the rumbling sound of a heavy diesel engine awakened Diamanté. He stumbled to his feet and went over to look out the window. In the moonlight, he saw a *Wehrmacht* transport truck making its way along the single gravel lane toward the farmhouse. It slid to a stop in the farmyard and positioned its low-beam headlights toward the barn. The vehicle's doors opened, and a swarm of shadows with round helmets descended quickly. They spread out, lanterns lit, rifles at the ready, and began methodically searching the outbuildings. In the surrounding woods, Diamanté heard the excited yelping of search hounds.

Bernard was standing behind him.

"Time to hide, *mon ami*," Diamanté whispered.

***

Downstairs, Guy de Noailles was also alerted by the rumbling. Fearing the pursuit of the flier would lead the *Boches* to his farm, he had kept vigil for the past few hours.

As had been planned, Bernard rushed down the stairs and ducked into the wine cellar where he had been instructed to hide behind a false brick wall.

Guy closed the door to the underground store after him, then went into the kitchen pantry to help Marguerite push a heavy storage cabinet against the entrance to the hidden passageway. In the garret above, the American lay in a fevered, semiconscious fog.

The sound of stomping boots and loud shouting came from outside in the garden, and eerie lights of moving lanterns flashed across the kitchen's shuttered windows.

Guy's frightened daughter, Nathalie, stood next to the pantry doorway, shaking and crying, her little fist balled and stuffed in her mouth.

"You and Nathalie stay in here," Guy whispered to his wife. "Bolt the door from the inside." He knelt and hugged the girl. "You must be very quiet now, *petite*," he warned.

"Will Hannibal be all right?"

"He'll be safe in the barn. *Je t'assure*." Guy put his index finger to his lips, and whispered as he closed the door, "Remember, now. *Silence*."

***

The barn door made a grating sound as one of the soldiers slid it open. From his upstairs window, Diamanté saw Hannibal emerge in the beam of the truck's headlights. The canine drew its lips back, bared its teeth in a snarl, then emitted a low growl.

The soldier took a threatening step forward and raised his Luger.

The dog snapped his jaw and barked a warning.

The man cocked the gun.

At the sound, the Alsatian charged.

The sharp "crack" of a gunshot slashed the night air.

The dog staggered backward and fell to the ground whimpering.

Diamanté froze. "*Merde alors!*" he exclaimed under his breath. Scrambling to get his Walther PP from his pack, he loaded it and returned to the window.

***

Hearing the gun blast, Guy moved as quickly as he could into the darkened salon. He felt for his small loaded pistol on the mantel and slipped it into his belt.

***

Diamanté ducked away from the window as a floodlight clicked on, spreading an intense, blinding light over the entire farmhouse façade. Next came a thunderous pounding on the heavy wooden front door. He held his breath and listened.

Below in the foyer he heard Guy holler, "*Warten Sie. Ich komme an. Attendez! J'arrive.*"

***

Guy unbolted the front door, opened it, and stepped onto the stoop. A semicircle of steel rifle barrels faced him, all pointing in his direction.

"*Guten Abend*," he said politely. In the bright light, he recognized the twin lightning bolts on the soldiers' helmets—*Schutzstaffel* – Waffen-SS. "*Was die Mühe ist?*" What seems to be the trouble?

An officer in SS collar patches and shoulder stripes shoved the point of his rifle into Guy's chest. The man's large head sat solidly on his neckless, barrel-chested body. The muscles in his thick jaw bulged. "*Ein Pilot*," he grunted. The pair of fierce black eyes bore into Guy's. "*Wir suchen einen Piloten.*" We are looking for a flier.

Guy flinched. "*Es gibt keinen Flieger hier,*" he said, shaking his head and holding his breath. He hoped they would believe him that there was no aviator in his house.

The officer barked a command in German. His meaty hand shoved Guy aside and pushed through the door.

***

Diamanté heard the bone-crushing sound of hobnailed jackboots on the tiled floor of the foyer. A door slammed; a piece of furniture crashed to the floor. A flash of light roamed the stairwell. Sweat poured from his brow. Breathing fast, he pointed his pistol and crept out into the dark hallway.

***

The officer stood by the door, nonchalantly smoking a cigarette while two of his SS men searched the interior of the farmhouse. "You speak excellent German," he said to Guy de Noailles, a tone of arrogance in his voice.

Guy's heart thudded in his chest at the sight of one of the soldiers thrusting his lantern through the door of the wine cellar where the Jew was hiding. "Until recent events, my wife and I lived in Alsace," he replied, forcing himself to remain calm.

No-Neck took a puff on his cigarette. "*Ja?* My parents were originally from Alsace. Strasbourg, actually. Where did you live?"

Guy didn't look at the man. "Riquewihr."

"Ah." The officer nodded his head. "Pretty little village. Excellent wines." Then his hard eyes focused on Guy. "Your wife, you say? But where, *mein Herr,* is she now? *Hier?*" He pointed to the level above with his cigarette.

Guy watched his furniture being tossed about by the second soldier. He wanted to take the gun from his belt and shoot all three of them, but he knew there were more of the hated *Boches* outside in his farmyard. Even with the help of the stranger upstairs, they would be outnumbered. He shook his head. "*Nein,*" he said. "My wife has gone to live with her sister in the unoccupied zone."

The officer frowned and narrowed his eyes. "And why would she do that? *Jüdin?*"

The first soldier emerged from the wine cellar. "*Nichts,*" he said, shaking his head and slamming the door shut. He pointed his gun barrel toward the pantry. "*Was innen hier ist?*"

"Rats, hopefully dead ones," Guy answered matter-of-factly. "We put out poison. It is very toxic. It will kill humans, too." He raised an eyebrow. "Instantly."

The officer glared at Guy. "And if we don't believe you?"

Guy shrugged, looking the man directly in the eye. He reached into his shirt pocket and handed over a key. "*Hier, bitte.* You are welcome to open it if you don't believe me."

The other soldier, who was about to climb the stairway to the floor above, stopped and turned around. "*Scheiße.* We use that poison on *our* farm. He's right."

The three soldiers looked at each other. No-Neck turned the key over in his palm as if trying to decide if it was a trap.

Guy turned and hobbled as calmly and slowly as he could toward the front stoop. "I'll just step outside," he said. "I personally advise you not to breath in the fumes." He could feel their eyes boring into his back.

***

With his loaded Walther PP, Diamanté listened intently to the exchange from the top of the stairs. The roar of an airplane over the rooftop startled him. He moved cautiously back into his room and peered out the window.

He heard the "tat tat tat tat tat" of the approaching machine guns first, then he saw the planes. Two British fighters flew so low over the farmhouse that he could see the roundels on their sides and wings. The Spitfires riddled the *Wehrmacht* transport truck, blowing out its head beams. In the darkness, Diamanté saw the shadow of a man falling from the cab. A strong smell of diesel fuel permeated the night air.

The officer in charge emerged from the house and barked a command to his men as he climbed into the cab. Two of them hoisted the wounded soldier into the truck, and the rest piled quickly into the back. The vehicle sped off. Diamanté watched as it raced down the dirt pathway in the dark. Minutes later, he heard the roar of a plane and more gunfire followed by a huge explosion. The woods lit up, and the random sound of ammo cooking off went on for several minutes. Finally, all was quiet. He heaved a huge sigh of relief when he heard the heavy front door of the farmhouse slam shut.

Downstairs a single candle was burning, but it illuminated the shambles. Lamps had been tossed aside, chairs upended.

Guy de Noailles was knocking lightly at the door of the pantry. "*Ils sont partis*," he whispered. From inside came a sob. Then the door opened, and Marguerite and the child fell into his arms.

Diamanté went into the wine cellar.

"All clear, *mon ami*," he said in a low voice.

Bernard pushed a rack of wine bottles aside and emerged from the back of the false brick wall.

"The dog was shot," Diamanté said as they came back into the kitchen. "I'm going out to try to find him."

"We can't risk it," Guy said, shaking his head. He looked at his daughter. "Hannibal is brave. He'll survive. I know it."

The little girl held onto his hand.

Guy turned to Diamanté. "You are a courageous man, but this is not the time. The SS may return. We could all be killed. We can't risk everything."

Diamanté and Bernard went upstairs to their room. Still concerned, Diamanté peered out the window toward the barn. In the moonlit farmyard, there was no sign of Hannibal.

Chapter Twenty-Five

On July 18, a crumpled envelope was left in the lobby of the Hôtel Saint-Jacques in Paris. Marcel never saw who delivered it. By the time he reached the front desk, the person was gone.

"This arrived for you today," he said, handing it to Ferdinand later as they ate their midday meal.

Inside was a note from Sara, Bernard's girlfriend.

> *Bernard told me to let you know if I am all right since you are his only trusted friend.*
>
> *The day after he left, the police came pounding on the door of our apartment at dawn, and they arrested me. We were taken on buses to the Vél d'Hiv where we have been ever since. I say "we" because there are hundreds of us. Women and children, too. Entire families. Our neighbors in the apartment building. All Jews! We have no water or food. The heat is stifling, and the sanitary conditions are deplorable. The stench is unbearable. Some have committed suicide by jumping from the upper gallery. Rumors abound that we are to be deported. I never believed the French police would arrest women and children.*

If you see Bernard, please inform him about my predicament, and tell him that I love him. I have searched for him here in despair and hope he is safe. I will now give this note to someone who is determined to escape from this hellish place. If he succeeds, he will deliver it to you in person.

The note was signed S. Leszczynski. Ferdinand's hand trembled as he passed it over to Elise. "This is terrible," he said. "We have to try to do something."

Elise read quickly, tears filling her eyes. "*Oh là*. Those poor people. What can be done?"

Ferdinand was already out the door.

Chapter Twenty-Six

Ferdinand stood outside the Vélodrome d'Hiver in the fifteen arrondissement. The enormous indoor arena on rue Nélaton was reserved for cycling competitions, but on this stifling hot day in July 1942 it was a scene of misery and chaos. There were throngs of people detained inside behind barbed-wire fences, all of them with yellow stars sewn on their clothing. Women, their eyes white with fear, screamed in desperation as they begged for food and water for their crying children. He nearly gagged at the overpowering stench.

French police in their dark-blue knee-length capes and high, round caps stood around the perimeter, pushing back anyone who tried to escape. Ferdinand realized that there wasn't a gray-green uniform in sight. Not one round helmet. The Germans were staying away while the French did this to their own.

He recognized one of the policemen. He was young like himself, just over twenty. He had even chatted occasionally with the *flic* on rue Saint-Jacques. The man's forehead glistened with moisture.

"Can you help me?" Ferdinand asked. "I've come to find someone."

"Go home," the officer growled as he dabbed at the moist patch under his nose. "It's none of your business."

"But…" Ferdinand tried to think. "I…I have a message for a girl whom I believe to be inside."

"Then give it to me," the man said gruffly. "I'll see to its delivery."

The coldness in the policeman's eyes told Ferdinand a message would never be delivered. As he looked over at the writhing throng of humanity behind the cruel barrier, the face of a young woman stared at him. Was it Sara?

He walked a few steps forward, but another policeman grabbed his shoulder and shoved him harshly backward. He caught himself before he lost his balance.

The woman was still staring at him. He had always been struck by Sara's beauty—her alabaster skin, hazel eyes, curly light-brown hair. This woman's face was dirty, her hair in disarray, and her eyes looked sallow and circled with black as if she had not slept for days, but it was Sara. He was certain of it, and she was mouthing a question to him: Bernard?

Ever so slowly, Ferdinand moved his head up and down. She smiled.

Ferdinand had an orange in his pocket. How, he wondered, could he get it to her? With all these desperate people, she would surely be trampled if he tried to toss it over the fence. He went around the side of the stadium, looking for another exit. Maybe he could get closer, he thought.

Sara moved her way through the crowd, watching him, keeping up with him. On the far side of the stadium, he stopped. Police were everywhere. The yelling and screaming was deafening. Those who tried to escape were beaten back. It made him sick to his stomach. He took one last look at Sara. Her sad eyes were filled with tears.

"He…loves…you," he mouthed. Then he quickly tossed the orange over the fence to her.

Tears streamed from her eyes.

A policeman pulled Ferdinand to the ground and whacked him with his baton. "*Con!*" he said, kicking him in the hip. "Damn fool! *Allez! Foutez le camp!*" Get the hell out of here!

***

"What will happen to them?" Elise asked Ferdinand later as she cleaned and bandaged the cut on his forehead.

Ferdinand shook his head. "Marcel says they are to be deported."

"To where?"

Ferdinand looked at her with great sadness in his eyes. "To the camps."

Chapter Twenty-Seven

The rumble of thunder jolted Diamanté awake. He had slept fitfully overnight, listening as SS patrols roamed the countryside. At the sound of a vehicle pulling into the farmyard driveway, he picked up his Walther and rose quickly from the bed.

Bernard was standing by the window. "It's Lemonier," he said.

Outside, the sky was gunmetal gray, and heavy rain was falling. They watched the doctor climb out of his beaten-up old truck and scurry into the farmhouse under a black umbrella.

Minutes later there was a gentle tap on the bedroom door.

"*Oui?*" Diamanté said in a low voice.

"*C'est* Marguerite."

He opened the door. Guy's wife stood in the darkened hallway. The scent of lavender drifted into the room.

"You leave this morning," she told them after a quick *bonjour*. "Guy delivers fresh produce to the restaurant in Rouen today. Come down now and have something to eat before you depart."

"How is the American?" Diamanté asked as they descended the stairs.

"Not good." She sighed. "He hasn't awakened. Hubert has come again this morning to tend to him."

In the kitchen, Hannibal, his head bandaged, was asleep in the corner by the wood-burning stove. The girl, Nathalie, sat cross-legged on the floor next to him.

Diamanté went over and crouched beside them. The morning after the SS raid, Diamanté had searched for Hannibal everywhere and had finally found him curled up behind a rabbit hutch. The bullet had grazed his head and part of an ear was missing, but he'd survived. Diamanté patted the dog's paw. The canine opened one soulful eye.

Guy de Noailles looked up from his newspaper. "We have just had some news from Lemonier," he said. "The search for the aviator apparently has been called off. A British flier was arrested last night in the nearby woods."

Diamanté sat down at the table next to Bernard. He picked up a piece of bread and spread a generous helping of sweet butter and fruit preserves over the length of it. "Unfortunate for the Brit," he said.

Outside the storm hadn't let up. Cracks of thunder chased bright flashes of lightning in the darkened sky, and rain streaked across the windowpanes.

Marguerite set cups of cider in front of them. "There's coffee, too," she offered. "That is, if you want some."

Diamanté and Bernard shook their heads. For the past two days, they'd tried the bitter-tasting liquid chicory that substituted for real coffee. "The cider will do," Diamanté said. "*Merci*."

Guy leaned forward and looked over his reading glasses at Diamanté. "Lemonier said the patrols found a parachute hidden in some bushes near the clearing not far from the house." He paused. "Next time you rescue someone, bury the evidence, *mon ami*."

Diamanté wiped his forehead with the palm of his hand. "I should have thought of that."

"If it hadn't been for those Spitfires," Guy lamented, "we might have all been shot. As it is, we are on high alert. It's unknown whether all of the members of the patrol were killed when the truck exploded." He shook his head. "Now, *mes amis*, finish your breakfast. We should be on our way."

***

In the barn, Diamanté and Bernard helped Guy load the back of the truck with crates of fresh vegetables; baskets of apples, turnips, and potatoes; and a cage of live rabbits. Guy motioned for Bernard to fit himself into the open space in the middle. Then he placed flats of fresh eggs over him.

"Climb into the cab," Guy said to Diamanté as he tossed a canvas over the entire top of the truck bed and tied its corners securely to the sides.

"What if there are checkpoints?" Diamanté asked.

Guy shook his head. "With the rain, there will be very few today." He hoisted himself into the driver's seat and started the engine. "On a stormy day such as this, the *Boches* generally pass the time drinking beer in the local bars, but have your papers ready just in case. As far as we are concerned, I'm making my weekly delivery to the restaurant in

Rouen. Remain calm and don't say anything. I often have riders. I generally offer anyone dressed in *feldgrau* a rabbit or some apples," he chuckled, "whatever they choose. Marguerite puts the rotten vegetables on the top. Then they let me pass without any trouble." The truck's engine sputtered and died. "*Merde*," he said. "The Nazis have taken all the gasoline for their military, so we improvise."

Guy started the engine again, put the truck in gear, and let out the clutch.

"What are you running on?" Diamanté asked.

Guy winked. "You don't want to know, but you will notice a terrible smell once we get going."

Chapter Twenty-Eight

The dirt road was muddy and full of ruts, and a light mist fell as they approached the outskirts of Rouen.

"There is always a checkpoint just before entering the city," Guy warned. "Let me do the talking."

Ten minutes later, Guy slowed the truck as two Nazi soldiers, rifles pointed directly at them, appeared in the fog just ahead. A third armed soldier, his face expressionless, held up his hand.

Guy pulled up and shut off the engine. "This isn't normal," he said to Diamanté in a low voice. "Gestapo. They're looking for someone."

The officer came forward with his rifle pointed at them. "*Ausweis*," he demanded, his eyes darting back and forth between Guy and Diamanté.

Guy handed over his papers while Diamanté assessed the scene. On the right side of the road, two soldiers sat inside the cab of a *Wehrmacht* transport truck. On the left, another leaned against the back of a Czech-made Skoda automobile, the preferred vehicle of the Gestapo. His foot was on the running board, and he was smoking a cigarette. All six were in SS gray uniforms, but the collar patches were plain black without insignias, as were the cuff bands, and they wore the police-pattern shoulder boards of the Gestapo.

The officer glanced at Guy's permit briefly then returned it to him. "*Wie wärs mit passagier?*"

Guy nodded toward Diamanté. "Show him your identification," he instructed.

Diamanté handed over his papers.

The man studied them briefly. Still holding them, he walked to the back of the truck, untied one corner of the canvas, and peered underneath.

"*Ich habe Kaninchen heute,*" Guy hollered. "*Auf der Käfig. Helfen dir.*"

"*Ja?*"

Curious, the officer untied the other corner, then lifted the entire canvas to expose the produce. After carefully selecting an apple from one of the baskets, he began prodding the crates with his bayonet.

Thunder rolled in the distance.

Diamanté felt for the Walther in his pocket.

"Remain calm," Guy whispered under his breath. "We're outnumbered."

One of the trays in the center, under which Bernard was hiding, tipped dangerously. Eggs rolled and tumbled over the edge. The officer plunged his bayonet into the space below.

Meanwhile the sky continued to darken, the wind picked up, and there was a sudden flash followed almost immediately by a deafening clap of thunder. Then the rain fell, sheets of it, mixed with pellets of hail.

"*Scheiße,*" the officer said as he quickly opened the cage of rabbits and selected a fat hare. He went around to Diamanté's side of the cab, tossed his identity papers to him, and said, "*GehenSie,*" as he headed for the shelter of the transport truck.

The two soldiers who had been standing guard in the road waved them through and deserted their positions.

Guy started the engine and coaxed the truck into gear. As soon as they were out of sight of the checkpoint, he pulled over and stopped.

Diamanté climbed out, wrenched the canvas back over the produce, and quickly retied the corners. Peering underneath, he whistled a short high-low, two-tone signal.

From under the center of the truck bed, there came a soft response. Smiling, Diamanté climbed back into the cab and winked at Guy. "Our friend is OK. He was whistling 'La Marseillaise' just now."

***

They followed the quay along the Seine until they reached rue Jeanne-d'Arc. Just short of the rue du Gros-Horloge, Guy made a sharp turn into a back alley and came to a stop behind a restaurant. Through the streaks of rain on the windshield, Diamanté could see the double towers of the great Rouen cathedral, looking exactly like one of Claude Monet's paintings.

A stout woman in a long gray apron met them. "*Vite vite!*" she called, shouting orders to her assistants as she pulled the canvas from the truck bed.

While the kitchen staff unloaded the baskets and crates, Diamanté carefully lifted the trays of eggs from the center.

Bernard climbed out of his hiding place. Wet and covered with broken eggshells and yellow yolk, he removed his splattered wire-rimmed glasses and wiped them with his shirttail.

"*Oh là là*," the woman exclaimed when she saw his trousers caked in dried blood. "You are injured."

"It's nothing. Just a scratch."

"*Merde*. The bastard got you with the bayonet," Diamanté said.

"*Oui mais*, I was lucky," Bernard said. "It barely grazed my leg."

The woman shook Guy's hand, then introduced herself to Diamanté. "Marie-Thérèse La Forêt," she said. "Come quickly." She hurried them through the doorway and down the back stairs of the restaurant.

A familiar odor, a musty combination of mildew and fermenting wine, greeted them.

Marie-Thérèse led them into a small space and lit a candle. One wall of the chamber was lined with wine bottles. A table with two wooden chairs sat in the middle. She set the candle into a holder on the table and instructed Bernard to have a seat on a cot in the corner. "Wait here. I'll be back to have a look at your wound." Then she motioned to Diamanté and Guy. "This way," she said as she pushed aside a large barrel. "They're waiting for you."

They slipped behind a deliberately deceptive brick wall into a cavernous room. Stacks of huge wine barrels lined the walls. A single lantern on a crude wooden table in the center illuminated the faces of a small group of men who had gathered to meet them.

A short, thickset man wearing the traditional double-paneled white coat and apron of a sous-chef rose and came forward. He shook Guy's hand.

"This is Jacques Gérard," Guy said to Diamanté, "the man who is responsible for saving our country's wine."

Jacques chuckled. "With wine and hope, anything is possible." He shook Diamanté's hand. "I understand you are from Corsica," he said. "*Moi aussi.*"

Diamanté's eyes brightened. "*Ié,*" he affirmed in his native *Corsu*. "Castagglione."

"*Ah bon. Moi*, I come from Ajaccio, birthplace of Napoléon."

Diamanté smiled.

Guy nodded to a stocky man in a suit who was having trouble standing upright due to his height. "This is Léo La Bergère."

Diamanté shook the man's hand.

"Léo is a stockbroker," Guy said.

"He is also our financier," Jacques added.

"In addition to being the restaurant's most loyal customer," Léo added with a wink. "My first love is food."

Diamanté laughed.

Pierre Truette was introduced next. The thin priest, dressed entirely in black, bowed in greeting. "I am pleased to meet you," he said to Diamanté.

The men returned to their places at the table. Jacques invited Guy and Diamanté to sit with them.

Jacques cleared his throat. Directing his comments to Diamanté, he said, "The reason we've asked *you* to join us is this: using fishing boats to escape via the channel is getting too dangerous. We need to organize an alternate route."

Diamanté's eyes lit up. "To the south."

"*Oui. Exacte.*"

Diamanté leaned forward. "*Eh bien,* the Maquis is setting up safe houses in the unoccupied zone now. We deliver the evaders to the Basques who then lead them over the Pyrenees. It is a perilous journey, but it seems to be the only alternative."

"Can we count on you to coordinate a southern route for us?" Jacques asked.

Diamanté looked at them a moment, then nodded and said, "*Mais, bien sûr.*"

The group let out a collective sigh.

Jacques tapped the back of his knuckles on the table. "That is just what we hoped. Now then…" He fished a map of France from his pocket and spread it in front of them.

The others listened intently as he explained the desperate need to set up an escape line from the German-occupied zone in the north to free France in the south.

Diamanté moved his index finger across the map, zigzagging from Paris to Bourges, Lyon, Avignon, and Marseilles. "We have to get them to here," he said, drawing his finger straight west across the entire width of the country. "From here," he said, pointing to the city of Dax, "they go on foot to Spain."

While he was talking, a man entered the cellar. Without greeting any of them, he pulled a chair from the back corner, placed it by a wine barrel, and sat down.

Jacques looked up. "How did it go, *mon ami?*" he asked.

"A success," the latecomer said in a low, raspy voice. "It will be in all the papers. There is no question of retaliation." Twitching his mouth nervously from side to side like a rodent, the man scanned the faces around the table and stopped abruptly at Diamanté. His eyes narrowed behind his thick, square, dark-rimmed glasses.

"Ah, as you see, we have a visitor," Jacques said. He turned to Diamanté. "This man is known to us only as *l'Écureuil*. He does not wish for his true identity to be revealed."

Diamanté stared at the man known as the Squirrel. He didn't need to know his real name; he already knew it.

***

A half hour later, the meeting ended, and Guy stood. "I must leave," he said. He shook Diamanté's hand warmly. "*Bon voyage, mon ami.* I'll see you again soon, I hope?"

"I'll be back for the American when he is well enough to travel," Diamanté said.

"*À bientôt, alors. Au revoir, mes amis clandestins.*" Guy waved to the others.

"*Les amis clandestins*," Léo repeated enthusiastically. "That's it! Our name. We'll call ourselves Les Amis Clandestins."

Heads bobbed in agreement, and there was handshaking all around. The mood in the cellar changed from serious to buoyant. Jacques opened a bottle of red wine and poured a round of the thick *vin du pays* for everyone. They held their glasses high in the air and toasted in unison. "France *Toujours* France."

***

Diamanté and the latecomer remained in the cellar after the others departed.

"I didn't expect to see *you* here, André," Diamanté said finally.

The man removed his eyeglasses, then snatched a handkerchief from his pocket and began to wipe them. He took his time, not looking at Diamanté. Finally, he slowly placed the spectacles back on the bridge of his nose. His thick eyebrows rose slightly. "Nor I you," he sniffed.

Diamanté had not seen André Narbon in three years, but his hatred for his half brother had never waned. He cleared his throat. "I barely recognized you."

"Ah, the glasses, *oui*. I had bad luck. I lost part of my sight in a grenade attack a year ago. Shrapnel." André looked up. "How is it you are with the Maquis now?"

"*Bon bref,* I was working in a factory in Marseilles. A month ago, the Vichy issued the first decree for obligatory labor conscription, the STO. I went to my boss, demanded the wages owed me, and fled into the countryside to join up."

André Narbon rubbed the stubble of whiskers on his chin. His black eyes, magnified to at least twice their size by bottle-thick lenses, glared at Diamanté. "*Eh bien,* which of you was it? You or Ferdinand? The coward who killed my father?"

Diamanté studied the rows of bottles, weighing his answer. "I did," he said finally.

André raised his eyebrows as if surprised. "*Tiens*," he said. "Really." He curled his lip. "I don't believe you." He stood and spat into a bucket. "You wouldn't have had the courage." With that, he left the cellar.

***

Jacques came for Bernard just after midnight. He was dressed entirely in black and had rubbed soot on his face.

"*C'est l'heure*," he announced, handing Bernard a hooded, waterproof jacket and black rubber boots. Time to depart.

Bernard put on the gear and bid Diamanté a nervous farewell. "The butterfly has found the sunflower," he said. "That will be my message. If you hear it on the wireless, you will know I have joined de Gaulle." He took a step up the stairs, then stopped. "When you return to Paris," he said, "will you go see Sara?" His voice caught. "Tell her that I love her."

Diamanté nodded and wished him *bon voyage*.

***

Diamanté slept fitfully that night. A moonless sky along the coast, Bernard climbing into the fishing boat, the rough channel crossing, all played out in his dreams. Repeatedly the hateful eyes of his half brother appeared, staring at him through the bottle-thick lenses. Then, abruptly, the eyes would change to those of his stepfather, lying lifeless in the maquis. Larenzu's dead eyes, gazing at him through André's square, dark-rimmed glasses. Awakening each time, soaking in sweat and in a state of panic, he would go back to sleep only to experience the recurring nightmare. By morning, he was exhausted. All he wanted to do was return to Paris and hold Elise in his arms.

Chapter Twenty-Nine

Epinay

Stu Ellis awoke in a place he didn't recognize. He looked around the small dormer room. It reminded him of the one he had grown up in on the farm back home in Wisconsin. The air was stuffy, he felt claustrophobic, and his head ached. Midday light streamed through the slats of the partially closed shutters. He coughed, and the pain in his side almost made him pass out.

"Jesus Christ," he swore.

With his left hand he pulled back the white linen coverlet. His right arm was in a sling, his right leg immobilized in a splint. Except for a pair of undershorts, he was naked. He looked around the room for his clothes. There was an armoire and a small chest. On the table beside the bed lay his personal items: the escape kit he thought he'd never need, his dog tags. He tried to raise himself, but the pain was too great.

A woman opened the door, entered, and came over to the bed.

"Ah, *vous vous réveillez*," she said when she saw he had awakened. "*Bonjour, Monsieur*."

"No speak French," he grunted.

She put up an index finger. "*Oui oui, Monsieur. Un moment.*"

"Well, that much French I understand," Stu said to himself, fingering his bandaged side. He winced in pain. What he wouldn't give for a cigarette.

***

Marguerite descended to the kitchen where Guy was sitting at the table reading the latest issue of *L'Action Française* that had been secretly delivered during the night.

"The American has awakened," she announced.

"Ah *bon!*" he exclaimed, putting the paper down. "Can he talk?"

"*Oui, mais*, he doesn't speak French."

Guy smiled. "*Tiens. Alors*, I'll be able to practice my English."

He got up and put his arms around her. "Are you feeling better this morning, *mon coeur?*"

She patted his shoulder. "It's nothing. Merely fatigue from the pregnancy, *chéri. C'est tout.*"

He bussed her cheek. "Nevertheless, you are so pale. I worry about you."

She smiled and brushed him away. "Don't fret over me, *chéri*. Go, see to our guest." She handed him a bottle of the region's strong apple brandy and a glass. "Give him some of this. It will make him feel better."

He disappeared through the pantry door and climbed the wooden steps to the room above.

Stu was sitting up, staring at a map of France spread out on his lap. He raised his head when Guy entered the room but said nothing.

Guy poured a glass of the brandy and held it out to him.

"Here. Drink," he said slowly in English. "Is good for the pain."

The young pilot's eyes opened wide. "You speak English?" he mumbled.

Guy nodded. "Not too much."

"Where…am…I?" Stu asked, pointing to the silk map the US Army had provided in his escape kit.

"Epinay," Guy said, "in Normandy. Your plane crash near to our farm."

Stu ran his fingers through his short, cropped, sandy-blond hair. "The last I remember I had to bail out. The engines were on fire."

Guy shook his head. "You were hanging in a tree. Man who save you not here. He cut you down and carry you to house before *Boches* find you."

"I owe him a great deal." Stu offered his left hand. "By the way, I'm Stu Ellis. I'm not a Brit."

"You are Yank. I see your papers," Guy said, shaking his hand and noting that, in spite of his injuries, Stu Ellis had a very robust handshake. "Welcome."

The pilot took the glass. "What is this?" he asked.

"Calvados. Local cider."

Guy sat down on a wooden chair by the bed. "My name is Guy de Noailles," he said.

Stu took a sip of the liquid and choked.

Guy chuckled. "I know, is strong."

"I need to leave at once, ah, *Monsieur*—what did you say your last name was again?"

"Noailles, but just call me Guy."

"Guy," Stu nodded, directing hazel eyes at his host. "There's a problem. I don't have any clothes."

Guy laughed and stroked his handlebar mustache. "*Oui*. I agree. Is problem. But you not ready to leave yet. When you are, we have clothes for you." He motioned to the glass. "Now drink. And then you need rest. My wife, Marguerite, bring you food."

Stu smiled for the first time. "How about a cigarette?"

Guy nodded. "I think I can manage that."

Chapter Thirty

Jacques stood at the counter in the kitchen of Le Canard à la Rouennaise. A flat sous-chef's cap sat on the back of his head, and he was noisily chopping vegetables with a huge kitchen knife. Behind him, a kitchen assistant scrawled the menu items for the day on a blackboard hanging beneath a high shelf: *le plat du jour* (salmon with grilled tomatoes) and a five-course *prix fixe* menu consisting of cold gazpacho soup, a first course of *filet de sandre*, a freshwater fish, and a choice of main dishes (fricassee of summer vegetables, duck breast in honey lemon sauce, or rabbit stewed in wine), followed by salad, goat cheese, and wild plum *clafouti* for dessert.

Diamanté leaned against the massive fruitwood bar just outside the kitchen door watching Jacques and his assistant. To his left was the *salle*, the dining room, with its tablecloths the color of marigolds, cushioned wooden chairs, and lace-curtained windows. An antique chestnut sideboard, its worn and much-scarred top covered with bottles of wine, stood against one wall.

Seeing him, Jacques paused, set down his knife, and motioned for him to enter the kitchen. "*Du café?*" he offered, giving Diamanté a hearty handshake.

Diamanté raised his eyebrows.

"I get the real thing on the black market," Jacques whispered.

Diamanté noted that Jacques had switched to their native Corsican. He smiled, hoisted himself onto a tall stool, and leaned his elbows against the work surface. An ancient set of well-used copper cookware hung above them. "Did Bernard get off OK last night?" he asked, continuing the exchange in *Corsu*.

Jacques slid a small cup of coffee in front of him and poured hot milk into it.

"As far as we know, he did. The trip to the coast went smoothly. We won't hear soon if he made it all the way to England."

Diamanté took a sip of the *café au lait* and nodded his head in approval. "It's good."

Jacques smiled and returned to his task.

Diamanté looked around the kitchen. The crates of fresh vegetables Guy had delivered the day before lay all over the hard tiled floor. The door to the cellar was open, and he could see baskets of apples and fresh herbs. A steaming soup pot on the stove filled the room with a mouthwatering aroma. "This is the first real restaurant kitchen I've been in," he said. "I have a dream to own one of my own someday."

Jacques cocked his head. "*Ah bon?*" He offered Diamanté a croissant. "The first time I saw this place…" He drew in his breath. "I stood outside and just looked at it. I said, '*C'est ça qu'il me faut!*' I had to have it, and I will one day." He shrugged. "For now, I work."

"What's your specialty?"

"Duck. The name of the place, you know. *Le Canard à la Rouennaise*. It has to be."

Diamanté was intrigued. "How do you prepare it?"

Jacques wagged an index finger at him. "Ah, *mon ami*, it's a long process." He removed his white sous-chef's cap, then untied his apron and hung both on a hook by the door. "But for now, you need to catch the train. I'll see you to the *gare*. It's in the center of the city, not far from here."

Minutes later, they were walking down the rue du Gros-Horloge. The ancient clock for which the street was named towered overhead. They turned onto the rue Jeanne-d'Arc and passed the Palais de Justice. Jacques stepped up his pace at the sight of the Nazi flag flying over the front entrance of the historic Gothic structure. He spat, then spewed a string of expletives under his breath to punctuate the way he felt about the invaders.

Diamanté listened, amused. The man was thickset and built like a bull. It was no wonder the others called him *le Taureau*.

"Does everyone have a *nom de guerre?*"

Jacques nodded. "*Oui*. So no one can trace our real names or families. All animals. You met some of the group last night. Léo, for example, goes by *le Lion*. By the way, he is contributing his own personal fortune to make this escape line possible."

"*Admirable*," Diamanté said.

"*Oui. Très*." Jacques continued. "Then there is *Père* Truette who is known as *le Lapin* and Marie-Thérèse who wishes to be called the Hedgehog, *le Hérisson*." He laughed. "I don't know why. She doesn't look like one at all." He cleared his throat and went on. "And l'*Écureuil*. Now, that man looks exactly like his *nom de guerre*. Did you notice how he keeps twitching his nose from side to side like a squirrel?" He clucked his tongue. "He does a lot of the so-called dirty work for us. To tell the truth, he seems to enjoy killing."

"Always did," Diamanté mumbled to himself.

Jacques looked at Diamanté strangely.

"Do you two know each other?"

Diamanté shook his head. "I know the type," he said.

Jacques shrugged and nodded. "Do you have a name in mind? For you, I mean? With those eyes of yours, you should call yourself *le Loup*."

Diamanté chuckled. "Someone else told me that recently. A girl."

"*Your* girl?" Jacques asked.

Diamanté nodded and adjusted his beret lower on his forehead.

"What's her name?"

"Elise."

"Pretty?"

Diamanté nodded again.

"You going to marry her?"

"Someday, I hope."

They turned onto rue Verte. In front of them, a patrol of armed SS soldiers stood sentry over the large railway station.

"*Oh là là. La guarde*," Jacques said. "Here's where I bid you *au revoir. Bon courage, mon ami*." He held out his hand. "I hope to see you again soon."

Chapter Thirty-One

Paris

Diamanté and Elise strolled arm in arm along a meandering gravel pathway in the Luxembourg Gardens. They came to the Grand Bassin, the octagonal pond in the center of the park, and watched a group of children guiding wooden sailboats over the surface of the water. Late-afternoon sunlight filtered through the trees, and the fragrance of flowers floated on the warm summer breeze.

Elise sat down on a bench. Diamanté seated himself close to her.

"It's so peaceful here," she said wistfully. "I wish the war weren't…"

A butterfly fluttered around them for a moment, then drifted toward a colorful bed of flowers just behind the bench. Reminded of Bernard's message, Diamanté said, "The butterfly is looking for its sunflower, but I have found mine." He kissed her hand.

She turned suddenly to face him. "I don't want you to leave, *Lobo*." A fearful look crossed her face.

"What's wrong, *chérie?*" he asked. "Is something troubling you?"

She sighed. "*Oh là*. It's just that I…someone…"

"What is it?"

"Someone followed me this morning. A man. I feel him watching us now."

Diamanté turned to look behind them. "Only women and children are in the gardens," he said. "I don't see anyone suspicious."

"Maybe I'm being silly, but I was sure there *was* someone." She cleared her throat. "No, I'm certain of it. He followed me when I walked back to the hotel from the market, but he stayed at a distance."

Diamanté's brow furrowed. "What did the man look like, *chérie?*"

"He was short and wiry. That much I could tell. He moved very quickly, too. Every time I turned around, he darted into an alleyway."

"Would you recognize him? That is, if he *were* here in the park today?"

"*Oh là. Absolument*. He wore dark, square-rimmed glasses and had a pointy nose. Strange-looking man…like a rat."

Diamanté's pulse quickened. Only one person he knew could possibly fit that description, and it disturbed him. What was André up to? He scratched his cheek. Somehow he had learned about the Hôtel Saint-Jacques. Was it Marcel's involvement in the Résistance that had led him to Ferdinand? He felt the hair stand up on the back of his neck. If André were to harm Elise, he would kill him.

Elise buried her face in his shoulder. "I was so frightened. I think he must be a Nazi spy; he wasn't wearing a uniform. What do you suppose he wanted? Following me like that?"

Diamanté kissed her neck. "It's probably just a coincidence, *chérie*. Did you mention it to Ferdinand?"

She shook her head. "He's been preoccupied with the partisans. I didn't want to worry him."

He pulled back and looked into her eyes. "Have you told him yet? About us?"

"No, but I think he suspects."

"Why do you say that?"

She giggled. "He told me to put my best dress on today because you were returning to Paris."

"But how does that translate into suspicion?"

"He made that little kissing noise you Frenchmen make. You know." She pursed her lips. "He was suggesting to me that I would be doing a lot of it."

Diamanté chuckled. "And you are, too." He stood, pulled her to her feet, wrapped her in his arms, and kissed her for a long time.

A uniformed German officer sauntered casually along the pathway around the pond.

Diamanté cast a wary eye toward him as he approached and studied the lovers briefly, then moved on.

"Don't trust anyone," Diamanté whispered in Elise's ear.

Her bright blue eyes sparkled, and she nuzzled her nose against his. "Hurry back to me, *Lobo*."

He bussed her forehead. "*C'est promis*."

Chapter Thirty-Two

Late that evening, Ferdinand and Diamanté walked to the Gare de Lyon under the dim blue light of painted streetlamps in Paris's twelfth arrondissement. The day's stifling heat lingered, and both of them sweated profusely.

"Bernard made it to England, I assume?" Ferdinand asked.

Diamanté nodded. "We'll know for sure when we hear his message over the wireless."

"Message?"

"*Oui*. Just as he was departing, he said, 'If you hear the butterfly has found the sunflower, you will know I have joined de Gaulle.'" Diamanté sighed and added, "Too bad about Sara."

Ferdinand lit a cigarette. "I returned to the Vel d'Hiv a second time, hoping to see her, but it was deserted. She's likely been sent to the camps." He paused, a look of pain in his eyes. "You should have seen them. I can't get it out of my thoughts."

They crossed the Pont d'Austerlitz, followed the quay, and turned onto boulevard Diderot. Just past the rue Audubon, a Gestapo checkpoint had been set up. They watched from the shadows as two soldiers pulled a man out of line and shoved him against a wall. One of them raised his pistol. They heard a loud pop and then a thud as the man fell lifeless to the ground.

Ferdinand grabbed Diamanté's arm and whispered. "It's a sweep. Come on. I know a shortcut."

They ducked into a dark alley. Halfway, Ferdinand stopped and rapped three times on a recessed door. They waited, nervously looking around them. The dark shapes of boxes and stacks of rotting garbage formed shadows that seemed to move in the moonlight. A rat made them jump as it scurried from behind a bin and ran down the alleyway. Finally they heard the click of the bolt, and the portal opened just wide enough for two suspicious eyes to scrutinize them. A hand hurriedly pushed the door wider and motioned for them to enter, and almost immediately the door slammed shut, and they found themselves in total darkness. The space reeked of sweat and garlic, and someone breathed heavily next to them.

A second later, the bolt clicked loudly back into place, and an interior door opened. Bright light flooded the small passageway.

A rotund man with a grizzled beard and wiry salt-and-pepper hair wiped his hand on his soiled gray apron before extending his hand. "Ferdinand!" he exclaimed. "*Salut, mon ami.*"

Ferdinand shook the man's hand. "Henri is the proprietor of this bar," he explained, adding, a touch of sarcasm in his voice, "It is frequented by the Boches, so it's safe."

Henri sneered. "*Ah oui, mes amis.* They're always here. They love the Alsatian beer I serve." He leaned toward them, held his hand to his mouth, and winked. "To which I add my own secret ingredient." He spat. "Pthooey."

Diamanté and Ferdinand chuckled.

Henri showed them to a table at the back of the rowdy, smoke-filled bar. "Do you want a beer? I promise I won't…" He spat and winked again.

Diamanté looked warily around the room. Most of the patrons wore gray-green uniforms. In the corner, a group was singing a German drinking song and swinging mugs of lager high into the air.

Henri returned with two heavy beer steins and placed them on the table. "The sweep is just about done," he whispered. "They'll come in here afterward. I'll keep watch. You should leave as soon as I give you the signal."

"Who are they searching for?" Ferdinand asked.

"*Bof*. There was a high-level official murdered night before last in Normandy. His staff car was stopped on a bridge. All three occupants were killed. The *Boches* have proclaimed a curfew, and they're looking all over Paris for the assassin." He leaned forward. "*Merde*. So far, they've shot five suspects."

One of the patrons shouted in German from the zinc bar.

"*On arrive*," Henri grumbled. "That one," he whispered under his breath, "he's getting three doses of my special ingredient."

Diamanté lifted his beret and wiped the perspiration from his brow. The place was stuffy, and the raucous atmosphere made him nervous.

Ferdinand took a sip of his beer and glowered at the crowd.

"Elise told me today she thinks she is being followed," Diamanté said.

Ferdinand raised an eyebrow at the mention of Elise.

"She described the *mec*," Diamanté continued. He paused and sighed. "I have to tell you. It could be André."

There was a sudden outburst of laughter in the bar. Ferdinand frowned. "André Narbon, our half brother?"

Diamanté nodded. "The same. He has surfaced. I saw him in Rouen." He shrugged. "He was barely recognizable. Wore thick glasses. He said his eyesight was damaged in a grenade attack."

"*Merde alors!*" Ferdinand lowered his voice to a whisper. "Why was he in Normandy?"

"He's joined Les Amis Clandestins. They call him *l'Écureuil*."

"Do you think he's the assassin they're looking for here?"

Diamanté took a sip of his beer and leaned forward. "It's possible, *mon frère*. He's well trained, and we know he's capable of it."

Ferdinand's eyes widened. "Why do you believe he's the one who's following Elise?"

"The description she gave matches perfectly. *C'était lui. J'en suis certain*."

Ferdinand downed a gulp of his beer and set the heavy stein on the tabletop. "He's after me, isn't he?"

Diamanté considered his brother for a minute. Ferdinand's black eyes blazed at him like a bull's. Finally, he said, "He asked which of us killed old Larenzu."

"And what did you tell him?"

They were interrupted by the "tat tat tat" of rapid machine-gun fire outside in the street. The door opened, and five men in Gestapo uniforms entered the bar.

Ferdinand and Diamanté lowered their heads so they wouldn't be seen.

Henri nodded in their direction, then spat twice and winked.

Ferdinand grabbed his beret and slid out of his seat. "Come on. Let's beat it."

They ducked around the back of the zinc and left as they had entered.

***

They arrived at the Gare de Lyon a few minutes later.

"I'll return to Paris soon," Diamanté said. "Once I have things in place in Marseilles."

"There's much to do, *mon frère*. We're setting dynamite tonight…in the freight yard."

Ferdinand turned suddenly to Diamanté. He clenched and unclenched his fist. "There's something we need to discuss before you leave."

"It's about Elise, isn't it?"

"I would punch you in the face if you weren't my brother." Ferdinand's jaw tightened, and his eyes bore into Diamanté's.

Diamanté pulled back. His brother had a fiery Corsican temper, and he rarely let his anger show, but tonight Diamanté had seen it erupt twice. Both times it had been directed at him.

"Have you proposed marriage?" Ferdinand asked.

Diamanté shook his head. "*Non*. Not yet."

Ferdinand's eyes narrowed. He shoved his hands into his pockets and turned to walk away. "*Alors*, you've won this battle, *mon frère,* but the war isn't over. *Au revoir.*"

Diamantè lit a cigarette and waited until Ferdinand disappeared into a side street. As he turned to walk into the train station, he saw a dark figure watching him.

Chapter Thirty-Three

Two Months Later

Stu Ellis sat in bed thinking about Claire, his girl back in the States. She had probably been told by now that he was missing in action. "Presumed dead," he said aloud. What must she be feeling? He combed his fingers through his hair. Maybe he shouldn't have been such a hotshot, breaking ranks like that, abandoning formation just to pursue that goddamned *Messerschmitt*. He threw back the bed linen and eased his leg over the side. The cane Guy had given him was propped against the wall. He fingered it. Would he ever be able to walk without help again? He stood, lit a crumpled rolled cigarette, and inhaled. *Ingenious, these frogs. Who would have thought dried rose petals would make a pretty good smoke?*

Just then, he heard the sound of a vehicle pulling into the driveway. The farm's droopy-eared German shepherd barked. Taking one painful step at a time, Stu inched his way slowly over to peek out the open window. Heeding Guy's warning not to allow himself to be seen, he stood back a few feet from it.

The air was still, and the sun shone brightly in the midday sky. Below he saw a truck parked in front of the farmhouse. On its side panel was a graphic of a man's suit with large hand-painted letters *Tailleur à la Mode – Service 24 heures*. A curious black metal unit hung off the side. Stu guessed it was one of those wood gas generators Guy had talked about.

He watched as a short, white-haired man opened the door and stepped from the cab. He was wearing tan trousers, a black vest, and a white shirt. At the same time, Madame de Noailles came from the garden carrying a huge basket filled with fresh fruits and vegetables. After some discussion, the man loaded the basket into the truck bed, then in turn handed her a bundle wrapped in brown paper and tied with twine. They had made an exchange of some sort. Stu watched as the man climbed back into the truck, put on his beret, waved, and drove off.

Seconds later, there was a knock at his door. Stu dove for the bed.

"*Oui?*" he said, covering his bare legs quickly.

Marguerite came into the room carrying the package she had just received from the visitor. "*Pour vous, monsieur*," she said with a smile. She placed the parcel on his lap and motioned for him to untie the string.

Folded neatly inside the paper was a pair of dark-blue cotton work pants. He held them up.

Marguerite's eyes sparkled. "*Un moment.*" She put up an index finger and hurried out of the room. Within seconds, she returned with her husband.

"My wife work on surprise for you," Guy told him in English.

Marguerite placed a pile of clothing on the bed and a pair of well-worn shoes at the foot. Finally, she produced a black beret that she proceeded to position on Stu's head. She stood back and scrutinized him, making further adjustments and mumbling to herself until, at last, she seemed satisfied that he looked just right.

Guy chuckled. "She is *perfectionniste*, my Marguerite, when it comes to *la mode*. My friend, the tailor Christophe, made you trousers. He measure you while you were still *inconscient,* how you say, not conscious. The shirt is an old one of mine. Marguerite say it fit you." He looked down at the shoes. "Those may be too tight." He shrugged and played with his mustache. "If so, we try find someone else your size." He chuckled. "Then, too, you might want to try our wooden clogs."

"Damn. Wish I could just wear my flight boots," Stu said.

"They would immediately identify you as American," Guy responded. "We had to bury them with your flight suit." He studied Stu's chiseled chin, sandy-blond hair, and hazel eyes. "As it is, we have our challenge."

After Guy left the room, Stu inspected the pile of clothing. There were two pairs of French undershorts with buttons, a light-blue cotton shirt, and a short wool jacket. He pulled on the baggy trousers. A rope had been provided for a belt. Next, he put on the shirt. The fabric was rough and old, and the wool jacket, too, was moth-eaten and crumpled.

"I look like a goddamned frog," he grumbled aloud as he studied himself in the mirror over the washbasin.

Behind him, Guy chuckled.

Stu jumped. "Oh sorry," he mumbled. "I didn't know you had come back."

Guy put up his hand. "*Ça suffit*," he said. "I understand. It is not your style, but you must blend in as much as possible. Marguerite bring something to make your hair a bit darker.

We see what we can do to transform you into *authentique*…" he chuckled and his eyes twinkled, "genuine frog, as you say." He handed over a set of papers.

Stu studied his new identity card. The photo on it had come with his evasion kit.

"Albert?" he said. "What kind of French name is that?"

"Is pronounced *Ahll-bear*," Guy corrected him. "The 't,' it is silent."

"Alber…" Stu repeated.

"The last name is Delon."

"Alber Delo."

"The address can not be traced. The village, how you say, *détruit,* destroyed by *les Boches* two years ago."

"What's this?" Stu asked, holding up another paper.

"Show it if you are stopped. It say you are *sourd et muet,* deaf and dumb. That way, you don't have to speak or understand, and it will guarantee that you won't be sent to forced labor in Germany."

Stu nodded in approval. "Clever."

Guy handed Stu a handful of French coins and instructed him not to jangle them in his pocket.

"Why is that?" Stu asked.

"Only Americans do that. The French don't want anyone to know they have any money."

Stu studied the coins in the palm of his hand. "Guess I've got a lot to learn."

Guy turned toward the door. "Come down to the kitchen when you ready. I have someone for you to meet."

Stu raised an eyebrow. "Who is it?"

"The man who saved your life."

***

Downstairs in the kitchen, two men sat with Guy at the table having a glass of Calvados. They wore black berets, crumpled overalls, and a bandolier of rifle cartridges strapped across their chests. Both had a hard-eyed look.

Stu gulped.

"Ah, *le voilà notre Américain*," Guy said.

The men stood. The taller of the two smiled and offered his hand. "*Bonjour*," he said. "Loupré-Tigre."

"Stu Ellis. Er," Stu looked over at Guy. "I mean Alber Delo." He flashed a wide smile. "Glad to meet ya."

The second man offered his hand. "Jacques Gérard."

"Which one saved my life?" Stu asked Guy in English.

"The one who is known as *le Loup*," he replied, pointing at Diamanté. "The Wolf."

"Ze Wolf," Stu repeated, imitating Guy's accent. "Well, *merci*, Monsieur Wolf, for savin' my life."

Diamanté chuckled. "You look *beaucoup* better."

Stu grinned at him. "I owe you, sir."

Diamanté lowered his eyes. "It was nothing."

"These two men will take you to the South," Guy explained, "to the unoccupied zone. You must do exactly as they tell you."

Stu smiled. "How soon can we leave?"

Guy laughed at his youthful eagerness. "Tomorrow. But first, there are a few things you need to know. Have a seat, Albert."

Over a country dinner of stewed chicken and vegetables, Stu was given his last-minute instructions. They would go on bicycle in single file, he was told. He was not to talk or make any noise, stay close and not fall behind.

"Follow orders," Guy admonished, "and keep your beret on."

Chapter Thirty-Four

Stu had passed a restless night, and he was anxious to be on his way. When the first light of dawn began to peek through the shuttered window, he was already dressed.

"Now for the final touch," he said as he sniffed the contents of a jar Marguerite had given him. The odd-smelling paste she said she had made from blueberries and carrots was supposed to tint his hair a shade or two darker. With a finger, he scooped up a small amount and combed it in.

"Well, I'll be," he exclaimed. His sandy-colored hair had turned brown. He put on the beret and studied himself in the mirror. "*Bonjour, Albert Delon.*" The image, looking almost French, grinned back at him. He pursed his lips like he had seen Guy do. What was it they said? The equivalent of "pleased to meet ya." Oh hell, he couldn't remember.

He folded his new identification papers and placed them in the pack Guy had given him. After one last look around the room where he had spent the past eight weeks convalescing, he shut the door and descended the narrow stairway to the first floor.

Marguerite was working at the kitchen sink. She smiled when she saw him and wiped her hands on her apron. "*Bon-

jour, Albert," she said, nodding her head in approval as she checked out his hair color and fussed with the placement of his beret. "*Ils vous attendent*."

Stu looked confused.

She laughed and pointed in the direction of the front door. "*Là-bas*."

They were set to depart just after daybreak. It was the first Stu had been outside since the night he'd been shot down. He lit a crumpled rolled cigarette, looked up at the sky, and breathed in the fresh morning air. The farm dog wagged its tail and came over to greet him. Stu patted its head, and it licked his fingers.

Diamanté and Jacques pushed two bicycles from the barn. Guy was behind them with a third.

"You ride my daughter's *bicyclette*," he said to Stu.

Stu scratched his head. The bicycle had no center bar. "A girl's bike?"

"It better for your leg."

Marguerite came from the house and handed him an item of clothing. "*C'est pour vous*," she said with tears in her eyes.

Stu held the soft white shirt up to his chest.

"My wife had it made for you," Guy said, "with the silk from your parachute."

"Well, I'll be." Stu smiled at her. "Thanks. I mean, er." He scratched his jaw and corrected himself. "I mean, mercy, Marguerite. This will be my good luck charm."

Marguerite beamed and hugged him goodbye.

Guy patted his shoulder and wished him courage. "Come back and visit us," he said, "after war is *fini*."

Stu promised he would.

The three mounted their bicycles. Diamanté led the way; Jacques brought up the rear. In between, Stu struggled to keep his bike from toppling over. "Goddamn leg," he mumbled under his breath, wondering if he would have the strength to go on all day.

"No talk," Diamanté hissed.

***

They rode through gently sloping hills and dense forests, past small farms, cows, and orchards of apple trees. Occasionally they would enter a centuries-old village. In the square, there was always a stone church, a town hall, and a monument to the soldiers who had died during the Great War. The Nazi flag flew from the government buildings, and patrols passed.

The danger of being discovered was constant. They walked along with their heads down, and Diamanté carried two dead rabbits over his shoulder, *assurance*, he had said with a wink.

More than once when they were stopped and asked to show their papers, he and Jacques were questioned about the rifles they carried. Diamanté would smile and produce the rabbits as proof that they had been merely out hunting for the day. At one checkpoint, a guard wasn't buying their story and seemed about to blow his whistle when Diamanté handed him one of the animals. To Stu's relief, the peace offering was accepted, and they were allowed to move on.

Stu kept his head down, remembering to not look toward noises or up at passing airplanes until the others did for fear of blowing his cover. His instructions had been clear: don't look them in the eye. He produced his *carte d'identité* only after Diamanté and Jacques had shown theirs and never muttered so much as a sigh, though his heart beat fast and he could feel beads of sweat trickling from his armpits.

After a day's ride, they arrived at a farmhouse. The farmer, his face weathered from exposure to the elements and too much wine, showed them where to hide their bicycles, then fed them soup, bread, and cheese. That night, they climbed a ladder to the hayloft where Stu spent another restless night. Just before dawn, they were awakened and provided a breakfast of coffee, eggs, and sausages. Then they were off again.

After a morning of riding, Diamanté noticed that Stu was rubbing his leg and having difficulty keeping up. He stopped, motioned for them to pull off the path, and pointed to a small tree-shaded pond a short distance away. He recognized the marsh. They were only a short distance from Brignancourt and Doctor Lemonier's house.

"Wait over there," he said. He and Jacques exchanged a nod, and then he left.

Stu limped over to the pond, washed his face and hands in the cool water, and collapsed on the bank. Jacques stood his rifle against a tree trunk and slid to the ground. "We wait," he said. "You rest now."

Stu nodded and placed his beret over his eyes. He dozed off almost immediately.

The rumbling of a vehicle jarred him awake. Alarmed, he sat up abruptly. How long he had slept he had no idea, but the sun had moved so that he was no longer in the shade.

Jacques was standing with his rifle in his hands. Stu rose as Doctor Lemonier's familiar old truck came up the dirt road toward them and stopped. Diamanté climbed out of the cab and fetched a picnic basket from the back.

Lemonier shook Stu's hand. "How are you feeling, *mon ami?*"

Stu smiled. "Could be better. My leg's giving me a lot of pain."

The doctor examined the wound. "It's still healing," he said. "The bicycle has made it bleed again." He turned to Diamanté and said in French, "This man can't continue."

Diamanté nodded. "We need to get him to Paris."

Lemonier thought briefly. "I will try to arrange for you to ride the rest of the way in a delivery truck from Brignancourt. Give me an hour or so. You'll be safe enough here. I'll be back as soon as I can."

Diamanté waved as the truck drove off. Then he picked up the picnic basket and went over to where Stu and Jacques were seated under the shade of a large tree. "*Eh bien,*" he said. "Let's see what Madame Lemonier has prepared for our *piquenique.*"

The doctor's wife had packed a whole roast chicken, some Roquefort cheese, a crusty baguette, bottle of wine, and apples.

Stu devoured the food and then lay back with his hands behind his neck. "I like it here in Normandy," he said.

Diamanté thought about the shortages and rationing that the Parisians were going through. Marcel's family was starving, and along with them, Elise. He wished he could bring her here to the country where the food was more plentiful. She was too thin, and he worried about her, but no place was safe now.

His thoughts were interrupted by the roar of a plane flying low over the marsh.

Stu's eyes opened wide. "Son of a bitch!" he exclaimed. "It's German...a *Messerschmitt*."

"*Aérodrome* nearby," Diamanté said.

Jacques pointed an imaginary anti-aircraft gun in the air. "*Ack ack ack!*" Then he chuckled.

Stu stared into the sky. What he wouldn't give to be in his plane again chasing the bastards.

Chapter Thirty-Five

As promised, Doctor Lemonier returned an hour later. He spoke in excited, rapid French to Diamanté and Jacques.

Stu struggled to understand what was being said. It alarmed him when he heard the man say "*l'Américain.*"

Seeing a distressed look on Stu's face, Lemonier patted his shoulder. "Don't worry, *mon ami*. There is a change of plans. We have an arms drop tonight. A big one. A plane is coming in, and you are in luck. There will be room for a passenger."

Stu raised his eyebrows.

Lemonier smiled. "*Oui.* You are going to England."

A wide grin flashed across Stu's face. He wiped the sweat from his forehead and said, "I thought you were going to turn me over to the Gestapo."

Diamanté chuckled. "Just to the Brits."

They loaded the bicycles into the truck bed. Stu was instructed to climb into the cab; Diamanté and Jacques rode in back.

They drove south, then southwest, along narrow roads, through the lush rural countryside, passing fields of wheat and clusters of apple orchards. It was dark by the time they reached their destination, a timbered farm building. They were led immediately inside where a small group of men had congregated. The air was thick with cigarette smoke, and the place had the strong odor of fermenting fruit.

Stu stared at the men scattered about the room, smoking and speaking to each other in hushed voices. Guy, dressed in a wide pin-striped suit, was seated on an oak barrel talking to another man. He held a torch in his hand that illuminated the entire space. There were ten of them. Some were not yet twenty, others were much older. A few were dressed, like Guy, in pressed suits; others wore crumpled overalls and muddy boots.

Diamanté and Jacques went over to greet Guy. The others surrounded them and took turns shaking hands. There was an air of excitement in the room.

"Ah, Stu, *mon ami,*" Guy said. "I didn't think I would see you again so soon. My friends here are known collectively as Les Amis Clandestins. They have regular jobs by day, but," he wagged a finger and chuckled, "by night, they blow up trains and bridges."

A tall man in the back added, "Along with an occasional *Boche.*" There was laughter and another round of handshaking.

Jacques opened a bottle of apple brandy and poured glasses for all.

Guy produced a small box camera, and they snapped photos.

The group left the building after midnight and followed Guy's dog, Hannibal, down a path into the woods. They moved quietly. There was no moon. Frogs croaked; crickets chirped.

Just as they arrived at the edge of a clearing, they could hear the muted drone of a plane's engine in the distance. The small group spread out and quickly lit flare pots to illuminate the open space. As the sound came closer, the men tensed and looked up into the sky.

An RAF high-wing Westland Lysander made a low pass over the short makeshift airfield, its exhaust ports heavily muffled.

Jacques signaled to it in Morse code with his flashlight.

It circled to the west, gained altitude, and disappeared from sight.

Minutes later, they heard the plane approaching again. This time it came in low at near stalling speed and landed almost immediately. The men ran to it. They worked silently and swiftly. In less than five minutes, heavy canvas panniers were unloaded and passed from man to man to the edge of the clearing where a farm wagon, pulled by two oxen, awaited.

When the last of the stores had been unloaded, Diamanté gave Stu a gentle push and said, "Go now."

Guy handed him the roll of film from his camera. "To remember us by," he said, and he shook Stu's hand.

Before he climbed into the small cockpit, Stu stood erect and, filled with emotion and admiration for the courage of this small army of fighters, he saluted the group in formal military style.

***

Diamanté and Guy watched until the plane was off the ground. They breathed a sigh of relief; then they turned and joined the others. There was much work to be done before dawn.

Inside the distillery, working by the light of lanterns, the panniers were opened and the contents separated for distribution. They found Sten guns, .38 Llama pistols, boxes of ammunition, and bundles of plastic explosives along with fuses and timing devices. There were also bread and meat ration stamps and counterfeit franc notes.

Diamanté thought, *Bernard is behind this. I know it. Everything we talked about needing is here.* He felt certain his friend had made it safely to England.

"We'll hide the weapons in haystacks and root cellars around the countryside," he said. "Jacques and I will personally make a delivery to Marcel in Paris." He raked the group with his eyes. "If all of you agree, we will give them the ration stamps, too. The need for food is greater in Paris."

They nodded in agreement.

"*Bon alors.*" Diamanté glanced over at Jacques. "We leave before dawn."

***

Early the next morning, Doctor Lemonier, Diamanté, and Jacques arrived in Brignancourt with their truckload full of arms hidden under a layer of firewood. They stopped and waited in the alleyway behind Le Café de la Côte. A delivery truck was parked at the rear of the café with its back open.

Seeing them, the driver climbed out of the truck's cab and came around the side, pointing to the open trailer.

"*Allez allez*," he said. "*Vite!*"

Diamanté recognized the man. It was the same man who had brought Bernard and him to Brignancourt from Paris in July. This time, the camion was loaded with rows of empty wine bottles, baskets of apples, and huge rounds of cheese.

They shoved the crates of weapons into an open space at the far end of the trailer just behind the cab, covered them with burlap sacks, and piled the firewood high to the ceiling to conceal them. Then they lowered the door with as little noise as possible and crowded into the front.

At the checkpoints, the driver handed over apples and generous amounts of cheese to the guards who knew him by now. Each time, he promised wine on his return trip, and they were waved through. In that way, they made it to the outskirts of Paris without incident.

The driver stopped abruptly just outside the city. "There's a Gestapo checkpoint just ahead," he said. "I'll be able to deal with them better if I am alone." He motioned for them to get out. "Go on foot, about a kilometer. Stay undercover, away from the road. Wait at the junction. I will blink my headlights if I am going to pick you up. If not," he shrugged, "you're on your own."

Diamanté and Jacques climbed out. The truck accelerated and moved on.

***

It was some time before the headlights coming toward them blinked on and off three times and stopped. The driver, cigarette dangling from the side of his mouth, motioned to them. They climbed quickly back into the cab and took off for the Hôtel Saint-Jacques.

Chapter Thirty-Six

Diamanté draped his arm around Elise's shoulders and kissed her ear as they strolled along the Quai d'Orsay at sunset.

She pulled away from him and kept walking.

"Is something bothering you, *ma chérie?*" he asked. Ever since he returned to Paris, she'd seemed distant. She was very thin, and she appeared haggard. He couldn't help wondering what was going on with her.

She sighed. "*Oh là.* It's too hard here in Paris. There's not enough food. Everyone is starving and afraid." She glanced behind them nervously. "We can't trust anyone."

They stopped to watch two young boys chasing hoops. The river glowed like molten gold in the low setting sun.

"I have some news," she continued. "Marcel is sending Françoise and the children to live with Tante Amélie in Marseilles. He thinks it will be better for them in the South."

"He's probably right. Madame Boulon will take good care of them." He chuckled and added, "She has a way of finding food."

Elise glanced over at him. "There's more. I'm to accompany them."

Diamanté smiled. "*Mais c'est merveilleuse*! I always stop to see Madame every time I'm in Marseilles. I can visit you often." He took her hand and kissed it. "When do you leave?"

"We're to depart in two days," she said, withdrawing her hand from his. "Ferdinand is to accompany us."

"I could go with you. I'm headed to the South anyway."

She shook her head. "No. Ferdinand is going. It's been settled."

"Don't you want me to go?"

She looked up at him sheepishly. Then she lowered her head and started walking again.

So that was it, Diamanté thought as he followed her. His brother had made his move. "Are you telling me you and I are…are?" He couldn't say it. He didn't want to say it. He clenched his fists in anger. Finally he stopped in front of her and blurted out, "I love you, Elise. I don't want to lose you."

"*Écoute,* Diamanté, you haven't lost me. It's just that I haven't made up my mind about either of you." She pushed him aside and continued walking. "*Oh là*, I'm so confused. I need some time away from you both to think about it."

He hurried to keep up with her. "But why can't I go with you to Marseilles, then, instead of Ferdinand? Isn't he needed here?"

She clicked her tongue, but she didn't answer. She was watching behind them again.

"Why do you keep looking back? Do you still feel you're being followed? Have you seen him even once since we've been walking?"

She turned to him in anger. Her eyes flared. "Feel? Feel? I know it, Diamanté." She threw up her hands in frustration. "It's *toujours* the same man. No matter where I go."

Diamanté stopped, surprised at her sudden outburst. He put up his hands. "I didn't mean I doubted you were telling the truth, *chérie*. I just asked."

"Well, the answer is yes," she said. Tears glistened in her eyes. "I'm scared, Diamanté."

The sun had set, and there were shadows in the streets. It was a cool autumn night. Merchants were pulling down the gates to their shops. People hurried to be home before curfew.

"It would be best, then, if we return to the hotel," Diamanté conceded with a shrug. They turned a corner and headed down the boulevard Saint-Germain. The thoroughfare was wide, and it would be difficult for anyone following to stay hidden long. *If he is following us*, Diamanté thought, *let's make him show himself*.

Elise shuddered. "*Oh là.* I just want this all to end."

They took a detour, passed the Sorbonne, crossed the boulevard Saint-Michel, and continued past the École de Médecine. Just as they arrived at the place de l'Odéon, Elise sucked in a breath and grabbed his arm. "I see him," she whispered.

Diamanté glanced behind. "How far back?"

"The church," she said. "He's hiding near the front entry."

Diamanté saw a shadow move slightly next to the entrance to Saint-Germain-des-Prés. He thought quickly. They had stopped near a bookstore that was still open. "Wait in there," he instructed Elise. "I'll be right back."

"Be careful," she whispered.

He watched until she had entered the bookstore, then he doubled back toward the church and crept along the abbey's outer wall until he reached the main entrance. Peeking around the corner into the dark space, he came face to face with a man hiding in the shadows.

Diamanté was the taller of the two. He grabbed the stranger with both hands and pulled him onto the brick pavement.

"Why are you following us?" he asked, trying to get a good look at the man in the faint light. He wore an oversized beret low over his forehead. "Tell me." He shook him roughly. "*Hein?*"

Before Diamanté could stop him, the man raised his fist and punched him hard in the face. He reeled, stumbled backward, and fell. Blood spurted from his nose. *The* mec *knows how to fight*, he thought as he struggled to get up. As soon as he was upright again, his swift opponent thrust out a leg and kicked him in the groin. Diamanté staggered in shock as excruciating pain spread to his spine, chest, and belly. He grunted and dropped to his knees. Then, using all the strength he could muster, he formed a fist, came in low, and punched hard into the man's stomach, causing him to double over in pain.

The two men went after each other like angry bulls, and the struggle continued until a passerby yelled to them, "*Foutez le camp!* The Gestapo is coming."

Diamanté grabbed his opponent by the collar, pulled off the beret, and stared into his face. As he'd suspected, he recognized him. The stalker was his half brother, André Narbon. "You?" he said, letting go. "Why were you following us?"

André pushed Diamanté away and adjusted his thick, dark, square-rimmed glasses. "Her name's Elise, isn't it? I've been watching her. She's your girl, *non?*" He let out a hateful laugh. "Or was. She's Ferdinand's now, but I'm going to steal her away from you both."

"By stalking her?"

André shook his head. "By doing something worse."

The pounding sound of jackboots marching in unison hammered the air.

"Stay away from her," Diamanté warned. "Or you'll have me to deal with."

"You can't keep me from her," André sneered. He turned and ran quickly into the shadows just as Third Reich soldiers rounded the corner.

Diamanté hid in a hollow of the abbey wall until the army had passed, then, holding his nose to stop the bleeding, he headed for the bookstore.

Elise put her hand to her mouth in horror when she saw his bloodied face. "What happened?" she screamed.

Diamanté grabbed her arm and pulled her outside. "Let's get out of here."

He needed to warn Ferdinand. André was obviously planning to avenge his father's murder with the worst possible consequences. He remembered the old gypsy saying about vengeance: kill the one they love. His mouth went dry. Elise was in great danger, and so was Ferdinand. And it was all his fault.

Chapter Thirty-Seven

Later, when Diamanté shared the details of his violent encounter with André, Ferdinand's reaction was immediate and emotional. "Elise shouldn't leave the hotel until we depart for Marseilles," he said, pounding his fist on the table in anger.

Marcel nodded in agreement. "It would be best if she isn't left alone either."

Diamanté and Ferdinand exchanged a glance, each of them secretly delighted at the thought of getting her undivided attention. Over the next two days, however, neither brother would allow the other to be alone with her. Predictably, a fierce competition developed.

Diamanté started it when he decided to prepare Elise's favorite meal, a traditional rustic Portuguese soup made with chouriço sausage, kale, and potatoes. While she was occupied with the children, he made a quick trip to the central market. With some of the ration stamps from the drop in Normandy, he purchased all the ingredients.

"This is wonderful!" Elise exclaimed as she savored his flavorful stew that evening. "I've never tasted a better *caldo verde*. Not even in my native Portugal." She blew Diamanté a kiss from across the dining table.

Ferdinand, seated next to her, leered at his brother. "I think it has too much salt," he smirked.

After dinner, they gathered in the salon. Ferdinand left and returned two minutes later carrying a small steamer trunk. "I just finished it," he said with pride as he set it down in front of Elise. "It's to pack your things in…for the trip."

The trunk was made of canvas with wood bracing. Elise ran her fingers over the handcrafted leather trim and side handles. "*Oh là!*" she exclaimed with delight as she opened it. The interior was lined in white muslin. "It's beautiful, Ferdi!"

Diamanté bristled at the affectionate name she had called his brother.

Ferdinand's eyes sparkled. "See here." He showed her the interior. "There's a little fitted basket for…" He looked at her and blushed. "It's where you can keep your special things."

Diamanté groaned inwardly. His soup was forgotten.

The next afternoon, while Elise was again occupied, Diamanté walked down the rue Saint-Jacques until he found the only open florist's shop on the street.

An elderly woman hollered from the back of the store, "*Un moment.*" Then she came forward wiping dirt from her hands. "*Oui?* What can I do for you?"

He looked around the nearly empty space. Pots were stacked along the walls, and the shelves were bare except for a few green plants and some curios. "I want to purchase a bouquet," he said, adding, "of flowers."

The woman shrugged. "As you can see, *Monsieur*, we don't have any flowers. Everyone is growing vegetables. All the garden space in the city is used for food." She saw his disappointment. "*Tiens*, I do have some dried cuttings, mostly lavender and herbs. I could possibly make up a small bouquet."

His face brightened. "That, Madame, would be nice. *C'est pour ma petite amie.*"

She studied him and finally said, "It will cost you a franc."

He handed over the coin and also a meat ration stamp. "Could you possibly, *chère madame*, also find a fresh rosebud or two to add to it?"

The woman's eyes widened at the appearance of the coveted food stamp. "You must really love her to give up that." She snatched his offering. "*Attendez,*" she called behind her as she disappeared into a workroom at the back of the shop.

***

Elise buried her nose in the sweet-scented bouquet. "How on earth did you manage to get roses?" she asked.

He shrugged. "I picked them myself."

Ferdinand countered that afternoon. They were working in the courtyard vegetable garden when he handed Elise a small covered wicker basket. "*Un petit paquet de joie,*" he said, "a little package to make you happy."

Elise raised her eyebrows. "*Eh bien,* what is it?"

He laughed. "Open it."

She wiped her hands on her apron, raised the cover, and peered inside. "Oh, Ferdi," she exclaimed as she lifted out a scrawny kitten. She rubbed the little ball of white fluff against her cheek, and it let out a soft meow.

"I found her scrounging for food in the alley behind the restaurant next door," Ferdinand said, smiling.

"I'm going to name her Mirabelle," Elise exclaimed.

Merde, Diamanté thought. *That was a surprise. Ferdinand hates cats.* "You'll have to keep it hidden on the train," he sneered, exchanging a glance with his brother.

Elise flashed a sweet smile in Ferdinand's direction "She can travel in my new trunk. They'll never know she's there."

Diamanté secretly wished the cat would smother in that trunk.

***

Late that evening, Françoise and Marcel sat on a loveseat in their bedroom. They shared their final moments together over a quiet glass of cognac.

"I'm concerned about Elise," Françoise said, clucking her tongue. "They're courting her, you know."

"Who?"

"Haven't you noticed? The Loupré brothers. They're in love with her, both of them."

Marcel took a sip of his brandy. "How did you conclude that?"

Françoise starred at him in disbelief. "Are you blind? Have you seen how they act around her? They won't leave her alone. Not even for a moment." She paused. "Then there's that horrible man who's been following her. The one who fought with Diamanté." She sighed and shook her head. "*Mon Dieu!* The poor girl's a nervous wreck."

***

Elise, Françoise, and the children were to depart by the first train of the day from the Gare de Lyon.

Diamanté couldn't sleep. Worried that there had been no sign of André since the night of the encounter, he rose and stood guard in the dark corridor outside Elise's room. Just before dawn, he heard her moving around. This would be his last opportunity, he thought, to get her alone. When her door opened and she pulled her packed trunk into the hallway, he showed himself.

"Can I come in?" he whispered.

She jumped in surprise. "You startled me."

"Sorry. I just wanted to speak with you for a moment."

She lifted her chin. "I know what you're going to ask," she said as she went back into her room. "And I don't have an answer for you."

He approached her and took her into his arms.

She didn't resist.

"I just wanted to tell you," he kissed her forehead, "I'll always love you."

She patted his still swollen and bruised cheek. "And I you, *Lobo*," she whispered.

Diamanté's heart leapt. She hadn't used the Portuguese pet name she had given him for some time.

Just then, Ferdinand barged in. "It's time to go."

Elise pulled away from Diamanté. "I'm all packed," she said, and she hurried out of the room.

Ferdinand glared at his brother.

"I'm not giving her up," Diamanté warned. A ball of anxiety stuck in his throat.

Ferdinand raised his eyebrows. He lifted Elise's trunk to his shoulders and went into the corridor.

***

Downstairs, Pauline and François jumped up and down with excitement. Marcel's wife fidgeted nervously. Elise buttoned her cloth coat. She was wearing a hat, and she had tied a scarf around her neck.

"You look very nice," Diamanté told her.

She picked up the kitten and the bouquet he'd given her and kissed him lightly on both cheeks. "*Au revoir*," she whispered.

Françoise hugged Diamanté. "Will you be going through Brignancourt?" she asked.

"Most likely," he replied.

She handed him an envelope. "Could you deliver this to my parents?"

He took the envelope from her and stuffed it into his shirt pocket. "I will be happy to do it."

She smiled. "Assure them not to worry. The children and I will be all right."

Diamanté glanced over at Elise and said, "I hope to see you soon."

While Diamanté and Ferdinand stood lookout for any signs of André, the women and children climbed into a bicycle taxi in the back alley behind the hotel.

Ferdinand shook Diamanté's hand. "I'm going to go see *Maman* in Corsica before I return to Paris," he said. "Do you have a message for her?"

Diamanté shook his head. "It will be enough for her to know that we are both still alive."

Ferdinand patted his shoulder. "Be safe, *mon frère*," he said.

The bicycle taxi departed, and Ferdinand followed on foot.

Diamanté stood alone in the middle of the alley smoking a cigarette.

Chapter Thirty-Eight

After Elise and Ferdinand's departure, Diamanté occupied himself for the better part of the morning digging root vegetables from the hotel's garden. He tried not to think about Elise and Ferdinand traveling south together. Initially, he fantasized that Elise would break away at the last minute and come running back to him, but as the morning went on, he lost hope and began to fear that he would never see her again.

By noon, he had finished storing the vegetables in Marcel's cellar. He sat down on the bench in the courtyard and lit a cigarette. Birds chirped, and a slight wind rustled in the trees. He looked up into the sky. Low, iron-gray clouds boiled across the heavens. There would be rain soon. The leaves had begun turning, and the cold weather and dark days would set in. If he had been at home in Corsica, he thought, he would be out hunting in the maquis. He could always find solace in the wild. What did he have to stalk now? It occurred to him that he could go out searching for Nazis. He chuckled to himself, briefly picturing them as wild boars in the undergrowth, tracking them down and killing them with his hunting rifle.

His hatred for the invaders had steadily increased—as had his resolve to do everything he could to defeat them.

He thought about his mother. Ferdinand would be seeing her again. That would make her happy. It was then that he remembered the journal she had sent him for Christmas the year he had left Corsica. What was it she had written in it? "Tell your story," he said aloud.

He ran upstairs and pulled the journal from the bottom of the pack he carried always with him. The black leather was not as shiny as it once had been nor did the binding smell new. The pages were slightly frayed but blank. In three years, he had not written a single word. He turned to the inside cover and reread his mother's message aloud, "*Chi va pianu va sanu E chi va sanu va luntanu.*" He who goes slowly, goes surely; and he who goes surely, goes far. He fished a pencil from his pack and began writing in his native Corsican.

> *Allow me to introduce myself. My full name is Diamanté Soudain Loupré-Tigre. I am known as* Le Loup *for I am told I have the eyes of a wolf, but within me is the soul of a tiger. This is my story.*

He went on to describe the event that had brought him to Marseilles in 1939. He had resolved never to tell anyone, including Ferdinand. This would be the only time in his life he would explain how and why he had planned and carried out the murder of his stepfather.

All afternoon he wrote furiously. He included loving thoughts about his mother and the hurt he had felt leaving her, details of his childhood fantasies during hours spent in the maquis, and he poured out his emotions over his country's current predicament and his resolve to resist the tyranny of the Nazis. He expressed his dream to have a restaurant of his own someday, in a free France, and allowed himself to speculate on what it would be like to raise a child or two. Then he described his unrequited love for Elise.

> *I am desperate to see her again. When I do, I will convince her that I love her.*

The sun was just beginning to set when a light knock at his door jolted him from his trance.

"Are you awake?" Marcel asked.

"*Oui.*"

"Jacques has arrived. Come down to the salon and join us for an aperitif."

Diamanté smiled. He liked Jacques. "Sure. I'll be down in a minute."

He stared at the journal. He had filled nearly half of it. On the last page, he wrote, "France *Toujours* France!" in bold letters, adding below, "Paris le 2 octobre 1942." Then, with a sigh, he put down his pencil.

Downstairs he greeted his friend with a handshake. "*Salut, mon ami.* I'm happy to see you."

Jacques stared at Diamanté's swollen and bruised face.

Self-consciously, Diamanté rubbed his cheek. He knew Jacques wouldn't ask what had happened. It wasn't the Corsican way to pry into private affairs. "It's nothing," he said with a shrug, adding, "I was in a fight over a girl."

Jacques chuckled. "I hope you won her."

Diamanté threw back his head. "*Enfin, merde, non.*"

Jacques grimaced. "*C'est dommage.*"

"How did the delivery go?" Marcel asked.

"Well enough. We made it through safely. The *Boches* didn't even suspect."

"Where are you headed to next, then?" Diamanté asked.

"I'm returning to Rouen. And you?"

"I had thought to return to Marseilles, but my plans changed." Diamanté hesitated. "I think I'll go with you. I've got a message to deliver to Doctor Lemonier in Brignancourt."

"*Très bien.* We'll leave tomorrow…early."

Diamanté's stomach growled, reminding him that he hadn't eaten all day.

Marcel entered the salon carrying a tray. "Are you two hungry?" he asked as he handed them each a glass of marc.

Jacques nodded. "Isn't everyone these days?"

"I think we have some leftover soup in the kitchen," Diamanté suggested.

"I have a better idea," Marcel said. He looked at Diamanté. "I'm in need of some cheering up. How about you?"

Diamanté nodded.

"*Eh bien,*" Marcel continued. "My Alsatian friend, Louis, has offered me private dining above his restaurant next door while my family is away. We'll have a room to ourselves; the *Boches* dine downstairs." He winked. "Because of them, the food is good. Louis gets it on the black market." He cleared his throat and became serious. "But first, I want to discuss something with you." He picked up his own glass and went over to sit in his chair by the fireplace. "The partisans could use your help," he said. "A *Wehrmacht* supply train is due to leave after midnight. Those explosives you brought were just what we needed." He smiled. "We're planning to blow a bridge." He lifted his glass. "Are you in?"

Jacques and Diamanté exchanged a glance and nodded.

***

At eight o'clock that evening, Diamanté, Jacques, and Marcel left the hotel, walked through the alley, and climbed the back stairway of the building next door. From the noisy restaurant below came the sounds of clicking silverware, animated voices, and laughter.

The private dining room was decorated in rich furnishings. The walls were covered in teal blue and taupe *toiles de jouy* fabric; an eighteenth-century wooden cherub stood on a pedestal in front of a gilt-framed mirror. In the center of the room, dark-gray silk-upholstered bergère chairs had been arranged around an oval table set with a white cloth and silverware. A crystal chandelier hung from the ceiling above.

Marcel's friend Louis was waiting for them. He was a big man, dressed in a white chef's coat, with plump cheeks, blue eyes, and a head of unruly light-brown hair.

He came forward and shook their hands warmly. "*S'il vous plaît,*" he said. "Please be seated, *mes amis.*" His accent sounded Alsatian, as if his cheeks were stuffed with food. Patting Marcel on the shoulder, he asked, "Did your wife make it off OK?"

Marcel nodded. "She said to thank you for the basket of food you sent for their train trip."

Louis smiled. "You should have gone with them."

Marcel shook his head. "It wasn't possible to leave the hotel."

Louis poured them glasses of Riesling, then moved to the buffet. On the sideboard, above which sat a glass-fronted cupboard filled with china and crystal goblets, was a steaming soup tureen.

"Our *plat du jour*," he said, "is *Filet de Boeuf Ficelle* served, *bien sûr*, on *choucroute* with just a touch of cream."

Marcel smiled. "I don't know how you do it, Louis."

Louis chuckled and pointed to the floor below. "*Merci aux Boches*." He promptly served three bowls of the first course *soupe*, bid them "*Bon appétit*," and closed the door.

Diamanté had just taken a spoonful when they heard the distant wailing of air raid sirens. Rising and falling mournfully in pitch, the two-toned warnings joined each other in chorus as the sound grew closer. In the distance, they heard the drumming of bombs exploding. The chandelier flickered above them, then went dark.

"Ah, *mes amis*, the RAF arrives," Marcel exclaimed. "The sirens have been more frequent since the bombing of the Renault factory in March."

Louis arrived with their main course, and they ate the rest of their meal by the light of a single candle in the center of the table.

***

The *Wehrmacht* transport train was due to leave Paris shortly after midnight. Below the high bridge, a small group of partisans spread out and waited quietly in the darkness. Earlier, they had set explosives under the railroad ties and at the base of the abutments.

Diamanté spotted a shadow moving stealthily along the top of the bridge. He recognized the slight profile with the oversized beret and the familiar square-rimmed glasses. It was André.

"What's *he* doing here?" he whispered, pointing him out to Jacques and Marcel. Henri, the rotund barkeep of spitting fame from boulevard Diderot, came to kneel beside them.

Marcel shrugged and shook his head.

They watched as the figure on the bridge stopped suddenly, looked around cautiously, and knelt down. A long cord dropped quickly to the ground below. The man hurried back along the bridge, reached the end, and ran down the embankment. He stayed close to the trees, stopping twice to lift his nose into the air, and then scurried quietly into the woods.

Diamanté was relieved that André hadn't followed Ferdinand and Elise to Marseilles, but seeing him just now was troubling. He hadn't attended Marcel's meeting, so how could he have known about the operation?

Seconds later, they heard the "chug chug chug" of the approaching train. It was a steam engine, and it moved slowly as if pulling a very heavy load.

Diamanté tensed; Marcel readied himself to push the plunger in front of him.

The locomotive came to a slow stop just before the trestle. Diamanté could see the swastikas of the Third Reich flags waving in the night breeze on either side of its dimmed front beam. Two armed SS guards descended from behind the coal car and inspected the track with their flashlights. They went as far as the center of the span then turned back and signaled to the engineer.

Diamanté held his breath. Whatever André had placed on the track, they hadn't discovered it.

Slowly the train pulled onto the bridge. The heavy wooden beams of the structure shook, and the pilings groaned. The guards stood sentry on either side.

A swift movement below the bridge caught Diamanté's attention. André had reappeared. Diamanté watched with curiosity as he quickly lit the end of the dangling fuse. They heard a soft hiss and saw the flicker of a flame traveling swiftly upward. It reached its destination at the same time as the front of the engine. There was a sudden flash followed by a whoosh, and the effect was as if fireworks had been set on the tracks. The locomotive squealed loudly as it came to a torturous halt. By then, several cars were also on the bridge. Soldiers descended from the open carriages with their rifles drawn. The guards ran ahead, shouting in German.

Marcel pushed hard on the plunger and then motioned to the others just as the first earsplitting detonation shook the ground. The explosion caused the front part of the engine to rise into the sky. Diamanté glanced over his shoulder as he ran. Deafening blasts followed as the explosives detonated and pounded through the air in a series of thunderous concussions. The bridge crumpled, and the locomotive plummeted over the side in a great ball of flame. *Wehrmacht* soldiers stumbled from the cars and leapt for safety as the falling train squealed and wailed, dragging the next few carriages with it into the ravine below. Car after car piled into the inferno of mangled steel and bridge pilings. The sound of rapid machine-gun fire followed as the partisans picked off any escaping soldiers.

The heat was intense, and the pungent smell of burning coal stung Diamanté's nostrils. Dirt and small rocks rained down on them.

Marcel pulled on his sleeve. "Come on," he shouted, "we need to get the hell out of here before they come looking for us."

Chapter Thirty-Nine

Rouen, France
Two Days Later

Le Canard à la Rouennaise was in total shambles. Jacques stood with his hands on his hips looking at the mess. "*Putain de merde.* What happened here?"

The restaurant's head chef, Jean Marc, was on the floor picking up shards of glass. "They came for the wine," he said.

Jacques's eyes opened wide. "Who?"

Marie-Thérèse piped in. "Who else? The *Boches*. Ordinary soldiers they were, too. No officers with them." She stood in the doorway with her hands on her hips, legs spread apart. Her eyes were wide, and her frizzy hair protruded from the sides of her head. "Those bastards were looting!"

"They discovered the cellar was nearly empty," Jean Marc added, "and they searched everywhere. They accused us of hiding all the best wines."

Jacques couldn't wait for the rest of the story. "And did they find them?" he asked impatiently.

"They went on an angry rampage," the chef continued as if he had not heard the question. "They broke up all the tables and chairs and smashed the windows with their rifle butts." He was nearly sobbing. "They even hacked at the artwork." His voice cracked. "My beautiful restaurant all destroyed."

Jacques was out of patience. "But did they find the wine?"

"*Non. Non*, they didn't," Marie-Thérése answered. She chuckled finally. "They carted away all the bottles we had in the cellar, and the barrels too, but they didn't know there was anything behind the wall with the cobwebs."

Jacques wanted to see for himself. Diamanté followed him as he ran down the stairway and into the wine cellar. The wooden tables and chairs had been smashed; shards of broken bottles lay in pools of red wine. They went behind the false brick wall and into the room where Les Amis had held their meeting. The space was empty. Only the musty smell reminded them that it had once held huge barrels of wine.

Jacques surveyed the far wall. "The webs were my final touch," he said. "I caught spiders and put them there after I sealed the last and largest chamber. Behind it are stored over ten thousand bottles of France's best wines." He breathed a sigh of relief and ran his fingers through his hair.

"The *Boches* would have smashed in the walls had they known," Diamanté said. "They're not likely to return now."

Chapter Forty

Diamanté, Jacques, and Marie-Thérèse spent the next day helping Jean Marc. By late afternoon, they had salvaged enough tables and chairs to seat a few guests in the bar, and the kitchen was repaired and back in operation. With the aid of Pierre Truette, the young priest at Saint-Maclou Church, Jacques had even procured a few bottles of sacramental wine. Le Canard à la Rouennaise was set to reopen the next day in time for the dinner service.

Jean Marc was replacing a broken windowpane in the front door when he noticed outside in the street a shiny black Third Reich staff car pulling up in front of the restaurant. "*Putain de merde.*" He spat and then threw up his arms. "Now they return to finish me off."

The others raised their heads in alarm. They watched as an officer, flanked by two guards, stepped from the back of the big Mercedes-Benz. With his chin regally thrust into the air, he looked up and down the rue du Gros Horloge. Then he removed his peaked hat, slipped it under his armpit, and entered the restaurant.

Jean Marc, his eyes narrowed, stood in the middle of the room with his arms crossed to face him.

Diamanté and Jacques joined Marie-Thérèse behind the bar. "He's high ranking," she whispered knowingly. "Look at the collar patch, the gold star, and that dark-blue ribbon on his cuff." Her head bobbled up and down. "Silver eagle. Luftwaffe special command."

The German, handsome and slender with wavy blond hair and thin lips, glanced around the restaurant. His eyes came to rest on the three behind the bar. "Please accept my personal regrets, *Messieurs et Madame*," he said to them in French. He focused on Diamanté for a second, seeming to study his eyes. "The soldiers who did this damage to your establishment will be punished, I assure you," he continued, turning to the chef. "Can I offer you help with the cleanup?"

Jean Marc, his mouth open in astonishment, acknowledged the proposal with a polite nod. "That won't be necessary," he answered finally, adding, "My staff can finish the task."

"When will you reopen then?"

"In two days' time."

"*Das Gute*. In that case, I request to make a reservation."

Jean Marc stared at the man.

"I wish to bring some of my friends for dinner. Can you accommodate a party of twelve at, say, midnight Saturday?"

Jean Marc said that he could.

"I noted the name of this restaurant is Le Canard à la Rouennaise," the officer continued. "I assume you serve duck?"

Jean Marc glanced at Jacques. "*Oui*," he answered. "*C'est notre spécialité*. That is, when we can get it."

The officer clicked his heels together sharply and bowed slightly at the waist. "Well then, we shall have your specialty." He looked over to the bar. "I'm sure you'll find the ducks somewhere." He put on his hat and positioned the visor low over his forehead. The silver bullion eagle caught the sunlight streaming from the windows. "We shall bring our own Champagne," he added with a slight smile. With that, he tossed his hand into the air in a casual Nazi salute. "*Heil* Hitler."

They stared in disbelief as they watched him leave the restaurant and climb back into the big roadster.

"*Nom de Dieu.* Was that an apology?" Jacques asked.

Jean Marc scratched his head. "I believe so."

"*Eh bien,*" Jacques chuckled. "He'll get his duck, and a bloody story to go with it."

***

Les Amis Clandestins met that night in the sparsely furnished rectory of the Church of Saint-Maclou just across the rue de la République from the Rouen cathedral.

The quiet-spoken Father Truette welcomed the small group and invited them to have a seat. He placed a tray with several glasses of Calvados in the center of the table and joined them.

In addition to Diamanté, Jacques, and Marie-Thérèse, there was Léo La Bergère and one other individual whom Diamanté had not met previously. He had a thick Breton accent and smoked a pipe, but no one bothered to introduce him.

Léo had just begun the meeting when André Narbon made his appearance. He glanced around the room suspiciously, his mouth twitching nervously from side to side. When he saw Diamanté he hesitated, then he took a seat at the end of the table nearest the door.

Diamanté glared at him; the others acknowledged him with a slight nod.

"Two men parachuted into Normandy last night," Léo was saying. "They are just outside the city now at a safe house." He leaned forward and whispered, "And they are not pilots."

Eyebrows raised in surprise.

Marie-Thérèse asked, "*Mais*, who are they *alors?*"

Léo's eyes twinkled, and he tapped his fingers together. Finally, he said, "They did not say exactly, but I believe they are spies."

Father Truette cocked his head to the side. "What makes you say that?"

"*Eh bien*, they are British, that is certain, but they speak fluent French. And…" Léo rapped his knuckles on the table, "they are not in a hurry to get out of France."

"*Tiens*. What do you think they are doing here, *alors?*" Jacques asked.

"Normandy is dotted with Third Reich aerodromes," Léo continued. "They're camouflaged extremely well. My guess is," he lowered his voice so they could barely hear him, "the Brits are in need of more intelligence so they can send in their bombers."

"So what is the plan, then?" Diamanté asked.

"Can you leave tomorrow?"

Diamanté said that he could.

"*Bon alors.* You will take the two men as far as Guy's. Stay the night. Lemonier will pick them up the next day."

At that, André rose abruptly and departed.

Diamanté excused himself and followed André down the stairs, through the cloister, and out into the dark courtyard known as the Aître that had once been a graveyard for victims of the plague. Deathly carvings, skulls and bones, eerily decorated the wooden beams of the surrounding buildings, evidence of the churchyard's darker past. He pulled up his collar. The air was cold, and it was beginning to rain. André had disappeared.

I don't trust the bastard, Diamanté thought. *Whatever he is doing, it can't be honorable.*

***

That night, in the empty wine cellar, Jacques and Diamanté listened together to the BBC broadcast. A bridge in Paris had been destroyed, the report said. The main rail route into the city for German troops and equipment had been shut down.

Diamanté clapped his hands together, and Jacques slapped him on the back.

Next, as the broadcast crackled, they strained to hear the announcer read the quaintly coded messages meant for those in the war zone.

Jacques nodded at one and smiled. "A drop," he whispered.

The last was barely audible. Diamanté's eyes widened. "Did I hear that correctly?" he asked in disbelief as Jacques switched off the wireless. "The butterfly has found the sunflower?"

Jacques cocked his head to the side. "That's what I heard."

"It was Bernard's message. He's joined de Gaulle!"

They shook hands. "Come on," Jacques said, "I've a bottle of cognac stashed in my apartment above. We'll celebrate."

Chapter Forty-One

As they approached the old stone farmhouse, Diamanté put up his hand to warn the two men behind him. Something about the scene was bothersome; it was too quiet.

The three dismounted their bicycles and crept alongside the barn. Diamanté tried the small side door. It squealed as he pushed it open and then peered inside.

The ground floor was empty except for a stack of feed bales and some tools. There were no animals in the stalls. Guy kept his truck in here. It too was gone. *Maybe he's out making deliveries*, Diamanté thought. He leaned his bicycle against a wall and motioned for the other two to push their cycles inside. Then he climbed the ladder to the hayloft. There was evidence that evaders had been hiding in the space recently. Loose straw was piled around the perimeter for sleeping, and a table and chairs sat in the center. Leftovers from a partially eaten meal suggested the lodgers had recently made a hasty departure.

At that moment, he heard the familiar sound of German military motorcycles approaching. They regularly patrolled the Normandy countryside looking for downed fliers, and they frequently executed the French citizens who were suspected of sheltering them. Diamanté became concerned as the rumbling grew louder. "*Merde*," he said. There was only one road, and it ended at Guy's farm. This could be a trap. He broke out in a sweat. Were they already surrounded? He looked around for an escape route. Behind him, at the gable end, was a large swing door used for loading hay into the loft. The apple orchard was just a short distance from the back of the barn. A jump and they would be able to make a run for it.

The two men who had accompanied him were still on the lower level. "*Vite!*" he hollered to them. "Close the side door!"

One of the men climbed to the loft; the other concealed himself in the stack of feed bales below. All three listened, their pistols at the ready.

The loud military bikes entered the farmyard and came to a stop; hobnailed jackboots pounded the earth.

There was a lot of shouting. They heard doors slam, the sharp crack of a shotgun, the sound of a vehicle entering the farmyard. Then the track-and-wheel hardware of the heavy barn door slid open. Diamanté and his companion peeked through gaps in the floorboards and saw, framed in the opening, the shadow of a German soldier wielding a rifle.

The figure stepped inside. Several more armed men filled the space behind him. Diamanté held his breath. They wore *feldgrau*, and the twin lightning bolts on their helmets and collars caught the sunlight streaming through the barn door. Waffen-SS.

The soldiers kicked over the bicycles, and hollered, "*Drei! Es gibt drei davon.*" There are three of them.

They prodded the stack of feed bales with bayonets. A shot reverberated throughout the barn. Suddenly the Brit sprang from his hiding place and bolted for the side door.

Diamanté blenched. The man didn't have a chance. From outside came the loud "errrt" of machine guns followed by agonized screams.

Diamanté heard the officer yelling, "*Wo sind die anderen?*" There was a moment of silence, then a single pistol shot rang out.

The lead soldier fired in the direction of the hayloft and barked a command. "*Kommen Sie mit Ihren Händen! Mach schnell!*"

Diamanté and his companion remained stock-still.

Outside, an army truck rumbled to a stop, and an officer, in collar patches and shoulder stripes, stepped onto the running board and hopped to the ground. He casually lit a cigarette and barked a command. More soldiers descended from the back of the truck.

A salvo of gunfire pierced the floorboards. Diamanté fumbled desperately for the box of matches in his pocket. His hand shaking, he struck a match and held it to the dry straw that quickly caught fire then immediately went out. *Merde,* he thought. Another barrage of bullets sprayed the old wooden beams. One grazed his arm, and he winced in pain. He struck a second spark. This time, there was a flash, and the straw exploded. Diamanté pulled off his ammo belt and tossed it into the blaze. The heat scorched his face, and he coughed from the smoke as he ran to push open the big loading door. It swung out and landed with a loud thud against the side of the barn.

The two men leaped to the ground. Diamanté stumbled, then ran. Noticing the Brit wasn't following him, he looked back over his shoulder.

The man lay on the ground where he had landed, writhing in pain and holding his ankle.

Diamanté looked down and saw drops of blood on the gravel next to his feet. His arm was bleeding from the bullet wound. With his heart in his throat, he considered his options. He could run away, leave this Brit whom he didn't even know by name to the same fate as his companion. Or should he help him? He shook his head. The answer was clear. He hurried back and hoisted the man to his feet.

They had just reached the edge of the orchard when from behind them they heard, "*Halten sie!*" Soldiers, alerted by the loud sound of the swing door, had come around to the back of the barn, their rifles at the ready.

Diamanté quickly pulled the envelope Françoise had given him from his pocket and stashed it along with his pistol behind the nearest apple tree. Then he turned around and put his hands in the air.

The upper story of the barn was now totally engulfed in flames, and popping sounds from the exploding bullets gave the effect of a battle going on inside. Diamanté and the Brit were dragged into the farmyard with their hands tied behind their backs and thrown against the stone wall next to the farmhouse. A short distance from them, their companion lay dead on the ground, a gaping bullet wound in the center of his forehead.

Diamanté became aware of blood-curdling screams coming from inside the farmhouse. His mouth went dry, and his heart pounded. Then he watched in horror as they dragged Guy's pregnant and bleeding wife, Marguerite, outside and threw her to the ground. She let out a gasp of horror at the sight of the burning barn. The soldier standing above her pinned her head to the ground with his boot and smashed her face with his rifle butt. Her body went limp. Blood oozed in big drops onto the gravel.

Chapter Forty-Two

Guy de Noailles was looking forward to returning home to the farm. After delivering his produce to Rouen, he stopped in Epinay to see Christophe, the tailor. There was to be a big drop later that night, one that would require the help of several men.

Guy's stomach growled as he made the turn onto the narrow dirt road. He wondered briefly what Marguerite was preparing for their dinner. They would have several at the table: Diamanté, along with the men he was escorting, and, of course, the four fliers who had spent the previous night in the hayloft of his barn. All of these brave souls were due to depart in the morning.

Guy looked forward to seeing Diamanté again. He genuinely liked the young man, and he had good news to relay to him, too. Stu had sent word back that he had arrived safely in England. It would be a nice evening.

As the truck approached the farm, he became alarmed at the strong smell of smoke in the air. Around the next bend, he saw the origin. "*Nom de Dieu*," he said aloud. His barn was consumed in a raging fire. He pulled to an abrupt stop, grabbed his rifle from under the seat, and scrambled quickly out of the cab.

There were no vehicles in the farmyard. The only sound was the crackling of the burning timber. The smoke was heavy and black. Flaming cinders drifted from the air like snowflakes. Guy approached the farm with caution. His eyes stung. Where was Hannibal? And the others? He turned and headed toward the house, fear growing in his heart.

The body of a dead man lay in the farmyard. Guy raised his rifle and approached the body with caution. Was this a trap? The man's shoes were off, and his shirt was torn open. Guy knelt down to have a better look. The man had been shot and his body ransacked, then left for the locals to inter. He looked up toward the farmhouse. It was then that he saw Marguerite lying just a few feet away from the front door. He ran to her and dropped to his knees. Her face was swollen and covered in blood. He enveloped her in his arms and rocked her back and forth. "*Mon coeur, mon coeur*," he howled over and over, tears welling in his eyes. "What have they done to you?"

She moaned. Blood sputtered from her nose and mouth.

Guy looked up at the farmhouse. A paper sign, in French and German, hastily tacked on the heavy wooden front door read: "This house has been requisitioned for the purpose of billeting soldiers of the Third Reich. All inhabitants are ordered to vacate in two days."

"*Salauds*," he swore under his breath. He lifted his wife and rose to his feet. Carrying her, he stepped onto the stoop and winced at the excruciating pain in his crippled leg. He hesitated and drew in a breath. Was it safe to go inside?

"*Ils sont partis*," she mumbled. They're gone.

The salon was dark. He laid Marguerite on the sofa, lit a candle, and covered her with a warm quilt.

Choking sobs racked her body. She curled her small frame into the fetal position and held her swollen belly.

He hurried into the kitchen and wet a towel.

"Were they SS?" he asked as he gently cleaned the blood from her face.

She nodded and trembled violently in his arms. "They... they kicked me, and...and," she blubbered. "Oh, Guy." She cried out and buried her head in his shoulder. He held her tightly.

"You're safe with me now, *chérie*. I should never have left you alone, you and—" His eyes widened in terror. "Where is Nathalie?"

She looked up at him and screamed. "I don't know where she is! You've got to find her!"

Guy panicked. "But where? Where did you tell her to go?"

She shook her head. "I just told her to run and hide. And to not come out, no matter what, not until you came home."

He moved as quickly as he could through the rooms searching for the child and calling out her name. He checked the hiding place behind the brick wall in the wine cellar and entered the secret space above the pantry where Stu had slept. The farmhouse was empty.

He went out into the back garden and called out to Hannibal. If the dog were anywhere nearby, he would hear him. In desperation, he searched the outbuildings. The barn was almost totally incinerated. The roof had collapsed, and only the stone foundation and one outer wall stood. The smoldering, twisted skeletons of three blackened bicycles lay near where the side door had been.

He went around to the back. The heavy swing door from the hayloft lay on the ground. There were small droplets of dried blood in the dirt nearby. He shuddered. There were also the distinctive footprints of hob-nailed jackboots on the topsoil.

His rifle at the ready, he followed the trail into the orchard. A pistol lay at the base of a tree. He bent down and picked it up. With it in the dirt was a crumpled envelope with Lemonier's name written on the front.

Guy clenched the letter in his fist. His intense anger boiled over into a seething rage. A trap had clearly been set for Diamanté and the others. Who had betrayed them?

The sun was beginning to set. In desperation he called out his daughter's name. Walking further into the orchard, he saw two small figures—a girl and a dog. The canine's one good ear was up, and its tail wagged, but it didn't bark. It stood protectively in front of the child who held firmly onto its collar.

"Papa?" a little voice said. "Is that you?"

Guy knelt and held out his arms. "Nathalie, *ma petite*."

The Alsatian let out a low-pitched "woof" and bounded for him, followed by the girl.

Guy enveloped his daughter in his arms, sobbing and repeating her name.

"I'm all right, Papa," she assured him, patting his shoulder. "Are the bad men gone? *Maman* told me to run into the garden when they came. She said not to come back to the house no matter what. I was so afraid, Papa, but Hannibal went with me, and he protected me. We hid behind the stone wall at the back of the orchard. The one where we always find the runaway bunnies." She looked up at him, suddenly concerned. "What is wrong, Papa? Why are you crying?"

Chapter Forty-Three

Paris

His hands tied behind him, Diamanté stood facing the wall in the basement of the four-story French Gestapo headquarters at Number 93 rue Lauriston. Two other men flanked him in the small waiting room. The one on his right shook from terror; the other vomited. Diamanté tensed his jaw and gritted his teeth in a futile attempt to control his fear.

A door opened and a guard entered. "*Schnell. Schnell,*" he said as he roughly pushed the man on Diamanté's right into the hallway.

Shortly they heard screaming coming from the adjacent interrogation room. The man on Diamanté's left retched violently. Diamanté realized he was the Brit who had been with him when they were taken prisoner.

An hour later, only Diamanté stood facing the wall, listening to the sound of unmitigated horror coming from the next room. When his turn came, the guard dragged him down a long corridor and into a special chamber. The air was freezing, and an enormous tub of ice water sat in the middle of the room. Two men in black business suits entered. They took off their coats and rolled up their shirtsleeves, then they lashed Diamanté's hands and feet to a wooden beam and hung him upside down between two chairs.

Diamanté tried desperately to keep himself from panicking. He focused on André's hateful words that night when they had fought over Elise. "You can't keep me from her." A cold, steadfast resolve preoccupied his thoughts. If he ever found out that it was André who had betrayed him, he, Diamanté, would kill again.

Part Three

I have been to hell and back many times.
—Carl Sandburg

Chapter Forty-Four

Mauzac Concentration Camp
1943

Diamanté lay on the floor, drifting in and out of consciousness. Above him a ceiling lamp moved slowly to and fro, casting a wan, sinister light over the room. The wind blew through the barred window. Outside he saw heavy storm clouds forming in the foggy gray light of the winter afternoon.

He moaned and felt his forehead, then winced in pain as his fingers touched his right temple. His head throbbed. The rifle butt had nearly split open his skull. He had not broken, though. He had refused to give names. And it had cost him.

Cloudy, disconnected memories played in slow motion over and over in his mind, rekindling the horrors and setting off new panic attacks. Paris, just after his arrest, was the clearest. After being given nothing to eat for days, his torturers had plunged him into a bathtub of ice water with his hands tied behind his back. They had dragged him to the surface by his hair, gasping and struggling for breath. Because he refused to speak, they immediately plunged him underwater again.

After that, the memories became foggier and more disjointed. At one point, his nails had been torn out. He couldn't recall. Was it before or after the soles of his feet had been slashed with a razor and they had made him walk on salt? Hazy recollections of electric torture came to him, too. Was that after he had been transported to Montluc Prison? He remembered being in leg irons and manacles and more than once threatened with being shot on the spot. At one point, locked in a dark hut with a corpse, he had survived by concentrating on the comings and goings of a rat that he named André.

After Montluc, he was transported by train to Mauzac. The daily interrogations had resulted in more severe beatings. He tried to escape, but the camp was surrounded by three rings of barbed wire and heavily guarded. The consequence of his attempt was the rifle butt to his head. At least here he had some companionship, members of the Résistance who had gone through much the same treatment as he had. They were all starving to death, weakened by dysentery, and covered with lice.

Diamanté considered suicide. He even contemplated how he would carry it off. It occupied his thoughts constantly. It occurred to him that being shot on the spot would be easier.

As he lay now, slipping in and out of a dazed semiconscious state, he wondered vaguely what month it was. It was obvious it was winter. There was no heat, and he was shivering.

A man lay on a cot near him. He had just arrived. Diamanté tried to pull himself up to a sitting position.

The man turned his head. "So, you are alive after all. I thought they had put me in here with a corpse."

Diamanté coughed. "I'm alive," he answered in a raspy voice. "I wish I were dead."

The man rose from the cot and came over to kneel beside him. He was a large man with big feet. "*Écoutez*. You are *le Loup, non?*"

Diamanté recoiled in fear. His hands shook, and his eyes scanned the room. They were alone. "What do you want?" he mumbled finally.

"I am known as *l'Ours*," the man whispered in his ear.

Diamanté studied him through swollen eyes. The beating had caused him to have double vision, but the man kneeling beside him did indeed look like a bear.

"I bring a message from your friends."

Diamanté looked at him in alarm. "*Mes amis?*"

The man nodded. "Les Amis."

Someone had talked. That's how they knew about Les Amis Clandestins. "Is this a trick?"

The man pulled a piece of paper from his pocket. "Read this and then eat it." He chuckled. "Not much nourishment, but it will help with the stomach pains."

Diamanté took the paper and unfolded it. He tried to focus, but he was reading double. He closed one eye. The handwriting became clear enough to make out.

> *Get yourself admitted to a hospital somehow. In two days, we will help you escape. J.*

He read it again and then shoved it into his mouth. When he looked up, the man had disappeared. The piece of paper dissolved on his tongue. It had no taste. Had he dreamt the whole thing?

***

That night, Diamanté lay awake in the darkness. He knew the Dordogne well. The nearest hospital would be in Toulouse, twenty-eight kilometers away. He would have to be near death to be sent there.

Merde. He'd have to make it look good. No faking. *I've been considering this anyway*, he thought. *What do I have to lose? If I die, I die.*

At the first sign of daylight, he etched a *V* in the wall next to his cot. Inside the *V* he carved the double-barred cross of Lorraine. Then he picked up a shard of glass he had removed from the broken window and without hesitation jabbed it deep into his neck.

Chapter Forty-Five

A sentry, arriving to take Diamanté to his daily interrogation session, found him on the floor drenched in blood.

Medics from the camp infirmary were called.

In his delirium, Diamanté was vaguely aware of what was happening. Later it would seem as if he had watched it all from a distance, as if his body were that of a half-dead stranger being dragged onto a stretcher and transported through the night in an open vehicle over a bumpy dirt road.

***

Shuffling sounds. Footsteps, maybe? His eyes opened, closed, then fluttered open again. A darkened room. Diamanté swallowed. Pain. He moaned and raised a hand to his neck. A thick bandage. He coughed. More pain. His head throbbed. Where was he? He tried to sit up.

A woman in a nurse's uniform rose from the chair next to his bed. "*Allez doucement, Monsieur,*" she said, coaxing him back onto the pillow. "You have lost a lot of blood."

"*Où…Où suis-je?*" He barely had a voice.

She lit a candle on the nightstand. "Toulouse. *L'hôpital*."

Diamanté blinked and forced himself to focus. "The last thing I recall…" he rasped and then coughed again. A metallic taste flowed onto his tongue.

She took a tissue and wiped a trickle of blood from the corner of his mouth. She was young and pretty with rich chestnut-brown hair and eyes dark as espresso. "You tried to kill yourself," she said, finishing his sentence for him. She lifted an eyebrow. "*Bof*, you didn't succeed. You nicked an artery." She felt his forehead. "The surgeon sutured your wound, and you received a blood transfusion."

Over the medicinal hospital smells, he caught a trace of lavender perfume. Was he still dreaming?

The nurse lowered her head and whispered next to his ear, "You were apparently too valuable to be allowed to die."

"How long?" he murmured. "I need to get out."

"You are to be kept under surveillance overnight, then returned to the Mauzac camp tomorrow. We don't have much time."

"*Nous?*" He let out a deep breath. What did she mean *we*?

She leaned down to him again and whispered in Corsican, "Try to get some sleep. I'll come for you after midnight."

"*Corsu?*"

She nodded and then put her finger to her lips to indicate he shouldn't talk anymore.

***

Diamanté slept fitfully. Images of the torture of the past few months invaded his dreams, intermingled in a foggy, disconnected way with the glowering eyes of his half brother, André, in a Gestapo uniform. When he awoke, soaking in sweat, the reality of the shard of glass in his neck came back to him, along with the pain. He tried to calm himself, to keep from panicking, but he was apprehensive. Could he trust the nurse? Would the Gestapo come for him instead? He listened for footsteps. An hour passed, then two. No one came into his room. The hospital corridor remained quiet.

Sometime after midnight, she arrived with a pile of fresh linens, in the middle of which she had secreted clothing and a beret.

"Can you stand?" she asked as she unhooked the intravenous line from his arm and pulled back the coverlet.

He nodded. He felt weak, but his head had cleared some.

She helped him rise and change out of his hospital gown. "Guillaume, the night watchman who guards the service entrance, is old and hard of hearing," she said as she buttoned his shirt. "Don't kill him; he's one of us." She slipped a handful of pills into his pocket. "These will help ease the pain."

Together they crept through the dim hallways and descended the rear staircase. The door to the back exit was ajar, and Diamanté could see the shadow of a man just outside. The air smelled of cigarette smoke.

The nurse adjusted the oversized beret low on his forehead. "I'm Marie," she whispered. "Take the cane. Walk as far away from here as you are able. The Maquis will find you." She raised her chin and brushed his lips softly with hers. "*Vive Libre ou Mourir*," Live in Freedom or Die. Then she turned on her heel. He heard her bid him farewell. "*A'vedeci.*"

A stool sat just inside the door; a wooden cane was propped against the wall next to it. He picked up the cane and pushed open the exit with his foot.

In the quiet back alley, a rat skittered from behind a pile of crates.

The watchman turned his head slightly but remained calm with his back to him, smoking his cigarette.

Diamanté raised the cane cautiously above his head.

"*Laissez-le*," the old man spat. "It won't be necessary. I don't stop you."

Keeping the cane, Diamanté crept silently into the night.

The guard snuffed out his cigarette and nonchalantly shuffled back to his post.

An hour later, on an isolated dirt road outside the city, Diamanté collapsed against a tree.

***

At daybreak, a boy riding past on a bicycle stopped. He wore an oversized black beret with the cross of Lorraine embroidered on the front.

"Are you all right, *Monsieur*?" he asked in alarm.

Diamanté was shaking. He touched the blood-soaked bandage at his neck. In a barely audible voice, he murmured a single word: "Maquis."

The youth nodded and sped off. After a time, he returned with two men in a horse-drawn farm wagon.

Chapter Forty-Six

Castagniers, France

A desperate yowl erupted from Diamanté's throat, awakening him. He opened his eyes. He was sweating profusely; his heart pounded.

That dream…again. He had been in the Cistercian convent in the Italian-occupied demilitarized zone north of Nice for over two months, and the recurring nightmare persisted. Always a variation of the theme: His tormentor standing over him with a rifle butt raised into the air, the force of the blow splitting his head open, splattering his brain to the floor like the flesh of a melon. Strong hands shoving him down into a sea of blood, the thick red liquid filling his mouth, nose, running down his throat. Desperately trying to scream as he gasped for air and felt his lungs burst.

He sat up and looked around the room. The space was furnished sparsely: a small sofa, a simple wooden table and chair, and a well-worn rug. On the stand next to the bed lay a single book, a tome of philosophical writings by Jean-Jacques Rousseau. A ray of early-morning sunlight streamed through the slats of the shuttered window. Outside the wind howled.

He pulled back the duvet, rose from the bed, and shuffled slowly over to stand at the washbasin. In the mirror above the sink, he saw a man he barely recognized. Behind the beard was an emaciated face with hollow cheeks and sunken, red-rimmed eyes. His bony shoulders sagged. He touched the ugly scar at his temple and spat into the basin.

"Only nineteen years old," he murmured. His voice was hoarse and raspy, and his neck was still sore from the surgery that had closed the self-inflicted wound. "A useless, shattered wreck. Where do I go from here?"

Three soft knocks at the door startled him. "*Un moment*," he said as he pulled on his shirt and pants before opening it.

Outside in the hallway, a diminutive woman, her face framed in a black veil, peered at him through tiny wire-rimmed glasses. She carried a tray with a coffee pot and cups, a milk pitcher, a jar of preserves, and a linen-covered bread-basket. The aroma of strong coffee and fresh bread made his mouth water.

"*Bonjour, Monsieur. Votre petit déjeuner.*" She was young, barely twenty, he guessed. She wore a penguin-like habit and flat, black sandals. An ornate filigree cross hung on a long silver chain from her neck.

"*Merci*, Soeur Thérèse. *Entrez.*" He opened the door wider for her to enter.

"How are you feeling today, *Monsieur?*" she asked cheerfully.

He rubbed his forehead. "I'm alive."

She smiled and placed the tray on the table. "You have a visitor."

Had he heard her correctly? "*Comment?*" What did you say?

She turned to him. "A man is waiting just outside in the hallway. Shall I tell him he may enter?"

His hand trembled slightly. "Did he give his name?"

She shook her head. "*Non, Monsieur,* but he said he is a friend."

Finally he nodded, and she left the room.

Seconds later, a stocky man of medium height stood in the doorway. "*Nom de Dieu!* You look like *merde.*" He spoke in Corsican.

Diamanté chuckled at the sound of the familiar deep bass voice. "Worse than *merde*," he said as he went over to shake Jacques's hand. "It's good to see you, *mon ami*. How did you know to find me here?"

"The Maquis. It took a while, but they finally sent word to us where you were."

"I knew that they brought me here, but I don't remember it," Diamanté said. He pointed to the tray. "Do you want some *café?*" He peeked under the linen-covered breadbasket. "Soeur Thérèse seems to have delivered enough breakfast for a party this morning. Help yourself."

Jacques poured coffee into a large cup, added a generous amount of milk, then sat down on the sofa. "When they found you, you were half-dead. You were lucky to escape."

Diamanté plucked a slice of baguette from the breadbasket and joined him on the couch. "In Mauzac, I had a dream. Maybe it was a hallucination. I can't be sure. In it, I received a note signed *J*. It told me to find a way to get myself into the hospital. I didn't know the man who delivered it. He disappeared." He rubbed his neck. "And so did the note." For a moment he was quiet, and then he shook his head and looked up at Jacques. "They almost killed me, but I didn't talk."

"After we learned what happened at Guy's farm," Jacques said, "we held no hope of your being alive. Guy found his wife badly beaten and his barn burning to the ground when he arrived." His voice trailed off. "Then, the *Boches* requisitioned his farmhouse, and Marguerite lost the baby she was carrying."

Diamanté sighed. The memory of seeing Marguerite dragged into the farmyard came back to him. "I was responsible for the barn. I set fire to it trying to escape, but they caught us anyway. I wish I could have done something to help his wife." He wiped his cheekbone with a forefinger.

Jacques took a sip of his coffee and placed his cup on the table. "Do you know who betrayed you?" He held his arm out with his hand in a fist, then he smacked the other hand onto it just above the elbow. "Tell me. I'll kill the bastard myself."

Diamanté stared at the wall. "I have my suspicions."

Jacques shook his head and spat in anger. "Some of the others were set up, too. Christophe, the tailor, for one. Ambushed. The fisherman who delivered your friend Bernard was captured near the coast." He rolled a cigarette, offered it to Diamanté, and then fixed one for himself. "We can't trust anyone."

Diamanté's eyes narrowed. "What about the man who was called l'*Écureuil*, the Squirrel?"

Jacques shook his head. "Haven't seen him since the meeting at Saint-Maclou just before you were captured."

Diamanté furrowed his brows. He had chased his half brother André through the cloister that night wondering what he was up to. The next day, he and the others had walked into the trap at Guy's farm.

The two men lit their cigarettes and smoked in silence.

After a few minutes, Diamanté said, "Where is Guy now?"

"Do you remember the Luftwaffe officer who apologized for the destruction of the restaurant?"

Diamanté frowned. "Barely."

"*Eh bien*, as promised, the colonel brought his friends for dinner. I made up a bloody story about how the duck is prepared, and I thought that would be the end of it, but *non!* He came back. Brought his girlfriend. Turns out, he was originally from Alsace. Has a French mother." He hesitated. "He told me he joined the Luftwaffe merely because he wanted to fly a plane. Then the war started, and he was stuck." He paused and went on. "*Eh bien*, I managed to convince him Guy was an innocent victim, that it was purely coincidental there were enemy spies near the farm that day."

"And he believed you?"

"He was set on having his duck! I told him I couldn't get any more, that my source had been destroyed by his own people." He clicked his tongue and winked. "Of course, I embellished the story a bit. I told him our ducks are special, and not just anyone can raise them. I convinced him Guy was the restaurant's only supplier." He shrugged. "*Bof*. It was mostly true. Anyway, a few days later, we heard Guy and his family had been allowed to move back into their farmhouse."

Diamanté rose and went over to the window. He threw back the shutters and stared out over the small village. Tall pines danced in the strong wind. "I have to get to Marseilles," he said. "My girl is there."

Jacques took a drag on his cigarette. He tossed his chin in the air and exhaled a full breath. A white cloud of smoke trailed slowly toward the ceiling. "*Aïe, aïe, aïe.* How can I say it?" He sighed and spat out a shag of tobacco. "I doubt you will find her there. There's nothing left of Marseilles. The port was totally destroyed in January."

Diamanté looked up in horror.

"The *Boches* moved south in November. They took over the unoccupied zone. They evacuated the port and bombed Marseilles."

Diamanté clenched his jaw. All this had happened while he was imprisoned, and he couldn't do anything to help.

"What happened to Marcel's family? They were there."

"I heard they managed to escape to England after the order to evacuate was issued. Had something to do with Marcel's sister knowing a fisherman who had his own boat." He shrugged. "That's all I know."

Diamanté plucked the cigarette from his mouth and studied it. His shoulders sagged. Hopefully, Elise had fled with them. He hadn't been there for her when she needed him. He thought of his brother, Ferdinand. Where was he now? He'd never forgive himself if something had happened to them. Feeling suddenly weak, he returned to sit on the sofa.

"I nearly forgot," Jacques said as he got up and went over to the door. "There's a *mec* with me who's anxious to speak with you." He waved a hand into the hallway. "I believe you know him."

Chapter Forty-Seven

Diamanté rose slowly from the sofa. Was this the downed pilot he had rescued in Normandy? "Stu?"

"Bonjour, *mon ami*!" A grinning Stu Ellis set down his attaché case and gripped Diamanté's hand enthusiastically. "*Oui. C'est moi.*" He surprised Diamanté by speaking French with only a slight American accent. "*C'est bon de vous revoir encore.*"

"What are you doing back in France?"

Stu ran his fingers through his now-darkened hair. "You saved my life. I wanted to repay you by helping win this damn war."

Diamanté raised a dubious eyebrow and looked over at Jacques who was still standing by the door. "*Tiens*! One American is going to help all of France to free herself?"

Jacques shrugged and took a drag on his cigarette.

Stu ignored the Gallic skepticism and went on. "While I was recuperating at Guy's in the fall, my Eagle unit became the Fourth Fighter Group of the United States Army Air Force. I was eager to get back into action. Fly missions over Normandy again, shoot down those *Messerschmitts* and *Focke Wulfs*." He mimed being in the cockpit making the multiple sounds of a dogfight: whooshing interspersed with the "tat tat tats" of machine-gun fire, whizzing and hissing of bullets, planes rocketing and soaring.

He stopped suddenly and looked from one man to the other. Seeing no reaction, he wiped his brow and continued. "But, alas, I was barred from further fighting because I had been shot down and had a bum leg as a result." A glint of self-satisfaction flickered in his hazel eyes. "Well, to give you the shortened version, I wasn't going to let anything keep me from the fun, so I volunteered with the SOE."

Diamanté opened his mouth to ask a question, but Stu held up his hand and continued. "That's the Special Operations Executive. They call it Churchill's Secret Army. Espionage, sabotage, and reconnaissance to aid the resistance movements in occupied Europe." He smiled. "My commanding officers thought I was, how do you say it?" He put his finger to his temple and made a circle. "Crazy."

Diamanté smiled. "*Fou*."

"*Oui*, but they granted my request anyway. I went through a crash course in French and headed back to Normandy aboard a Lysander. *Bien sûr*, I spent a night with Guy and Marguerite before heading to Paris." He put up an index finger and went over to search inside his case. "Ah, here it is," he said with a grin as he lifted out the pistol. "Guy wanted me to personally deliver this to you. Said you had left it behind."

Diamanté took his Walther PP from Stu and ran his fingers over the smooth handle.

Looking over at Jacques, Stu let out a quiet laugh. "It was a challenge getting it here. Jacques and I, we made a good team.

You should have seen us parlaying it back and forth behind the backs of the sons of bitches who searched us on the train."

Jacques nodded.

"My brother gave this to me years ago," Diamanté said, swallowing hard, "to go hunting…"

"*Ah oui*. I was introduced to your brother in Paris actually. Ferdinand, is it?"

Diamanté looked up at him, suddenly fearful. "Is…is he well?"

"Very well," Stu continued. "As a matter of fact, he and his wife were kind enough to shelter me overnight in their apartment."

Diamanté's eyes grew wide. "His wife?" He looked over at Jacques. "Ferdinand is married?"

Jacques shook his head and shrugged.

"I understand they're newlyweds," Stu went on. "She's a pretty one."

"Did…did you catch her name?" Diamanté stared at him, his heart sinking.

"Umm, I can't quite recall. Lise or Lisa? Portuguese, I believe they said."

Diamanté's heart plummeted. Elise had chosen Ferdinand.

"I told them I was going to be seeing you," Stu went on. "They were both happy to hear that you are alive. Said to tell you they look forward to your return to Paris."

Diamanté went over to stare out the window.

Stu and Jacques remained silent.

Minutes passed.

"If you are feeling unwell," Stu said finally, a look of concern on his face, "I can come back later."

Diamanté turned to him. "*Non, non.* Sorry." He wiped his eyes and pinched the crook of his nose. "Please. Have a seat. Have some coffee. It's just that the news…"

Stu's face softened. "I have a brother, too," he said. "He's fighting in the Pacific. I worry."

Diamanté narrowed his eyes. "Why have you come here?" he snapped.

Silent, Stu studied him for a moment. His face grew serious, and he cleared his throat. "OK then. I have a proposition for you." He looked over at Jacques who was watching him. "We need intelligence to plan an invasion, and we were told you could be of help."

Diamanté sat down on the sofa and lit a cigarette. *This is absurd*, he thought. How could he, a broken-down ex-prisoner in poor health, be of any help? He inhaled a full breath and exhaled. "An invasion of what?"

Stu looked at him. "I'm talking about the liberation of Corsica."

Diamanté raised an eyebrow.

Stu pulled up a chair and straddled it, facing him. "With the fighting in North Africa, the Third Reich has its hands full. If the Allies can knock Italy out of the war and establish a staging point in Corsica…" He leaned forward. "We need someone like you who can speak the dialect, first of all. Second, provide us with inside information. Detailed maps of the interior of the island. Local citizen contacts. That sort of thing." He hesitated and turned his head toward Jacques.

"Finally, we'll need the support of the natives, those fighters you call the Maquis, who know the countryside."

Diamanté looked at Jacques. "What do you think?"

Jacques sat down on the foot of the bed. He sighed. "I'm in, but only if you are."

Diamanté lowered his head and closed his eyes.

The wind howled, and the open shutters banged loudly against the outside wall.

Stu rose from his chair and went over to look out the window.

Jacques sat patiently smoking.

Finally, Diamanté snuffed out his cigarette, stashed the butt in his shirt pocket, then rose to join Stu at the window.

"The wind doesn't seem to be letting up," Stu said.

"They tell me it blows a hundred days a year in this region," Diamanté said. "Like France, it refuses to go away." He turned to Stu and offered his hand.

Chapter Forty-Eight

Diamanté and Stu Ellis sat on a bench in the expansive courtyard of the Cistercian convent, a large map of Corsica spread out on a table in front of them.

It was late August, hot, and the leaves on the plane trees swayed in the light wind coming from the valley below. Stu was working on a drawing in his sketchbook.

"Jacques should arrive soon," Diamanté said.

Stu put down his pencil and fished a packet of cigarettes from his shirt pocket. "Castagniers seems so serene, so far away from the war." He offered a cigarette to Diamanté. "I think I'll bring my girl here someday after all this is over." He lit both their cigarettes with a lighter. "Her name's Claire. God, how I miss her." He inhaled a full breath, exhaled, then looked over at Diamanté. "Do you have a girl?"

Diamanté leaned forward with his elbows on his knees. He looked out over the valley below and shook his head. "I did. She married someone else."

Stu raised an eyebrow. "You're joking!"

Diamanté cocked his head sideways. "It couldn't be helped. I was captured and imprisoned. I've been gone for nearly a year now."

"And she couldn't wait for you?" Stu shook his head. "Or…" he hesitated, looking sideways at Diamanté, "was there someone else in the picture already?"

Diamanté took a drag on his cigarette and nodded. "She married my brother," he said with a sigh. "We were both in love with her from the first time we met her."

Stu completed the thought. "And when you were out of the picture, he made his move. Nice." He clicked his tongue in disgust.

"What's your girl, Claire, like?" Diamanté asked, changing the subject.

Stu smiled. He opened his sketchbook and thumbed through the pages. "She's terrific." He had said the word in English. "*Génial*, I think is how you say it."

Diamanté smiled.

"Ah, *je vous présente ma* Claire," Stu said, handing Diamanté the open sketchbook. He sat back, extending his legs, and put his hands behind his head. "I've been gone a long time myself. I hope she hasn't left me for someone else."

Diamanté studied the pencil drawing of the smiling young woman in a bathing suit, lying on her stomach on a sandy beach, knees bent and bare feet pointed skyward.

"I sketched that summer before last," Stu said.

"Where does she live?"

"In California. That's where I'm going after all this is over." Stu flipped back a page for Diamanté to see an architectural drawing of a sprawling one-story ranch-style house on a cliff overlooking the ocean. "That's the house I'm going to build there." He grinned. "I know just where it's going to be, too. In Laguna."

Sister Thérèse came from the convent carrying a tray of glasses and a pitcher of lemonade. Jacques was behind her.

Diamanté and Stu rose from the bench and shook his hand.

The nun placed the tray on the table, poured three glasses, then bowed slightly and left.

"How was your trip to Corsica?" Diamanté asked as he picked up one of the glasses.

Jacques was studying the map of Corsica. "The good news is, the local inhabitants, who call themselves the Service Maquis, are firmly united behind de Gaulle, and, despite the fascist police who repress them, they are gaining strength, especially in the countryside. The bad news is, there is a huge occupation force."

Stu nodded. "Our intelligence tells us that German troops have arrived on the island to reinforce the Italians. But with Mussolini now imprisoned, the Allies have a chance to knock Italy totally out of the war."

Diamanté took a long gulp of the lemonade. "Then the primary function of the Maquis in the countryside will be to prevent troop movements between the coasts."

Stu nodded in agreement. "They'll need to take control of the center of the island."

Jacques rapped his knuckles on the table. "The Maquis is ready."

"Excellent. Everything needs to be in place by early September. I'm heading back to Algiers. Can you be ready to leave immediately?"

Jacques and Diamanté both answered with an enthusiastic "*Oui!*"

"*Bon*. Make your way to Nice…to this address." He produced a piece of paper from his shirt pocket. "You'll be contacted there. We're arranging for the transport now." He winked. "You're in for a surprise!"

Diamanté took the paper from him.

Stu signed his drawing and wrote an address under his name. "I don't know if I will see you again," he said as he tore the page from the sketchbook and handed it over to Diamanté. He seemed emotional. "If I can ever do anything for you after the war is over, don't hesitate to write to me. I wish you luck, my friend."

CHAPTER FORTY-NINE

The Island of Corsica
13 September 1943

It was nearly midnight when they arrived in the port of Ajaccio. Diamanté breathed in the familiar herbal scent of the island. When he left in 1939, he had sworn to never again return to Corsica, but that had all changed when the American, Stu Ellis, unexpectedly appeared in Castagniers four months before.

Jacques stood next to him at the foot of the gangplank. Together they watched the members of the Fourth Moroccan Mountain Division disembark from the sleek ninety-two-meter-long Free French Forces submarine known as the *Casabianca* while crewmen unloaded radios, ammunitions, and small weapons, mostly American supplied. From the conning tower, the ship's commander, the inimitable Jean L'Herminier, oversaw the operation. Diamanté put his finger to his forehead and saluted. He had a lot of respect for the man.

L'Herminier smiled. A slight man in his midthirties, he had ignored the demands of the admiralty of Vichy France the year before. Instead of scuttling his vessel at Toulon, he had sailed for North Africa against orders and thus saved his ship and men from surrender to the Third Reich.

It was L'Herminier who had informed them of the details of Operation Vésuve once they had gotten underway—Vesuvius, named for the active volcano whose eruption had destroyed the ancient cities of Pompeii and Herculaneum. On the very same day as the *Casabianca*'s arrival in Ajaccio, the invasion of mainland Italy by the British and Americans was set to begin.

"I have to admit I'm happy to be on land again," Diamanté said to Jacques. It had not been easy being on the *Casabianca*. The sub rarely surfaced, spending most of the day waiting at the bottom of the sea and surfacing only at night to recharge her batteries for the electric motors. His tendency to be claustrophobic had nearly gotten the best of him.

"Let's go get a drink," Jacques said enthusiastically. "I'll introduce you to my Uncle Olivier."

The streets of the nighttime port were unlit, but along the waterfront, the bars were open and crowded. They passed a blind beggar playing "La Marseillaise" on his accordion.

Diamanté followed Jacques down a small side street to a smoke-filled bar just off the Quai Napoléon. "My ancient haunt," Jacques explained as they entered Chez Olivier. "The *propriétaire* is my uncle."

From the back of the bar, they heard, "Jacques? *Quelle bonne surprise!*"

Jacques's face lit up. "*Oncle* Olivier! *Salut!*" He went over and shook the hand of a middle-aged man with black curly hair and a goatee. The man threw his arms around Jacques and kissed him on both cheeks.

"This is my friend Diamanté," Jacques said. "We just arrived in port," adding in a whisper, "on the *Casabianca*."

His uncle's eyes widened; he sucked in a breath. "*Le Casa? Vraiment?* It is here in Ajaccio?"

Jacques nodded. "*Mais oui! Les Boches*," he said with an air of pride, "have never been able to capture her."

The small bar smelled of liquor and stale cigarette smoke. Giant unmarked barrels of wine lined the walls, and hams and salamis hung from the ceiling. Half-filled bottles of wines and liqueurs sat on the wooden countertops. On top of a cabinet, there was a bust of Napoleon.

Uncle Olivier motioned for them to take a seat at one of the overturned barrels being used as tables. "You want *un Cap?*"

Jacques slapped his uncle on the shoulder. "That's why we came to see you."

They sat down, and Olivier brought them two glasses of Cap Corse, the traditional Corsican aperitif, a dark-colored sweet wine served with a thin slice of lemon. "We've just had some good news," he whispered. "The Italians are now willing to fight on the side of the Allies!"

"*Tiens!*" Jacques exclaimed. "I guess that explains why the harbor was so easy to enter tonight."

His uncle smiled and thrust out his chest. "*Beh oui!* The Maquis controls Ajaccio. *Phfttt*."

Diamanté looked around the room. He smiled. It was indeed hard to believe, sitting here in this bar, that there was such brutality occurring all over Europe. In the far corner, a group of Corsican men with ruddy, weather-beaten faces carried on a heated discussion over glasses filled to the brim with red wine. There were two groups of soldiers seated at tables in the center. A third group of local girls sat at the table between them, giggling and flirting.

Diamanté stared at the bright red lips and bare legs. A momentary frisson of attraction ran through him, and he shifted uncomfortably in his chair.

"My uncle has offered to put us up tonight," Jacques was saying. "We can get a good night's rest and depart for the interior early in the morning."

Ajaccio made Diamanté nervous. He removed his beret and rubbed the scar on his forehead. "I'd prefer to leave immediately." Where were the Germans?

"Nevertheless, you need to rest. You look tired."

Diamanté didn't answer. He rarely slept well now. When he did, the hellish nightmares woke him.

Jacques took a sip of his aperitif and cocked his head toward the end of the bar where a young woman sat alone, her knuckles resting against her chin. A half-full glass of red wine sat on the counter in front of her. "That girl in the nurse's uniform over there is staring at you."

Diamanté glanced sideways. She was indeed eyeing him.

There was something vaguely familiar about her. She was slim, pretty, and her dark chestnut-brown hair was pulled back into a chignon.

He felt himself blush.

She lifted her glass of wine, swung her legs gracefully from the stool, and walked over to stand at his side. "You don't remember me, do you?"

"Have we met?"

She smiled. "I recognized you by the scar on your forehead."

Was this the way it was going to be from now on? Forever branded by the mark of the Gestapo? Diamanté took a deep breath and lowered his eyes.

She leaned over him.

He caught a trace of lavender perfume.

"The last time I saw you," she said, "you were in bad shape." Her eyes, dark as espresso, caressed his lips. "I kissed you goodbye. Don't you remember?"

He raised his eyebrows. "*Ah oui*! But, of course! The nurse in the hospital in Toulouse!" He remembered his manners and rose from his chair. "But what are you doing here in Ajaccio?"

"I returned to care for my father. I help out at the hospital, too. By the way," she extended her hand, "my real name's Clotilde Vergara. Marie was *mon nom de guerre* while I was in the Maquis in Toulouse."

He took her hand and kissed the back of it. "I owe you my life."

She placed her glass on the table. Then, as she had done before when she saw him out the back door of the hospital, she raised her chin and brushed his lips softly with hers.

The group in the corner began singing the national anthem of Corsica. "*Diu vi salvi Regina,*" they sang. "*È madre universale…Per cui favor si sale…Al paradisu.*"

"I was hoping I'd see you again," she whispered.

Diamanté pulled an empty chair up to their table.

"Join us, please," he said.

Clotilde looked at her watch, then back at him, and sighed. "I'd like to, but unfortunately it's very late. I should be getting home." She shrugged and added, "Sorry."

"Can I walk you home?"

She cleared her throat and looked up at him. "That would be nice. It's not far."

He smiled, slung his duffel bag over his shoulder, and extended his arm. "*Mademoiselle?*"

She slipped her arm through his.

Jacques stared after them as they left the bar. "*Merde*," he mumbled. "First she kisses him, then she takes the lucky *mec* home with her!"

Chapter Fifty

They strolled along the deserted waterfront. The night air was clean but still warm, and the strong rosemary and thyme-infused scent of the island mixed with the fishy, salty smell of the harbor. In the faint light of the crescent moon, they could see the shadows of fishing boats bobbing gently in the dark waters.

The slip where the *Casabianca* had docked was empty. The elusive submarine was off to deliver supplies to its next destination along the coast.

"Don't you worry about the curfew?" Diamanté asked, looking behind them, his eyes scanning the buildings of the port for any sign of movement. The shutters of the windows were all closed. No sounds came from within. The capital city of Corsica was hushed. Not even a dog barked. It made him nervous.

She shook her head. "I have a permit from the hospital."

An old drunkard staggered from an alleyway holding a wine bottle. Nearly colliding with them, he mumbled something unintelligible then lifted his hand in an obscene gesture.

Clotilde clutched Diamanté's arm. They waited.

"It's best we stay away from the port," Diamanté whispered, picking up his pace.

"It's not much farther," she said as she hurried to keep up with him. "There's a shortcut just ahead through that alley."

They ducked into the dark passage and stopped. A rancid smell hit Diamanté's nostrils. A few feet away, a rat scurried across the cobbles and a black cat leapt from behind a garbage can. The clatter of the overturning bin caused them both to jump.

He put his arms around her as if to protect her.

She leaned into him.

"I live just around the corner," she whispered. Her voice was so low he could hardly catch the words.

He did not know what to say. They stood very close, and he was aware of her warm breath against his cheek. The feeling of being watched and followed no longer meant anything. Everything he had gone through, the torture, imprisonment, all of what had happened in the past year smoothed away. His skin tingled. Nestling his nose into the crook of her neck, he smelled the musky scent of her. He wished he could crawl inside her and remain there.

She did not speak for a moment or two either. Finally she wrapped her arms around his neck and looked at him steadfastly. Her eyes, level and black, shone in the moonlight.

She seems so young and calm. He whispered in her ear, "Kiss me again like you did in the hospital."

She brushed his lips gently.

He waited for a few seconds, and then he kissed her fully on the mouth. Her lips were warm and soft, and, to his surprise, she let the kiss go on, not protesting, until it grew deeper and more tender.

The sound of distant rifle fire echoed through the streets, reminding them that this was wartime.

She broke away, breathless, and looked at him with tenderness in her eyes. "Are you afraid? You seem afraid."

"I am afraid for you." He touched her hair.

She took his hand. "Shall we go now? It's just around the corner. I'll fix us something to eat. Some soup and bread. It will be good for you to rest."

He followed her out of the alley and into a narrow, winding side street. Overhead, the crescent moon seemed to follow them. The silence was broken only by the rumble of a train far off in the distance.

At the last house, just before the street ended, up against a high stone wall, she stopped and fished a key from her pocket. She unlocked the heavy wooden door, paused to listen, then motioned for him to follow her inside. After she had closed the door and locked it, she said, "My father sleeps very soundly. We won't wake him."

Diamanté doffed his beret and followed her up the wooden steps. When they had reached the first floor, she went ahead of him and switched on a light. The dim ten-watt single lamp cast shadows around the room.

They were in a narrow foyer. A wooden bench sat against one wall; a mirror hung above it. Opposite sat a long black buffet and a rack filled with china plates. An ornate wrought iron chandelier hovered in the dark above.

Through an open French door, Diamanté could see a round wooden table and chairs in the kitchen. He stood in the foyer, awkwardly holding his beret and his duffel bag.

Clotilde kicked off her shoes and unpinned her chignon. Her hair fell to her shoulders in soft curls. "I'm going to fix us something to eat, but first we need to calm our nerves." She lifted a bottle of cognac and two glasses from the buffet then went into the kitchen and switched on another dim lamp above the sink. She glanced over her shoulder and smiled. "Put your duffel by the door and come take a seat at the table."

He did as ordered.

She poured two full glasses of the cognac and handed one to him. "*Santé.*"

"*Vive la France*," he added, touching his glass to hers.

She took a sip, set down her glass, and began to tie an apron around her slender waist.

He watched her, feeling awkward. The kiss in the alley had excited him. He wanted more kisses, more of her. He wondered why she had brought him here. What could she possibly like about him? Finally, he took a long swig of his cognac and asked, "Do you have a boyfriend?"

She sighed.

Catching himself, he shook his head and said, "Forgive me. It is not the Corsican way to ask questions."

"Jean-Bertrand was killed by the Gestapo two years ago. It was a random shooting. He was traveling to Paris by train. I only learned what happened because his cousin was with him, and he managed to get away." She picked up her glass and took a sip. "After that, I had to do something. I went to Toulouse and joined the Maquis." She put a pot of soup on the gas stove and fetched what was left of the morning's baguette from a cloth bag hanging behind the door. "Now I have my father to care for." She glanced at him through lowered eyelashes. "There is no one else." She placed the bread on the table and lit a candle.

He reached out for her hand. There were many things he wanted to know about her.

"What about you?" she asked him. "Do you have a girl?" She paused and bit her lip. "You called out for a woman...I think her name was Elise...when you were in the hospital."

"Elise is..." He studied his glass of cognac for a moment, and then looked up. "She is my brother's wife."

Clotilde raised her eyebrows.

He wondered briefly what else he had muttered in his semiconscious state but decided not to pursue the discussion.

She filled two steaming bowls of soup and placed them on the table.

"It's a fish stew," she explained as he studied the thick soup. "My uncle is a fisherman. He brings my father fresh catch every day. We haven't much to add to it now. Only beans and herbs from the maquis."

Diamanté's mouth watered with the sudden realization of how hungry he was. All he had had during the day was bad coffee on the *Casabianca*. "It smells of thyme," he said as he picked up his spoon, "and fresh sage. It reminds me of my mother's soups when I was growing up."

"Is she still living?"

He shrugged. "I don't know."

When they had finished eating, Clotilde stood and pulled him to his feet.

He put his arms around her and kissed her cheek.

She touched the stubble of beard on his chin and frowned. "You could use a shave. Would you like me to do it?"

He looked surprised.

She laughed. "I shaved you before when you were unconscious." She picked up the candle from the table and held out her hand. "Come with me."

A footed white porcelain tub, the outside of which had been painted a rich blue, dominated the center of the small bathroom. The checkerboard pattern of the floor was the same as that in the kitchen and foyer, but the tiles matched the blue and white colors of the tub.

Clotilde set the candle on a shelf below the mirror. Next she went over to the windowsill and lifted a heavy copper pot. "It's only lukewarm. I set the pot out in the sun during the day to heat it, but now the water has cooled." She set the pot on the floor, pulled the window shutters closed, then poured the water into the tub.

"It will be all right," he said.

She handed him a cake of lavender soap. "Go on. Climb in. I'm going to fetch my father's razor."

He hesitated.

She put her hands on her hips. "There's no need to be modest. You were my patient, *non*? It's not as if I haven't seen your body before."

He blushed. The thought of her seeing him nude sent an odd thrill up his spine.

When she had left the room, he undressed and stepped into the tub. The cool water felt good on his skin. Feeling suddenly very tired, he lay back and closed his eyes.

When Clotilde returned, she pulled a stool up to the side of the tub, sat down, and began lathering shaving cream on his face with her fingers. She hummed softly.

He closed his eyes again and felt the pleasant pull of the razor, flat and smooth, drawing down his cheek. The war seemed to him suddenly very far away.

When she had finished, she took the soap and worked it into a lather between her fingers. "Now I'm going to wash your back," she said. He sat up, and she massaged the foam into his neck and shoulders. When her fingers touched the scar where the shard of glass had been removed, he opened his eyes.

"Does it hurt?"

"*Non*, not really."

"The wound has healed nicely. It is barely noticeable."

"Not like the one on my forehead," he grumbled.

Her black eyes shone brightly. "No, I think you will have that mark all your life." She kissed the top of his head and lathered more soap into his hair. When she had finished, she poured cool water over him and wiped his face with a damp towel. Then she left the room again.

He stepped from the tub and was just finishing toweling himself off when she returned.

She held out a folded blue nightshirt. "Put this on. It's one of my father's. You are taller than he is, but you are both so thin. It should fit you."

He took it from her and pulled it over his head. It was made of soft, lightweight cotton. "I am very grateful."

She put her arms around his shoulders and murmured, "My bedroom is just across the hall."

He wrapped his arms around her waist, looked into her eyes, and whispered, "Are you sure you want me to stay?"

She nodded. "I think you need to rest."

He picked up his pile of clothing.

Clotilde's room was candlelit and smelled of lavender. A large feather bed covered with fluffy blue and white pillows dominated the center, and flowered curtains in the same colors draped the windows.

"I'll only be a few minutes," she said. She kissed his nose and quietly closed the door.

Diamanté placed his pile of clothes on an end table and looked around the room. His duffel bag was sitting at the foot of the bed. He went over to it and checked to make sure the Walther was still inside. Then he lay down.

Clotilde appeared some minutes later wearing a long white robe. She slipped it off and came over to the bed.

The sight of her naked breasts sent a frisson surging through his body.

She slid under the cover and lay close to him. "Ah, much better," she whispered as she nuzzled his smooth cheek.

She smelled of soap and herbs.

He touched her nipples and felt her body quiver. "I think your favorite color is blue," he said softly, kissing her forehead.

She nestled her face into the crook of his neck and put her arms around his waist. "*Oui*, blue is the color of the sea. I love it."

He smoothed his hand over her stomach, then ran it down her hips and legs. Her skin was soft and warm. He caught his breath. He had been fighting exhaustion, but suddenly he was wide awake. "Will your father hear us?"

"I checked on him just now. He is sleeping soundly."

"Is he very ill?"

"Yes, very. He was wounded badly in the Great War. He's been infirm ever since." Her hand slipped under his nightshirt. "Diamanté, *chéri*," she whispered, "no more questions."

***

Diamanté awoke at daybreak with Clotilde sleeping in his arms. He nestled his nose in her hair and breathed in her scent. *Whatever lies ahead for me*, he thought, *I will survive and return to her.* Becoming aware of a commotion outside, he repositioned her gently so as not to awaken her, then rose and went over to peer out the window. Carts and bicycles moved in the street below; the market across the street was just opening. He could hear people talking excitedly. Had something happened overnight? He quickly put on his clothing.

Clotilde opened her eyes and yawned. She smiled at him. "Are you leaving?"

"*Oui*. I've got to get going." He went over and sat down on the bed beside her. Enveloping her in his arms, he said, "I promise I'll come back to Ajaccio." He stroked her hair. "But it may not be for a very long time."

She placed her index finger against her lips and shook her head. "Let's not make any promises. With the war, it is a very uncertain time."

He kissed her long and hard, put on his beret, and stuffed his pistol inside his shirt.

"I'll see you out." She hurriedly threw on her robe and followed him down the stairs. Tears glistening in her eyes, she opened the heavy street door.

He embraced her one last time and walked away.

Chapter Fifty-One

A sea of Basque berets filled the streets of the port. *Maquisards* with rifles and ammunition belts slung over their shoulders stood around smoking cigarettes and speaking to each other in low voices. More combatants had arrived during the night. Now among the heavily armed guerillas and the Free French Forces were Italian soldiers and Breton sailors wearing the French navy's traditional blue Bachi berets with red pompons.

Diamanté shouldered his way through the angst-filled scene. At one point, he thought he caught a glimpse of André, his half brother, as he turned a corner, but the man disappeared quickly into a side street before Diamanté could be certain who it was.

Jacques stood on the sidewalk in front of his uncle's bar with an annoyed look on his face. "Where have you been?" he barked when he saw Diamanté. "We've been waiting for you. We need to depart."

"What has happened?"

"The Germans have invaded the southern coast."

Diamanté felt a hand on his shoulder. He turned to find himself staring into the eyes of his brother, Ferdinand. He narrowed his eyes and snapped, "What are you doing here? I warned you never to return to Corsica."

The smile of anticipation on Ferdinand's face faded. "*Çà y est, mon frère*. This is how you greet me after all this time?" He extended his hand. "I thought I would surprise you. You should have known I wouldn't stay out of *this* fight."

Diamanté and Ferdinand glared at each other.

"*Ça suffit*! There's no time now for a family squabble," Jacques growled. "I've arranged mules for us to ride into the hills. We'll have to go farther to the north than we planned originally. The *Boches* are headed toward Bastia."

Diamanté nodded and looked over at Ferdinand. "We'll take the lead. We know the countryside well."

***

They rode all day through difficult terrain. It was hot, and the heat of the sun made the scent of the maquis more intense. Diamanté reveled at the sight of wild boar, rabbits, hedgehogs, and weasels running in front of them. By nightfall, the buzzing cicadas had begun their song and the small brigade had reached the northern interior of the island not far from Castagglione. The mules were left in the care of a local blacksmith, who in turn supplied the men with a donkey to carry their food and wine up the mountainside. Diamanté and Ferdinand led the unit on foot through dense underbrush to a hillside hideout. Thick scrub covered the entrance, and it took some time before they were able to hack into it.

The cave was dark and musty smelling. "It's been a long time since anyone has been in here," Diamanté told Jacques.

"It will be safe enough for the night. The men can spread out, have their food and wine, and get some sleep. Tell them to try not to smoke too much."

Jacques relayed the message to the armed guerilla fighters who had ridden all day with them. The tired group took their crusts of bread and bottles of wine and settled in for the night.

Diamanté sat down, pulled a map from his duffel bag, and spread it on the ground under the light of a lantern. His hand shook slightly, and he felt drained. *I need to get some sleep,* he thought.

Ferdinand and Jacques joined him. The three lit cigarettes and passed around a bottle of red wine.

"There's a bridge a few miles to the north of here," Diamanté said, pointing to a spot on the map. "We'll need to get to it tomorrow." He looked up. "If it hasn't been destroyed, we will have to do the job immediately. The unit joining us tomorrow will be bringing the composition C-2."

After more discussion, Jacques stood. "I'm tired," he said. "If we have nothing more to decide, I'm going to get some rest now."

Diamanté and Ferdinand wished him *bonne nuit*.

When they were alone, Diamanté studied his brother's young face, younger looking now than himself, he thought. "I suppose *félicitations* are in order," he said flatly.

Ferdinand raised an eyebrow.

Diamanté hesitated. "I mean about your marriage, that is," he sucked in a breath, "to Elise."

Ferdinand frowned. "How did you know about that?"

"The American. Stu Ellis. He mentioned that he met you and your wife in Paris."

"I meant to tell you myself before you learned of it." Ferdinand studied his hands. After a pause, he looked up. "I hope there are no hard feelings. I mean, you were captured." He scratched his head. "*Mon Dieu*. We both thought you were dead."

Diamanté stared at him.

"Are you angry?"

"I was."

"Not now?"

"*Non*." Diamanté shrugged. "She chose you. I accept that."

"I love her."

Diamanté clenched his jaw and cleared his throat. He really didn't want to know any more details, but he was curious. "I don't mean to pry," he said, "but where were you married?"

"In Speloncato. The Germans were marching south to Marseilles. Marcel's wife and children left with Tante Amélie for England. I didn't want Elise to go with them." Ferdinand shook his head. "I guess I was selfish. We thought that if we were married, I could avoid the forced labor draft." He paused and added, "*En tout cas*, Elise met our mother."

Diamanté was intrigued. "How is she, our mother?"

Ferdinand lit another cigarette. "*Pleine d'entrain, comme d'habitude.*"

Diamanté chuckled. That was his mother, fiesty as ever.

Ferdinand rubbed the back of his neck as if to relieve the tension. "She has been hiding two Jewish children in her house all during the war."

Diamanté gasped. "*C'est incroyable.*" He hoisted the bottle and quaffed the wine.

"*Oui.* She's very proud of it, too."

"Is she happy?"

"I believe so."

Diamanté drifted off, exhausted, filled with thoughts of Clotilde. Her gentle touch. Her caring eyes. The lovemaking they had shared.

"*Bonne nuit, mon frère,*" Ferdinand whispered.

In the distance, they heard a burst of rapid gunfire followed by a loud explosion.

Diamanté sat up. "*Putain de merde.* What was that?"

The men in the cave shot to their feet and began loading their rifles.

Diamanté and Ferdinand ran to peer out the entrance. Bright flashes lit up the night sky accompanied by intense mortar fire.

"They are several kilometers away by the looks of it," Diamanté whispered.

Jacques joined them.

Diamanté started to say something when the deep foghorn call of a bittern filled the night air.

Jacques shushed him. "*Chut! Écoutez!*"

A second later, they heard it again.

"It's the other unit! That's the signal." Jacques stepped out of the cave and cupped his hands around his mouth; his long caterwaul sounded like a feral cat in heat.

They heard five slow, deep, resonant booms in response.

"Go see if they have the high explosive with them," Diamanté ordered. "If so, we'll set out immediately. The Barchetta bridge needs to be blown. It's a strategic pass."

Jacques saluted and disappeared into the darkness.

Diamanté and Ferdinand waited. The rest of the men squatted behind them, rifles at the ready.

When Jacques returned a few minutes later, he said, "They're not far from here, and they have the C-2 and the detonating cord."

"Have they spotted any *Boches* in the area?" Diamanté asked.

Jacques shook his head. "None nearby. For now, the local partisans have blocked any movement north with the help of Italian reinforcements. We won't have much time."

Diamanté put his arm in the air and motioned to the waiting men. "*Eh bien. Allons-y!*"

Chapter Fifty-Two

The maquis gave way to a dense pine forest and then to an open grade leading through a deep, narrow river gorge. Twigs broke beneath the men's feet as they made their way through the scrub. Dark outlines of mountains rose high on either side, and dense clouds partially obscured the full moon. In the distance, they heard an occasional burst of mortar fire.

"The one we knew as *l'Écureuil,* the Squirrel, is with the unit that's just joined us," Jacques whispered in the dark to Diamanté as they walked.

Diamanté turned his head and scanned the group nervously. "Are you certain?"

"*Oui.* I saw him earlier."

"Take the lead," Diamanté said to Ferdinand. "I need to check on something." He halted and allowed his men to pass.

The unit that had joined them was almost double theirs in size, and they were heavily armed. Several mules trudged alongside, large canvas bags strung across their backs.

Diamanté saluted to the leader and cast a wary eye over the band as he watched them pass by. At the rear, he saw a lone figure halt just a few steps away. The man abruptly pulled his oversized beret low over his forehead to obscure his face. Just then, the moon came from behind a cloud, and Diamanté caught the reflection of a pair of thick-lensed eyeglasses. It was his half brother. He spun around and hurried back to catch up with Ferdinand and Jacques. Nearly out of breath when he reached the front of the column, he said to Jacques, "You were right. He's here." Then he turned to Ferdinand. "Hold back a minute. I need to talk to you."

"What is it?" Ferdinand whispered. "*Les Boches?*"

"*Non.* André is here."

Ferdinand spat. "*T'es sûr? C'est vraimant lui?*"

"*Oui.* I'm sure. I saw him just now at the back of the column."

Ferdinand glanced nervously behind them. "*Le salaud.* What's the rat-faced bastard doing here?"

"*Putain de merde!* Probably recruited like we were because he's Corsican. Be alert."

"*Toi aussi,*" Ferdinand put his hand on Diamanté's shoulder. "You too, *mon frère. Fais attention.*"

***

They stood at the edge of the fast-flowing Golo. The vague outline of a Roman-style railway bridge towered high over the gorge above them. Stone arches extended from each bank, and two heavy pillars supported the center span over the river.

"It's like a fortress," Ferdinand said. "We'll be lucky if we can bring even a portion of it down."

"It will be daylight in two hours," Diamanté said. "We have just enough time to try."

***

They had just finished molding the high explosive around the rails at the tie when their attention was drawn to the low rumbling of a heavy vehicle's engine close by. With a noisy screech of brakes, a *Wehrmacht* truck stopped on the road on the other side of the river. They could see the silhouettes of a small group of Third Reich soldiers making their way down the embankment. When the soldiers reached the river's edge, they aimed their rifles and fired a barrage directly at the insurgents.

Ferdinand lifted his rifle and fired back. Motioning to the others, he lit a wooden match and hollered, "Get the hell out of here! We're ready to blow the bridge."

The first blast detonated just as the men retreated up the ridge. A second explosion followed, and then a series of thunderous concussions pounded through the air.

Diamanté glanced over his shoulder as he ran. Only one of the pillars had fallen, but it had been sufficient to send the center span tumbling into the river.

When the rubble settled and all was quiet, he heard shouting and the sound of the truck moving away. The Germans would send out a search party at first light. He looked around for Ferdinand.

At that moment, he heard a lone shot echo through the gorge.

Chapter Fifty-Three

Diamanté raced frantically down the embankment in a desperate search for his brother. In the gray light of predawn, he saw Jacques running toward him.

"Have you seen Ferdinand?" Diamanté shouted.

Jacques shook his head.

They heard a burst of artillery fire in the distance.

"*Fichez le camp!*" Diamanté yelled. "Tell the others to get out of here!"

Jacques saluted and ran off.

"Ferdinand?" Diamanté called out his brother's name. He stumbled in the scrub but regained his footing and kept going. The first light of day broke over the mountains. All of a sudden, Diamanté stopped and sucked in his breath. Ahead of him a man lay face down in the mud at the river's edge. The shadow of his half brother, André, with a pistol hanging from his hand, stood over the body.

Seeing Diamanté approach, André quickly turned his back to him and walked away.

Diamanté's heart pounded. It was surely one of the men who had accompanied them. He knelt down to have a closer look.

The back of the head was a bloody mass of brains and flesh. He wondered whether it had been blown away by the force of the explosion or the man had been shot. He turned the body over and gasped in horror. Ferdinand's open, lifeless eyes stared at him, the entry hole of a bullet between them.

Diamanté gently closed the eyes and then cupped his brother's face in his hands. For a moment he was quiet, and then a huge sob came from deep within his throat.

Part Four

Hope, like the gleaming taper's light,
Adorns and cheers our way;
And still, as darker grows the night,
Emits a brighter ray.

—Oliver Goldsmith

Chapter Fifty-Four

4 October 1943

Perched on a mountaintop six hundred meters above sea level, the village of Speloncato was a labyrinth of narrow streets, stairs, rock walls, and densely packed stone houses with tile roofs, all clustered around a single church with a steeple and bell tower.

Diamanté sat inside his mother's home listening to the roar of Allied bombers overhead.

"This is it," he said.

Tesa set a glass of lemonade on the table in front of him. The midday air was hot and still outside, but inside with the shutters closed it was cool and pleasant.

"Will the *Boches* be gone now? Forever?" a small voice asked. The girl, Simone, looked bright-eyed and hopeful.

Diamanté glanced over at her. "How old are you?"

"Twelve, next month."

Her younger brother, Emile, played with an improvised truck fashioned from two pieces of wood and four round disks cut from dried corn cobs for wheels.

"And your brother?"

"He's only seven."

"*Allez, les enfants*," Tesa instructed. "Let us talk. Play somewhere else, but stay indoors."

"We want to be in here with you," the little girl protested. "We're afraid of the airplanes."

"They won't hurt you," Diamanté said. "They've come to chase the *Boches* out of Corsica."

"And about time, too," his mother clucked. She took a seat at the table opposite him. Diamanté studied her face. In her black mourning dress she looked much older than her years, and more haggard. War and grief had given her eyes and cheeks a sunken look. Stray wisps of salt-and-pepper hair escaped from her tightly wound bun.

"Where are their parents?" Diamanté asked in their native Corsican dialect.

Tesa shrugged. "I don't ask. When suspicion fell on them, they were transferred to another village and given new papers. They left the children with me." She eyed the ceiling as another bomber roared over the house. "We will see them soon, I expect."

"Didn't you ever worry that you'd be caught harboring them?"

She chuckled. "Here in Speloncato? *Mais non!*" She waved her hand in an air of dismissal. "*Bof!* No one even knows we have any Jews on the island. Besides, everyone keeps *Omertà*."

Diamanté nodded. "Ah *oui*, the code of silence. Nevertheless, you are very brave to allow them to stay with you."

She smiled and patted his hand. "It is you, *mon fils*, who is very brave."

"Ferdinand was the bravest of us all."

Diamanté swiped beads of perspiration from his brow with his hand as he recalled the horror of seeing his brother's blank eyes staring up at him. It had been little more than two weeks since Ferdinand had been killed blowing the bridge at Barchetta. For several days, Diamanté had transported the body over the rugged, mountainous terrain of northern Corsica. Then, he and his mother had buried him alongside his father, Jean-Pierre.

Tesa got up and went over to the sink. "Will you go see his wife? She needs to know what happened."

Diamanté had been thinking about that. What, first of all, would he tell Elise? Would he let her believe it was the enemy soldiers? He had let his mother believe that.

"She sent me a letter," his mother was saying as she opened a cupboard. "It was written at the end of August, but it only just arrived on my doorstep a few days ago." She shook her head in disbelief. "Somehow, someone, I don't know who, managed to deliver it." She fingered the envelope then handed it over to him. "Two letters, really. There is one for Ferdinand inside, which I didn't open." She muffled a sob. "She must have written it right after he departed for Corsica."

Diamanté studied the return address on the envelope, an apartment number in the fifth arrondissement. He opened it and carefully removed the contents. The letter was written on very thin paper, and Elise's handwriting was small and crowded. He found the sealed envelope addressed to Ferdinand and looked over at his mother who stood by the window dabbing at her eyes.

"Life must be very hard in Paris," she said between sniffles. "She's anemic, poor dear. She should have been pregnant by now." She sighed. "Alas, you can't make babies when you don't have sufficient nourishment."

That piece of information briefly made Diamanté uncomfortable. He had believed, once, that Elise would be his wife. Now she seemed unreal. All that he remembered of those early days of the war in Paris seemed dreamlike. He shut his eyes, realizing that the life behind him was gone. Clotilde was his future now, if she would have him.

"That letter was the first I knew that you were alive," Tesa went on, interrupting his thoughts. "She said Ferdinand had hoped to join you." She looked over at him. "She's a nice girl, that Elise. Ferdinand was very devoted to her. You have to tell her what happened to him."

Diamanté wiped his eyes. "I promise I will go see her after the war is over," he said finally.

Bombers roared overhead again. The windows vibrated.

"The war *is* over," Tesa said. "Listen to that."

"Over for Corsica," he said. "But not yet for the mainland. The *Boches* have not surrendered."

"They will, *mon fils*," she said. "They will."

A small voice in the corner said, "What are you talking about? I don't want you to speak in Corsican." It was the boy, Emile. "I can't understand what you are saying."

Tesa bent down and patted his head. "*Je regrette, mon petit.*" She looked up at Diamanté. "My son and I were just saying how nice it will be after the war is over."

A few days later, Diamanté left for Ajaccio. As he bid his mother goodbye, it struck him that, in the entire time he had been there, neither of them had even once made mention of André or the vendetta.

Chapter Fifty-Five

It was just before dusk when Diamanté arrived in Ajaccio. The lights of the harbor glowed; a soft evening breeze blew. The city was teeming with Allied soldiers and sailors on R & R. Young couples walked arm in arm along the quay. Groups of small boys raced through the crowd shouting and rolling large hoops with wooden sticks.

Diamanté surveyed the port. In the vague light, he could see the shadows of cargo vessels flying the flags of Britain and the United States moored at the long docks, loading and unloading. Silver barrage balloons floated above the harbor, tethered with steel cables to discourage a low-level enemy aircraft attack. In the three months since he had first disembarked on the *Casabianca*, the island had been successfully secured by Free French Forces, the last of the German units had evacuated Bastia, and Corsica was liberated.

For Diamanté, the jubilant, bustling atmosphere of the capital city was bittersweet. He had witnessed the death of his beloved brother; his mother had suffered the loss of her first-born child. Elise, though she didn't know it yet, no longer had a husband. He wondered what Clotilde's reaction would be at the sight of him, and fearing rejection, he prepared himself mentally.

By the time he reached Clotilde's street, he was filled with self-doubt, convinced that she would slap him in the face and never want to see him again. Nonetheless, he knocked at the heavy wooden door. Minutes went by. He shifted his weight from one foot to the other. An old woman with a kerchief tied at her chin came out of the market across the street. She scrutinized him briefly then stopped to chat with a fisherman delivering his daily catch, all the time keeping one wary eye focused in Diamanté's direction. He turned his back to her and knocked again.

This time, the door cracked open, and two black eyes peered out at him over a pronounced nose. Diamanté knew at once it was Clotilde's father. He had seen a photo of him in a seafarer's knit cap on her nightstand.

The old seadog opened the door wider. He wore a faded blue bathrobe, and a long-stemmed pipe hung from the corner of his mouth. "Who are you?" he shouted. His face and hands were coarse from long exposure to wind and sea and sun. The bushy beard and mustache were white, but the unruly eyebrows above slightly sagging upper eyelids were coal black.

Diamanté took off his beret and extended his hand. "Monsieur Vergara?" he said. "I am Diamanté Loupré-Tigre."

The man sniffed. He didn't take Diamanté's hand.

"Is Clotilde here?"

The man cupped his hand to his ear and shouted, "Who?"

"Your daughter. Clotilde. I wish to see her. Is she here?"

"*Non*." The door slammed shut.

***

He found her at Chez Olivier, seated alone at a table with a half-full glass of red wine in front of her, one fist resting against her cheek and a sad, pensive expression on her face, much like the first time he'd seen her. Now she wasn't in a nurse's uniform, but in a short black skirt, white blouse, and a turquoise-blue headscarf around her neck. Her dark hair was cut slightly shorter; ringlets of curls framed her heart-shaped face. To Diamanté, she was beautiful.

The smoky bar was noisy and filled with laughter. Glasses clinked, and in one corner a young bearded musician strummed on a mandolin.

Diamanté made his way through the crowd and went to stand in front of her table. "Clotilde?"

She looked up and blinked her eyes in a momentary flash of recognition.

He grinned and held out his arms.

She remained silent, unsmiling, staring at him.

Stunned, he pulled up a chair and sat down at her table. "Don't you recognize me?" *Why is she so cold? Do I look so different?*

She lowered her eyelashes. "You have a beard," she said finally.

He rubbed his chin and chuckled. "I guess I *could* use a shave."

She stood and pulled her scarf up over her head. "Let's take a walk." She led him out of the bar and down to the pier where she stopped and turned to him.

He tried to put his arms around her, but she resisted the embrace.

"What is it?" he asked. "Are you angry with me?"

"I have something to tell you." Her face was very close to his. She placed her hand on his shoulder and gazed tenderly into his eyes.

It was a clear night. The sea breeze was fresh, and the full moon shone brightly.

His eyes drifted down to her breasts, and his loins tingled at the sight of her nipples beneath the delicate fabric of her blouse. He leaned in to try to kiss her.

She lowered her chin and pulled away.

"What is it? Has something happened?"

"*Oui*," she whispered, not looking at him. "Something has happened." She bit her lip. "I am—" She hesitated and took a deep breath. Finally, she blurted, "I am pregnant."

He jerked his head back. "But how?"

"The usual way!" She laughed nervously.

It didn't hit him immediately that she might be talking about them. "You mean?" He pointed to himself.

She nodded. Her shoulders sagged, and her arms fell to her sides. "Are you very upset?"

He felt dazed. "I...I don't know what to think about it." He removed his beret and rubbed the scar on his temple. Then he pulled a cigarette from his shirt pocket and lit it with a lighter. His hands shook. "I'm not unhappy," he said finally. He smiled at her. "Just surprised."

She seemed tense. "I was, too. *Bof*! I thought I had taken precautions." She turned sideways and stared out into the harbor. Tears glistened in her eyes, and he saw that she was trembling.

Diamanté took a drag on his cigarette and tossed it into the iridescent black water. "I think we should get married."

She turned back to him. "My father would not permit it."

"But why? After all..."

She put her finger to his lips. "He would want you to prove you can support me." She hesitated. "And even then he would make us wait. It's no use. This is Corsica. It's the tradition."

"I can cook!" he said. A thought occurred to him. "Maybe Olivier needs more help now that the bar is full of Americans and Brits."

She looked doubtful.

"It's been my lifelong dream to have a restaurant," he added. "No better time but now to start."

He put his arms around her waist and drew her to him. "Will you marry me?"

"You hardly know me."

He swayed a little, gently stroking her back. "I know how wonderful you are. I wanted to marry you the day I met you."

She smiled for the first time. Then she rubbed her nose against his and kissed him. "Time for that shave."

***

Diamanté propped himself on his elbow and studied Clotilde who lay naked next to him, her arms extended behind her head, her eyes closed, a sweet smile of contentment on her face. He smoothed the curls from her damp forehead. "You remind me of a Renoir painting," he whispered.

She opened her eyes.

He picked up a pack from the nightstand and offered her a cigarette.

She took one, studied it for a minute, then shook her head and handed it back to him.

He lit his, inhaled a full breath, and exhaled. Then he settled back against the pillows. "I've been thinking. We should find a priest and get married."

"Without my father's permission, a priest would never agree to it."

He took another drag on his cigarette and thought about what she had said. "Maybe," he said. "But it's worth a try, isn't it? We could explain."

She clucked her tongue. "The church won't accept an explanation like ours."

He rolled over on his side. "*Écoute*. What if we just walked in and asked? It's wartime. You're a nurse. I'm a member of the Maquis. *Phfft!* We want to get married, don't we? We wouldn't have to explain anything."

She nestled her face into his neck and remained quiet for a few minutes.

"*Chéri?*"

"*Oui?*"

"We'll have to tell my father about the baby soon."

"You haven't told him?"

"I was hoping you would come back."

"Were you afraid I wouldn't?"

She nodded, then took a deep breath and patted his cheek. "It would be best if we break the news to him together."

Diamanté groaned and stubbed out the cigarette in the ashtray on the nightstand. "He slammed the door in my face today."

"The crustiness comes from his years at sea. At least he's feeling better now."

"Well enough to come after me with a gaff hook?"

She laughed. "*Mon Dieu.* I don't think he'd do that."

"If I had work, he might be more agreeable. I'll go first thing tomorrow morning and speak with Jacques's uncle." He rested his head on her belly. "It doesn't seem possible. There's really a baby there?"

She caressed his temple. "If it's a boy, we should name him Diamanté *fils.*" Her voice was very tender. She wrapped her arms around him, and he kissed her. Her lips were warm and soft, and he felt all the intimacy of the kiss in the way she let it go on.

***

Early the next morning, Diamanté walked into Chez Olivier and approached Jacques's uncle who was sitting alone in the kitchen having a cup of coffee and a cigarette.

"Do you remember me?" he asked, extending his hand to the man. "I arrived here in September."

Olivier stood up. "Ah, *oui.* Certainly," he said. "*Le Casa! Superbe* effort chasing the *Boches* off the island!" He shook Diamanté's hand vigorously. "Want some coffee?"

Diamanté nodded and took a seat at the table.

Olivier poured a cup for him, refilled his own, and then sat down to join him.

Diamanté added some milk to his coffee and dropped in a couple of raw sugar cubes. "I was wondering," he said. "Have you seen Jacques?"

The middle-aged man with curly black hair frowned. "He came to say *au revoir*. I tried to convince him to stay and help me in the bar." He scratched his head. "*Mais non*, he would have nothing to do with that. He said he had an obligation to get back to watch over his restaurant in Rouen." He leaned forward and whispered, "And the wine!" He fingered the tuft of hair on his chin. "I warned him he might not have a restaurant to return to."

Diamanté nodded in agreement.

"He's stubborn as a bull, that one," Olivier continued, slapping both hands on the table. "Always has been." He focused his black eyes on Diamanté. "Have you seen that restaurant of his in Normandy?"

"*Oui*. And the wine cellar, too. It's quite amazing."

"The hidden bottles, you mean?"

Diamanté chuckled. "He's determined to save France's wine."

Olivier got up and went over to the sink. "Well, I wish him luck." He turned and placed his elbows on the counter. "Now, where are you headed, *mon ami*? Are you returning to fight the war in France, too?"

Diamanté shook his head. "For now, I stay here." He cleared his throat. "I'm looking for work."

"What kind?"

Diamanté shifted nervously in his chair. "Er...do you happen to know if someone, preferably around here, might be in need of a good chef?"

"You can cook?" Olivier looked surprised.

Diamanté nodded. "My specialty is *le lapin de garenne*."

Olivier smiled. "The bar is crowded every day now, and the patrons always demand food. I'm thinking of adding on more space." He tied a bar towel at his waist. "More and more sailors arrive, especially in the evenings. A big group came in last night from an American carrier out there." He cocked his head in the direction of the sea. "They were hungry. I cooked until I ran out of food." He threw up his arms. "I can't keep up with the demand." He handed Diamanté an apron. "Here, put this on. I don't have rabbit, but the sea is plentiful. I've just today received a crate of langoustines. See what you can do with them."

Excited at the prospect of cooking again, Diamanté tied the apron around his waist and went to work. In addition to the langoustines in the crate, he found sea bream and red mullet. He heated a stewing pot and added a splash of olive oil, then sautéed some garlic. In Olivier's kitchen garden in the back alley, he plucked a lemon from a tree and gathered a fistful of fresh mint. He went into the bar and poured a large wineglass of white wine. Back in the kitchen, he hummed to himself as he added the wine, lemon, mint, and a jar of tomatoes to the stew, then tossed in all the fish and shellfish, some sea salt and pepper, and covered the pot with a heavy lid.

An hour later, the mouthwatering aroma of the fish stew brought Olivier into the kitchen from the bar. He went over to the stove, lifted the lid of the pot, and dipped in a spoon to taste.

Diamanté held his breath.

Olivier took a second spoonful. Then he smacked his fingers with his lips. "*Formidable!*" he exclaimed. He went over to the chalkboard and scrolled SPÉCIALITÉ DU JOUR - RAGOÛT DES FRUITS DE MER.

"*Félicitations*," he said, putting down the piece of chalk and shaking Diamanté's hand. "You're hired."

Chapter Fifty-Six

Just before Christmas, Diamanté was chopping potatoes in the bar's small kitchen when Olivier entered carrying a bottle of Champagne. "I have some news," Olivier announced. His voice sounded excited, and his black eyes sparkled.

Diamanté looked up.

"You know that vacant building next door?"

Diamanté nodded.

Olivier set the bottle on the countertop. "It was once a restaurant. It has a kitchen that is," he looked around him, "twice as large as this one, and a big pantry, too, with a wine cellar. I've made up my mind I'm going to expand." He put his hands out in front of him and spread his arms as if picturing a sign above the door, "Bistrot Bar Chez Olivier." He grinned. "What do you think?"

Diamanté stopped chopping and smiled. "I think that is a very good idea."

Olivier slapped him on the back. "I've been considering something else. How about a partnership, *hein?*" He wagged his index finger back and forth between Diamanté and himself. "You and I."

Diamanté frowned and shook his head. "I don't have any money."

Olivier leaned over the counter. "Here's the deal. I fund the venture and run the bar as usual. You do the cooking and manage the restaurant. We split the profit. *Voilà*! We both win."

"Are you serious?" Diamanté was stunned. Was Olivier really offering him part ownership in a restaurant? He set the knife down on the counter and wiped his hands on his apron.

"I warn you," Olivier went on, "it will take a lot of work to make the place ready. We'll have to cut an archway between the bar and the restaurant, paint, build tables and chairs. A friend of mine, Antone, is a fine carpenter. You know him."

Diamanté nodded. Antone hung around the bar every evening, playing billiards and sharing war stories with his cronies. Having lost a leg in the Great War, he hobbled around on an intricately hand-carved mahogany peg he had fashioned for himself.

"He's willing to do the work in return for his daily meals and a bottle of wine."

"I…I don't know what to say."

Olivier picked up the Champagne and deftly popped the cork. "Before I forget." He winked. "The apartment on the floor above the restaurant is vacant, and it's included with the deal. You and Clotilde could live there, if you like."

Diamanté's eyes brightened.

"It needs painting, of course." Olivier pulled at his goatee. "But it's sufficiently big enough," he paused and grinned, "for a family."

Diamanté felt his face flush. One evening, when Olivier discovered him sleeping on a cot at the back of the kitchen after the bar had closed, they had had a glass too many of Ricard. Diamanté had confided that a baby was on the way, but Clotilde's father was refusing to allow them to be married until, as he put it, he could prove he owned his own restaurant.

"Go on. Have a look at it now," Olivier encouraged.

Diamanté removed his apron and threw it on the counter. He hurried through the bar that was already full of patrons.

The vacant two-story building next door was dirty and run down with holes in the walls, mouse droppings on the floor, and empty crates scattered throughout. Diamanté peeked into the kitchen. The zinc sink was corroded, and the cupboard doors hung off the hinges. The carpenter, he thought, would have steady work.

A stairway at the back, next to the pantry, led to the apartment above. He ascended the creaky wooden steps and found himself in a narrow hallway. To his left was a small kitchen with a black-and-white tiled floor, to the right a salon with built-in bookshelves and French doors leading to a tiny balcony overlooking the street. He went down the hallway and opened two more doors, a bedroom and a bathroom with water closet. At the far end of the hall, there was one more door. It opened into a space not much larger than a tie stall for a horse. He sat down on the floor. In his mind, he imagined the room painted blue, and in the center a baby's cradle.

Back in the kitchen of the bar, Olivier poured two glasses of Champagne and handed one to Diamanté. He lifted his own into the air and asked, "Do you like it?"

"It is a dream."

"To our partnership, then."

Diamanté clinked his glass to Olivier's. He couldn't wait to show the place to Clotilde.

***

"This seems too good to be true," Clotilde exclaimed. "No one just hands you your own restaurant."

They stood in the middle of the large kitchen.

"Olivier said he had planned to have Jacques join him, but Jacques turned him down. He's had his eye on taking over the restaurant in Rouen for some time, if it survives the war. Olivier said he couldn't convince him to give up the idea."

"This place is filthy." She crossed her arms and shook her head in disgust.

"It's been vacant for years."

She walked into the pantry, plucked a jar from the shelf, and blew the dust from it. "It's mustard," she said, "from Dijon." She handed it to Diamanté. "Do you think it's still good?"

The faded and dirty label had been partially chewed away. "Probably. It's still sealed tightly." Setting the jar on the counter, he took her hand. "Come with me. I want you to see something."

He opened the door next to the pantry and led her up the stairs to the apartment above. "Not only am I going to own a restaurant," he said as they entered the narrow hallway, "we're going to have an apartment to live in, too."

"What?" she gasped.

He chuckled. "That's the best part, Clotilde. Olivier says it comes with the deal."

Before he had even finished his sentence, she had begun inspecting the rooms. "The *séjour* is going to need new wallpaper," she said of the salon. "The kitchen will do." When she reached the bedroom, she turned to him and exclaimed, "It has an outdoor terrace with a view of the port!"

He enveloped her in his arms and kissed her. Finally, he said, "There's one more room for you to see. It will make a perfect nursery."

Old Vergara, he thought, *won't be able to prevent us from getting married now.*

Chapter Fifty-Seven

On the first of January 1944, Diamanté and Clotilde walked arm in arm through the Place du Diamant where a crowd had gathered to celebrate the new year. A brisk wind whipped the fronds of the palm trees like feather dusters, and the deep-blue Gulf of Ajaccio sparkled in the bright winter sun. At the north end of the square, a band was playing under the shadow of the equestrian monument to the glory of Napoleon, and a circle of young couples performed a lively folk dance to the music.

Diamanté smiled. He was in a festive mood. It was his twentieth birthday, Corsica was liberated, he owned a restaurant, and Clotilde's father had finally given them permission to marry.

As they made their way toward the Palais des Congrès, he pointed with pride to the tricolor with the cross of Lorraine flying prominently above the façade.

Dozens of members of the Maquis had gathered in front of the palace, many of them holding submachine guns. Those who had accompanied Diamanté into the interior in September acknowledged his arrival.

Throngs lined either side of the boulevard. Suddenly wild cheering and clapping erupted as an open car made its way slowly toward the palace. Brandishing the tricolor from doorways and windowsills, the jubilant citizens of Ajaccio hung out of the windows and waved from the building tops. Boys in short pants ran alongside the car, and mothers lifted babies to get a better view.

The small parade pulled to a stop directly in front of the palace, and a tall, distinguished-looking man in full military uniform descended along with the mayor and prefect of Ajaccio. The soldier was General Charles de Gaulle of the Free French Forces.

A young woman in native dress and kerchief came forward to present him a huge bouquet of flowers, and he bent to kiss her on both cheeks.

Diamanté stared at a member of de Gaulle's entourage, a short, gaunt young man with a prominent nose, black hair, and eyes framed in wire-rimmed glasses. "See that man over there?" he whispered to Clotilde. "The one just now getting out of the front seat of the second car? I recognize him. We worked together in the factory in Marseilles."

"Do you think he will remember you?" she asked.

"I'm not sure."

Her question was answered when suddenly Bernard made straight for them, a wide grin on his face.

"Diamanté!"

"*Salut*, Bernard."

Bernard put his arms around Diamanté's shoulders and embraced him warmly. "I'm so happy to see you," he said. His voice was emotional. "If it hadn't been for you, I wouldn't be here today."

"It is good to see you," Diamanté said. "This is my fiancée, Clotilde."

Bernard smiled and held out his right hand. "*Enchanté*," he said smiling. "*Et félicitations.*"

Clotilde put her hand in his, and he kissed the back of it.

Turning to Diamanté, he asked. "How is your brother, *mon ami?*"

Diamanté shook his head. "Ferdinand was killed in September."

Bernard's eyebrows furrowed in pain. He tried to say something more, but all of a sudden there was a general shushing around them. The crowd quieted down and craned their necks to listen.

De Gaulle began speaking from the steps of the palace. There were cheers and applause as he praised the splendidly organized resistance movement that had resulted in the liberation of Corsica. At the end of the short speech, the general held his hand aside the visor of his kepi and saluted the members of the Maquis.

Diamanté left Clotilde's side to join his fellow *maquisards*. When it came his turn to shake de Gaulle's hand, he saw Bernard come forward and murmur something in the man's ear. De Gaulle nodded and extended his hand to Diamanté. "We need you, all of you, if France is to be freed. Keep fighting until the final day, until the day of total and complete victory."

Diamanté felt his throat constrict with emotion. He nodded, shook the giant's hand, and said, "*Vive la France.*"

After the entourage departed, the band in the square started up again, and couples began forming a circle. Diamanté grabbed Clotilde's hand. "Come on," he said. "Let's join them. I feel like dancing."

Chapter Fifty-Eight

Two weeks after de Gaulle's visit, Diamanté was stocking the pantry in the kitchen one morning when a stranger appeared in the doorway. Reaching for his pistol, Diamanté hollered, "The restaurant is closed."

The man entered and placed a small green suitcase on the floor. He hesitated, then said, "They told me in the bar I could find you here. Are you *Le Loup?*" The stranger was dressed in civilian clothing and appeared to be in his early thirties, tall, trim, athletic, with a strong chin and intelligent blue eyes.

Uneasy at the casual mention of his *nom de guerre,* Diamanté turned to face the man. "What do you want with him?"

"Name's Butch," the man continued. "SOE. I was asked to deliver something to you. Sorry, I don't speak much French. Stu Ellis sent me." He chuckled and ran his fingers nervously through his mop of light brown hair. "He warned me you might shoot me."

Diamanté set his pistol on the counter. "You know Stu?"

Butch came forward, extended his hand, and pumped Diamanté's enthusiastically. "Same unit. Algiers. He says to say *baan jur* to you."

Diamanté noted the Texas accent. *How do I know he is who he says he is?* "How is Stu?"

"Still pissed that he can't get back in the cockpit." Butch scratched his head. "But he's needed more now where he is." He paused. "He told me how you saved his life when he was shot down in Normandy. Said to say *mercy* again."

Diamanté chuckled and relaxed. *The mec knows Stu if he told him about that.* "What can I do for you?"

Butch nodded and grinned. "Yes, right to the point. Stu told me that about you, too." He stared Diamanté in the eye. "I have to admit, though, I expected a much older man."

Diamanté frowned. "I don't understand."

Butch cleared his throat. "Sorry. Let me explain why I'm here. I was instructed to deliver a radio set to you personally. My orders are to contact Algiers immediately when your station is set up and operational."

"Instructed by whom?" Diamanté asked.

Butch looked through the doorway to the wine cellar. "We need an isolated room." He shook his head. "That won't do. No window for the antenna."

Diamanté nodded. "*D'accord.* Follow me, then." He climbed the stairs to the apartment and led Butch to a nearly empty, musty-smelling storage space on the second floor. The room was accessible by a ladder from the back of the apartment and had a small window that overlooked the back alley.

Diamanté opened the window to let in some air.

Butch walked around mumbling. Finally, he said, "It will do."

They sat on two overturned wooden vegetable crates. Diamanté pulled up a third for them to use as a table.

Butch opened the suitcase and lifted out twin black boxes, each no bigger than a shoe. "This is the transmitter," he said handing it to Diamanté. "The other's the receiver."

Diamanté picked up a third box. It was the same size as the other two but twice as heavy. "Power supply?"

Nodding, Butch proceeded to connect all three devices with thick black power cords, then he ran a length of thin bare wire from the set out to the plant shelf on the windowsill. "Your station will be known as Dionysus," he said while he worked.

Diamanté chuckled. "The god of wine."

"Yep." Butch looked over at Diamanté. "OK, now give me the code name of someone we can send a test message to. Unrestricted. No top-secret stuff."

Diamanté thought for a moment. Jacques's *nom de guerre* was bull. Les Amis Clandestins had a radio set. "Try *Taureau*."

"Toro? T-O-R-O?"

Diamanté shook his head.

Butch pulled a pad of paper and a pencil from his shirt pocket. "Here," he said, handing both to Diamanté. "Write it out."

Diamanté complied.

"Got it."

There was an assortment of knobs, dials, and toggle switches on the faceplates, and at the bottom right-hand-corner a button-shaped key. Butch flexed his fingers, then set to tapping out Morse code. "From Dionysus station," he said as he tapped, "unrestricted. Begin quote. For T-a-u-r-e-a-u. Contact requested. Loup stands by. End quote."

"Can you teach me how to operate that?"

"That's why I'm here." Butch tapped out more code. "Dionysus going off the air in five minutes." Then he threw the toggle on the faceplate to RECEIVE. "Now we wait." Lifting a handful of code books from the suitcase, he handed them to Diamanté and said, "You'll need to memorize these."

Three minutes later, there was a response from Jacques. Butch wrote it out and handed it to Diamanté. "It's in French."

Diamanté took the paper and translated slowly as he read. "Rouen heavily bombed. Rue du Gros Horloge intact. Restaurant, though damaged, still in one piece, and—" Diamanté hesitated and furrowed his brows as he tried to decipher the last part. Then he chuckled. "Ah, *oui*. Hole-and-corner remains."

"What the hell does that mean?" Butch asked.

Diamanté laughed. "Nothing. It's personal." Jacques was still in possession of his secret wine cache.

Suddenly Butch jumped. There was another incoming message. Excited, he wrote out the content and handed the pad of paper over to Diamanté. "It's for you. Top-level priority," he said, pulling off his headset, "from someone code named." He rechecked what he had written and smiled. "Butterfly?"

Diamanté stared at the name, recalling the BBC message Bernard had sent after he had joined de Gaulle. "The butterfly has found the sunflower." The transmission was from Bernard.

Urgent. Unrestricted. For Loup. Begin quote. Please respond known whereabouts Sara. Butterfly stands by. End quote.

With Butch's guidance, Diamanté sent his first message.

From Dionysus station. Unrestricted. For Butterfly. Begin quote. Sara detained. Last seen July 1942 Vel d'Hiv. End quote.

"Excellent," Butch said. "You're slow and a bit awkward, but you've got it. Anybody else around here we can add for backup?"

"Backup?"

"You know." Butch made a pistol with his hand and pointed it at Diamanté. "In case, boom, something happens to you. We need to keep this station operating. It's part of the network now."

Diamanté knew just whom he would approach.

***

"Do you happen to know any Morse code?" Diamanté asked Olivier that night as they cleaned up the kitchen after the bar had closed.

Olivier stopped sweeping the floor and looked up. "Why?"

"I have received a transmission set."

Olivier's eyes opened wide.

"With accompanying code books," Diamanté went on as he put away a stack of plates and wiped the countertop.

"*Sans blaque!*"

"*Non*. It's not a joke."

Olivier scratched his head. "As a matter of fact, I do know it. I learned at sea when I was a youth."

Diamanté turned to him. "Do you think you can remember?"

"One never forgets. Where is the set?"

Diamanté smiled and took off his apron. "I'll show you."

Chapter Fifty-Nine

Saturday, January 29, 1944

Olivier and Diamanté finished loading Clotilde's feather bed, end tables, and armoire onto the back of the borrowed delivery truck.

The wind had picked up and heavy, dark clouds hung over the sea. The salt air smelled of rain.

"We'd better get moving," Olivier said. "Looks like a storm is coming in."

Upstairs, Clotilde closed the lid of the steamer trunk. "I can't believe we're finally making the move to the apartment," she exclaimed to Diamanté when he entered the room.

He went over to her and swung her around. "I can't believe we are to be married. You don't think your father will change his mind again, do you?"

She kissed his nose. "No. He'll go along with it this time. Besides," she gestured toward the empty room and laughed, "it's too late."

He hoisted the heavy trunk onto his back, and she followed him down the stairs.

By afternoon, the rain came in sheets, and angry waves tossed the ships in the port like tiny fishing boats on a pond.

The marriage ceremony was scheduled to take place at four o'clock in the tiny office of the mayor. Olivier and Antone stood behind Clotilde and Diamanté. Monsieur Vergara, Clotilde's father, sat in a chair near the door smoking his pipe. He wore an old suit for the occasion, but the dour look on his face revealed that he had not entirely made up his mind about his future son-in-law. Earlier he had insisted, much to Diamanté's disappointment, that he would give his permission only for the civil ceremony. The religious ceremony in a church with a priest would be deferred until later, he had declared, when Diamanté had proven himself.

The short, skinny mayor, dressed in a black suit, read from the time-honored script. He raised his eyebrows, glanced over his spectacles at Clotilde's slightly expanded waistline, then cleared his throat and made a few pointed comments about the responsibilities of marriage and family life. Finally, he posed the question.

Clotilde, radiant in a light-blue two-piece ensemble with white lace collar, smiled and answered with a calm "*oui.*"

A nervous Diamanté, in the suit and tie Olivier had lent him for the occasion, turned to her, took her hands in his, and merely nodded his head. Then he placed a slim gold band on the ring finger of her right hand.

The mayor pronounced, "*Je vous déclare maintenant mari et épouse.*" The ceremony was over; Diamanté and Clotilde were legally married.

As they opened the heavy wooden front door of the *mairie,* a cold wind whipped their faces.

Monsieur Vergara grumbled something, then he pulled his knit cap low over his ears and stepped outside.

"We'd better see my father home," Clotilde said to Diamanté. "I worry about him getting disoriented and losing his way in this storm."

"Of course," Diamanté said. He helped her into her coat and donned his beret. Then he raised a *parapluie* over their heads.

"Don't worry about the kitchen tonight," Olivier said. He glanced at Clotilde and grinned. "I'll do whatever cooking is required. We won't have many patrons with this weather anyway." He winked at Antone. "Plus, we have something planned for you two."

Antone nodded, his weathered old face aglow with anticipation.

The rain was coming down harder, and rivulets of water ran down the street. Monsieur Vergara harrumphed and set off without waiting for them. Diamanté grasped Clotilde's hand, and they hastened to catch up.

When they reached Vergara's house, Diamanté extended his hand to his father-in-law. "I won't disappoint you," he said.

The old man hesitated, then nodded, hastily shook his son-in-law's hand, and climbed the stairs.

Clotilde grabbed a seaman's heavy rubber mackintosh from the hook just inside the door and draped it lovingly over Diamanté's shoulders. "I don't want my new husband catching his death."

They set off at a run, but halfway down the street, Diamanté caught Clotilde's arm and pulled her under the shelter of a doorway. He slid his arms under her coat and around her waist. "I love you," he said, smothering her face with kisses.

She caressed his cheek and whispered, "*Moi, aussi, je t'aime.*"

He pulled the mackintosh over their shoulders, and they ran as one through the deserted, rain-soaked streets, laughing and stopping to kiss in every sheltered alleyway and doorway they came to.

As they neared the port, a fisherman in orange-hooded waterproof gear and black rubber boots trudged toward them hauling his catch. He paused to watch them, then shook his head and moved on.

The storm literally blew them laughing through the door of the bar a few minutes later.

"*Mon Dieu*," Olivier exclaimed when he saw their pink-tinged faces.

Clotilde kicked off water-soaked shoes. Diamanté shook off the mackintosh and helped her remove her coat. There were only a few patrons playing billiards at the back of the bar and a lone sailor having a drink at a table.

"I told you it would be light tonight," Olivier said. "Antone," he called out, "they've arrived."

Antone appeared in the newly cut archway between the bar and what was soon to become the bistro. He smiled and performed a little jig, his wooden leg making a tapping sound as he spun himself around the room. He came to a stop in front of Clotilde, bowed to her, and held out his hand.

Clotilde laughed, curtsied, and placed her hand in his.

Diamanté thought to himself that he had never seen her looking more beautiful.

"I have something special to show you, Madame Loupré," Antone said. He led her through the archway and into the dim candlelit room. What was to become the main dining area of the bistro had been cleaned and the hard stone floor polished. In the center, two chairs were arranged on either side of a single small wooden table. On it sat four crystal glasses and a bottle of Champagne.

"*Voilà*! The first table and chairs for your restaurant," Antone said to Diamanté. He pointed with pride to the grain of the wood. "I salvaged beams from the shipbuilding yard to make them. There should be enough to fill the room."

Diamanté ran his hand over the square tabletop. "It's just what I had in mind."

"Look at the chairs, *chéri*," Clotilde exclaimed, drawing Diamanté's arm toward her. "He's carved anchors on the backs."

Olivier popped the Champagne cork and poured them all glasses. "To your happiness," he said, lifting his glass into the air.

"And to the success of our bistro," a smiling Diamanté added.

Antone's face brightened. He put up an index finger. "*Un moment*," he said as he disappeared into the bar.

Diamanté raised his eyebrows and looked at Olivier who held up his hands and lifted his shoulders in a Gallic shrug.

A second later, Antone peeked around the corner of the archway and motioned to Olivier to come help him. "Close your eyes, Clotilde," he said. "And you, too, Diamanté."

Clotilde and Diamanté stood together, their eyes squeezed tightly shut. They heard shuffling, then the light thud of something being placed at their feet.

"*Bon*. You may open now," Antone said.

On the floor in front of them sat an intricately carved mahogany cradle.

***

Diamanté and Clotilde lay listening to the sound of the rain outside on the terrace. A candle flickered on the nightstand. Clotilde nestled into the pillows and stared at the canopy of netting above the bed that she had dyed sea blue to match the color they had chosen for the walls. "I love this room."

Diamanté drew her into his arms. "You looked *ravissante* today, *mon amour*." He kissed her and repeated, "*Mon amour, mon amour*. It sounds nice." Then he whispered in her ear, "*Je t'aime*."

She snuggled into him. "I wish my father had been more enthusiastic about the wedding."

"*Bof!* He didn't even look at me when he shook my hand. *Salaud*."

She laughed. "You don't like him much, *hein?*"

"He could have agreed to the priest, *non?*" He tossed a hand into the air in exasperation. "*Phfft*! He could have at least given us permission, even if he didn't want to attend the ceremony."

She patted his arm. "He will. Once the baby is born. You'll see. Be patient."

He blew air through his lips.

She shook her head and rolled her eyes. "You know the saying? Patience is bitter, but its fruit is sweet."

He nodded, remembering the tome he had read when he was recuperating in the convent in Castagniers. "Jean-Jacques Rousseau didn't know your father."

A sudden gust of wind blew the French doors to the terrace open. The angry rainsquall blasted into the room, snuffing out the candle next to their bed.

"*Merde*," Diamanté mumbled as he tossed the bedcover back and went over to pull in the shutters and close the doors. Lightning flashed, followed immediately by a deafening boom. Diamanté broke out in a sweat. His body started to shake. For a moment he couldn't remember where he was. Terrified, he put his hands over his ears and lowered himself to the floor. His mind flashed back to the concentration camp. His heart pounded.

Clotilde sat bolt upright in bed. "*Chéri?*"

Her comforting voice brought him back to reality. He stared at his hands, then gripped them to stop the trembling. Finally, he got up from the floor and returned to bed.

Clotilde put her arms around his neck. "Are you all right? You frightened me."

He rubbed the scar on his forehead. "The sound of the thunder reminded me of the war, that's all." He lit a cigarette and lifted his chin to look at her. "Clotilde," he said, "there's a lot you don't know about me, what I've been through."

She placed her index finger against his lips. "*Ah oui*, but I do know. That night in the hospital when the Mauzac guards brought you in…" She nuzzled her cheek against his. "You said things in your delirium, *chéri*."

His brows furrowed and he pulled back from her. "What things?"

"At first you rambled, and I didn't pay close attention, but gradually I heard it because, of course, you repeated yourself. You spoke of Elise, the gruesome torture you had suffered, your brother, the Maquis, and then," she paused, "a vendetta and…"

His eyes grew wide. Did she know about the murder of his stepfather? "What?"

"The reason you left Corsica."

Nom de Dieu. He *had* talked. "I've never told anyone. How can you possibly love me, knowing what I did?"

"It will be our secret."

He put down the cigarette and enveloped her in his arms. "Are you happy, *chérie?*"

She nodded and kissed him. "Are you?"

"More than I've ever been in my life."

She draped a leg over his thigh and drew his body close to hers. "Then you won't go back to it?"

He stared at her. "What are you talking about?"

"The war. When we saw de Gaulle and your friend, I thought maybe you would."

He wrapped his arms around her and kissed her. "I have you and the restaurant to think about now."

He closed his eyes and breathed in the scent of her. "*Mon amour*," he added. Then he kissed her again. And kissed her. And kissed her some more.

***

After Clotilde had fallen asleep, Diamanté lay awake, listening to the storm. The shutters banged against the windows, and de Gaulle's words echoed in his head. "We need you, all of you." He sat up and lit another cigarette. In many ways, he had to admit, he was no less attached to the war effort for having met and fallen in love with Clotilde; her presence, all-embracing as it was, couldn't make up for his desire to help free France. Sooner or later, he would be forced to choose.

Chapter Sixty

It was a warm morning in late March, and the port bustled with activity. Diamanté and Olivier were preparing for the opening of their new restaurant, scheduled to take place on April 9, Easter Sunday.

Diamanté balanced himself on the top rung of the ladder and hoisted a heavy navy-blue-and-white sign into place. "What do you think?" he asked Olivier, who stood in the street, his head cocked and arms akimbo.

Olivier squinted and lifted his hand to shield his eyes from the bright sunlight. "Higher." He shook his head. "*Non non non*, too high. *Oui*, a little more, *ah ça y est.* That's it." He beamed with satisfaction. "*L'Ancre Bleue*. It looks *magnifique*."

The bistro's name, The Blue Anchor, was Clotilde's idea. "Maybe a maritime theme would be nice," she had casually suggested one day, "with blue color scheme, of course."

Below the sign, Diamanté draped the banner announcing the grand opening: *Ouverture Pâques*.

With everyone's agreement, the façade of the building was painted white, and a new blue and white striped awning shaded the slatted wooden banquettes Antone had made for the outdoor terrace. A large anchor, salvaged from the ship-building yard, stood just outside the entrance.

Inside, ships lamps adorned the many small square wooden tables, and fishing nets hung from the ceiling.

Diamanté's greatest satisfaction was his new kitchen. He and Antone had repaired the wooden cabinets and painted them cerulean blue. They had cleaned the zinc counters and scoured the sink until it gleamed. Fresh herbs grew on the windowsill, and the pantry was stocked with dried herbs and spices, several varieties of oils and vinegars, jars of olives, mustards, beans of all types for making the native Corsican soups, potatoes and yams, and baking supplies. The Escoffier cookbook Marcel had given him on Christmas Day 1939, its pages now dog-eared and covered with food stains, sat on a special shelf above the stove. The cookbook had a history of its own. He had left it for safekeeping with Madame Boulon in Marseilles; Elise and Ferdinand had brought it with them to Corsica when they were married; and, to his great surprise, he had discovered it sitting on the countertop in his mother's house after Ferdinand's burial in Speloncato.

"The opening will be grand," Olivier declared. He scrawled *Plat du Jour: Cingale* on the black chalkboard. Then he stood back to have a look and added with a flourish: *Bon Appétit!*

The last of the planks installed, Antone stood, put his hands on his hips, and surveyed the handsome new wood floor. With a wide grin on his face, he said, "I think we are ready."

Diamanté bit his lip. *What if no one comes?*

***

By daybreak on the day of the grand opening, Diamanté had been up and working in the kitchen for hours. Chickens braised in the oven, a thick bean soup bubbled on the stove, and just outside the back door in the alleyway, a whole boar—the *cingale*—roasted over a fire pit. Fruit tarts fresh out of the oven cooled on a table by an open window, and platters of nougats made of a blend of almonds and honey, his surprise treat for each of the day's customers, sat on the counter.

The early spring day was fresh, and sunlight streamed through the open doors and windows.

Olivier entered the kitchen followed by two women and a boy of about fifteen. "Our volunteers have arrived!" he announced. He introduced them to Diamanté. "This is my sister, Noëlle, and her two children, Delphine and Philippe," he said. All three were dressed in black, neatly groomed, and their hair had been freshly cut. They lived in a nearby village and had been recruited to help with the opening.

Diamanté went over to the pantry, took out three clean white aprons, and handed one to each of them.

"You two will wait tables," Olivier said to the teens, "and, Noëlle, can you help prep?"

Olivier's sister was a slim, dark-haired woman of about forty with bright eyes and a quick smile. "Just tell me what to do," she said.

"Let me explain how it's going to work," Olivier began. "We will be serving only one meal. Six courses with wine. Prix fixe. *Suppa*, entrée, fish course, meat course," he kissed his fingers, "the spit-roasted *cingale*, then cheese, and dessert."

Diamanté chuckled. "All for ten francs." *We won't make any money,* he thought, *even if someone does show up.*

Clotilde entered, followed by her father who was wearing the same suit and dour expression he had worn for their wedding.

Diamanté went over to his wife and whispered in her ear, "What's *he* doing here?"

She caressed his cheek. "No need for the scowl, *chéri*. He's come to see for himself how successful you are going to be."

Diamanté frowned. *Or what a complete failure.*

By early afternoon, much to Diamanté's relief, the first of the day's diners began to arrive in a steady stream, and the kitchen was quickly in turmoil. Half-empty crates and sacks of produce cluttered the floor, and every surface was covered with plates of food in various stages of preparation.

Olivier looked like an orchestra maestro, directing all the activity with a spatula from his position in front of the stove where he was sautéing thinly sliced potatoes to accompany the meat course. His sister hummed quietly to herself as she ran water over a tub of fresh spring lettuce in the sink.

Diamanté shut his eyes and breathed deeply. He listened to the double "kerchunk" of the walk-in door opening and banging shut as Delphine and Philippe swept in with orders and out with the first entrées. From the bar came the clink of wineglasses and from the dining room the rattle of silverware and murmured conversation. He finished clipping the fins off the red mullet for the fish course, and hearing the chime of his pocket watch, he realized he had been working now for several hours. He was exhausted.

"I'm going out for a cigarette," he announced.

Olivier nodded. "Check on the boar. It should be just about ready."

Diamanté went out the back door. A gust of wind cooled his face, and the appetite-stirring aroma of meat roasting over an open fire filled the air. He took a deep breath. At least his paranoia about not having any customers had subsided. The tables were all full. If anything, they could have a new problem. *What will we do*, he worried, *if we run out of food?*

Just outside the door, Olivier's dog lay on its side in the sunshine. It opened one eye and lifted its head, then stretched, yawned loudly, and sat up.

Pirate wasn't exactly Olivier's. As far as they could tell, the dog had been a stowaway on a supply ship that had arrived from somewhere in the Mediterranean months before. The scrawny black Catalonian sheepdog with droopy ears and long, thick tail had followed Olivier to the bar one morning, and he had fed it. After that, it took up permanent residence in the alley, herding the stray cats out of the area and terrorizing the rats. As a result, Olivier had named it Pirate because, in his view, the plucky dog had captured the alley. It never entered the bar, nor did it demand more than a daily meal and an occasional bone. Olivier brushed its thick coat, and the two walked together early every morning surveying the ships in the port. Today, Pirate was faithfully guarding the fire pit from any and all intruders.

As Diamanté reached into his shirt pocket for his pack of cigarettes, he noticed a dark figure standing in the shadows some distance away where the alley joined the side street.

Alerted, Pirate sniffed the air and emitted a low growl.

Diamanté plucked a cigarette from his packet and lit it. He lifted his chin and blew a breath of smoke into the air. Then, with the cigarette dangling from the corner of his mouth, he turned the hand crank over the spit and checked the meat. The exterior was nicely caramelized, and the interior was juicy.

"Boar's done," he hollered to Olivier inside.

Diamanté noted that the man at the end of the alley hadn't moved. A beggar perhaps? He called out, "Can I get you something to eat?"

The man emerged from the shadows. Pirate jumped to his feet, his ears back and hackles up.

Diamanté felt a pain in the pit of his stomach. This was no mendicant. The malicious eyes, magnified to at least twice their size by bottle-thick lenses, were all too familiar. *How many more dead bodies,* he wondered, *has he stood over since I saw him last?*

The dog bared his teeth in a snarl, then barked loudly.

Diamanté held out his hand. He pointed toward the kitchen door and snapped his fingers. "Lie down, Pirate."

The dog emitted a low growl, then slogged back to its resting spot with its tail docked.

Diamanté stepped forward. "What are you doing here, André?"

André Narbon lowered his chin and glanced behind him.

Diamanté held out his pack of cigarettes and offered his own to light it.

André took a drag and exhaled. Finally, he said, "I heard you were opening your own restaurant." His eyes locked on Diamanté's.

"Diamanté!" The dog's ears perked up at the sound of Olivier's voice coming from the kitchen. "Are you going to bring that boar inside for carving?"

"*Oui. Tout de suite*," Diamanté called.

"I heard also that you married a Corsican girl."

How does he know all this? Diamanté nodded. "*Oui.* In January."

"I'm married myself," André went on. "She's from Marseilles."

"*Alors,* what brings you to Ajaccio then?"

André sniffed and took a drag on his cigarette. "I'm en route to Algiers." His eyes narrowed, and he turned to look down the alley then lowered his voice. "I understand you have a transmission set. I need to use it to send an urgent message."

Diamanté raised his eyebrows. "Urgent?"

"Important intelligence."

"I will have to get authorization."

André suppressed a smile.

Diamanté threw his cigarette to the ground and crushed it with the heel of his shoe. He clenched his jaw. Had that been a trick to get him to reveal the existence of the set? "Go around to the bar. Have a glass of *marc* and something to eat. You'll have to wait until after the bistro closes."

André nodded and walked out of the alley.

Pirate snapped his jaws and snarled until the intruder was out of sight.

Diamanté stood for a moment, his shoulders cramped and tense, thinking about what had just happened. Whatever reason André had for arriving on this particular day, it couldn't be good. What was all that about important intelligence?

From inside the kitchen came the sound of Olivier's voice hollering his name.

Merde alors! He'd forgotten about the boar.

***

Diamanté slid the roast onto a heavy wooden carving block, then he went through the double swinging door to the dining room in search of Clotilde.

A soft late-afternoon sea breeze blew in through the open terrace, and the table lamps flickered.

Clotilde and her father were seated at a small table in the corner. Spotting Diamanté, she smiled and beckoned to him. He checked the bar and saw that André had taken a seat next to the archway to the dining room.

"You look pale, *chéri*," she said. "Is something wrong?"

He leaned over her and kissed her cheek. "We have a visitor," he said keeping his lips close to her ear. "The man behind me, seated just inside the bar?"

She stretched her neck to peek over his shoulder. "*Oui.* Who is he?"

"He will need to use the *extra* room tonight," he said, giving her a knowing look. Thank God he had recently divulged to her the existence of the transmission set in the storage room.

She nodded. Then, directing her eyes toward her father, she said, "Your father-in-law has something to tell you."

Diamanté straightened. *What is the old man up to now?*

Monsieur Vergara rose from his chair and looked Diamanté in the eye. Then he cleared his throat and said, "You have proven yourself to be a worthy husband for my daughter. I give you my permission for your marriage in the eyes of God."

Clotilde grabbed Diamanté's hand and squeezed it.

Finally, you old bastard, Diamanté thought, but he nodded and placed a gentle hand on his father-in-law's shoulder. "I am truly grateful, *Monsieur*."

Philippe came through the swinging door carrying a platter of cheeses. As he passed behind Diamanté, he said in a low voice, "Olivier says to tell you he needs you in the kitchen immediately."

Diamanté pulled Clotilde's hand to his lips and kissed it, then he returned to a scene of complete pandemonium. He found Olivier in the pantry, mumbling to himself. "Is there a problem?"

Olivier flailed his arms in the air. "*Merde alors*! We are running out of food!"

Chapter Sixty-One

Just after midnight, Diamanté sat on a crate watching his half brother skillfully tapping out transmissions. The small storage room was stuffy, and he was tired. The first message, sent to headquarters in Algiers, was simple. It merely announced that André would arrive in two days on the *Casabianca*. The second was taking unusually long, and Diamanté was becoming concerned because he didn't recognize the encryption code André used. It definitely wasn't included in the manuals Butch had given him to memorize.

Finally, André threw the toggle on the faceplate to RECEIVE and sat back.

"What was that long message all about?" Diamanté asked. "I didn't recognize the code."

Suddenly the set started clicking again. André read the acknowledgement, then he stood and declared that he needed to depart immediately.

Diamanté's irritation grew as he followed him down the stairs and opened the front door. "Are you going to tell me what the transmission was all about?"

André lifted his shoulders and exhaled, then he mumbled in disgust, "It's none of your business."

"You used my set to send it. I have a right to know."

André tried to elbow his way past Diamanté. "You are as foolish as your brother."

The mention of Ferdinand incensed Diamanté. "What do you mean?"

"He shot my father and left him to die in the maquis."

Diamanté realized he was making a fist and forced himself to open his hand. But the indignation did not go away. "He didn't shoot him. I told you that before."

"It's over in any case. The fool got what he deserved." André put his hand on Diamanté's chest and shoved him aside. Then he positioned his beret low over his forehead and stepped into the street.

"*Espèce de salaud*," Diamanté hissed under his breath. *Bastardo*.

"*Enculé*," André mumbled as he walked away. Asshole.

Diamanté slammed the door and angrily snapped the bolt. His hands shook as he lit a cigarette. He went into the kitchen. Olivier had apparently finished up and gone to bed. All was quiet. He opened the door to check the alley. The fire in the pit had extinguished itself, and Pirate lay next to it snoring. He tossed his cigarette and bolted the door. Then he went upstairs, undressed, and slipped into the feather bed next to his wife. "Are you awake?" he whispered.

Clotilde turned toward him and patted her swollen belly. "*Mon Dieu. Oui*. I can't sleep. The baby is kicking too much."

He put his hand on her abdomen and felt a slight rolling movement just under the skin.

"Has that man departed?" she asked.

He heaved a huge sigh. "*Oui.*"

"I didn't like how he looked at me. Who is he?"

He put his arms around her. "He's with the Maquis, or was. I'm not sure now."

Clotilde sat up. "Is he Corsican?"

"*Enfin, oui.*"

"I overheard you call him André. Is he related to you?"

"What? Why would you think that? Do I look like him?"

She rubbed his cheek and laughed. "No, you don't look a bit like him, *chéri*." She kissed him. "It's because when you mumble in your sleep, sometimes you mention your brother and then you seem very angry at a person you call André. You grind your teeth and clench your fists. Then you yell something about skinning a cat and wake yourself up."

He sighed. "Apparently, I talk too much in my sleep."

She chuckled.

"It is a recurring dream, along with the one where I am being tortured in the concentration camp. Sometimes the two fuse into one gigantic nightmare so frightful I can't sleep for the next two nights."

She began to massage his neck. "Tell me about André."

He felt his tension release as she kneaded his shoulders next. "André is my half brother. We grew up hating each other. His father was a wealthy landowner by the name of Narbon. My father, Jean-Pierre Loupré, was killed just before I was born. My mother remarried two months after my birth, and André was born nine months later."

"But why did you hate each other?"

"When you were younger, did you ever play a game called The Seven Turns?"

"No, but I've heard of it. As I recall, it wasn't complicated. The player who is it gives a map to the others. Then everyone follows the map to the prize. Why?"

"Ferdinand and I dreaded playing with André because he changed the rules."

"How could he change something so simple?"

"When André was it, well…" He hesitated. "Once we found a dead rabbit, another time a strangled baby bird, yet another a puppy with a broken leg, which Ferdinand and I nursed back to health. When I discovered our beloved family cat at the end of one game—" he stopped and swallowed, remembering. "*Enfin*, he'd skinned it."

Clotilde gasped.

"*Oui*. I ran to tell our mother, but André lied and said I was the one who killed the cat. We were only about seven or eight years old. I wanted to beat him up, but he was stronger than I was then."

"I guess that explains your nightmare."

Only partially.

"What happened as you grew older?"

"We fought constantly. His father finally sent him away to a fancy prep school in France when he was thirteen. I didn't see much of him after that." *End this conversation*, he thought, *before I have to tell her about the fight over Elise.*

"It frightens me that he came here today of all days."

Diamanté was silent for a moment. *Why did he indeed just turn up out of the blue like that on the day of the grand opening?*

Clotilde yawned. "You told me before your mother is widowed. So this man's father is dead then?"

Diamanté felt himself breaking out in a cold sweat. "*Oui,* a few years ago."

Clotilde lay back. "She must be lonely. If it's all right with you, I'd like to write to her and tell her about the baby. After the birth, that is."

"I think she would like that very much."

After Clotilde had fallen asleep, Diamanté rose from the bed and walked through the open French doors out onto the rooftop terrace. He went over to the edge, leaned on the parapet, and breathed in the fresh salt air. It was a bright moonlit night, and he could see the harbor clearly in the distance. The sleek ninety-two-meter-long Free French submarine, the *Casabianca*, was now moored at the end of the pier, its black silhouette just barely visible in the dark waters.

Well that explains why André was in such a hurry to leave. He spat. *Was the sub sent to pick André up personally?* He pounded a fist against the parapet. Unlike Ferdinand and himself, André had had opportunities. He had been well educated, studied several languages, received top military training, and had money. He'd always been the best at everything, and the bastard had always looked down on his half brothers whom he considered inferior.

The sub departed just before dawn; André was gone.

Chapter Sixty-Two

"We have much to improve," Olivier said the morning following the grand opening. "*Merde alors*! We came very close to running completely out of food."

Diamanté was seated at the bar having a second cup of strong coffee. He had had no sleep at all for over twenty-four hours, and he felt groggy, unfocused, and sluggish. "We didn't anticipate so many, but I'm pleased they came just the same," he said.

Noëlle patted her brother on the back. "It wasn't so bad, Oli," she said. "We gave them all Diamanté's nougats, and they departed happy. We managed to feed everyone." She shrugged. "*Eh bien*, most of them *alors*. Some had to be satisfied with four courses at the end instead of six. *Mais, c'est la vie*. They have been through a war, *n'est-ce pas*? The price was right, and they were celebrating Easter. They'll come back again, *je vous assure*." She took her daughter's arm. "*Moi*, I'm tired. *Venez, les enfants*, we're going home to rest."

"I'm not leaving," Philippe piped in.

Everyone turned to look at the boy.

He shrugged. "I want to stay on to help Uncle Olivier."

Noëlle tossed her hands into the air and sighed. "What did I tell you? *Madonna Mia!* I was afraid of this. Just like my Jacques. The restaurant business is in the blood." She drew her youngest son into her arms and hugged him.

Diamanté realized suddenly whom she was talking about. It hadn't occurred to him that this woman was Jacques's mother and that the two young people who had helped out in the bistro on Easter Sunday were his siblings. Now that he thought about it, however, he should have realized sooner. Philippe was a slighter and somewhat taller version of Jacques.

"He can stay if he wants," Olivier said, looking over at Diamanté.

Diamanté agreed. "We could use the extra help."

Noëlle whispered a few parting instructions to her son, then she kissed Olivier, and she and Delphine departed.

Philippe watched them leave, then turned to his uncle and folded his arms across his chest. "I have two questions," he said, his face deadly serious. "How much will I be paid, and where will I sleep?"

Olivier raised an eyebrow. "I'll have to consult with my partner about the pay," he said, looking over at Diamanté.

Diamanté smiled and scratched his head. "The boy has a lot of Jacques in him."

Olivier nodded in agreement.

Just then, Clotilde entered the kitchen carrying a basket filled with freshly cut spring wildflowers. "I've just bid *au revoir* to Noëlle and Delphine," she said to Olivier. "I hope they will come visit us again soon." She looked over to Philippe.

"I heard the wonderful news that you're staying on to help us out."

Philippe blushed and nodded his head.

"Only one little problem," Diamanté said.

Clotilde gave her husband a questioning look.

"He needs somewhere to stay," Olivier piped in. "I don't have room in my small apartment."

Diamanté glanced at his wife's expanded figure. "And in less than two months we won't have a spare bedroom either."

Clotilde smiled. "I have an idea," she said, taking Philippe's arm and leading him out the door. "Come with me."

***

"I can't believe your father agreed to take Philippe in," Diamanté said as he unpacked crates of produce in the storeroom the following week. "Your idea was good."

Clotilde was seated at the kitchen counter shelling peas. "So far, it's working," she said with a shrug. "He even seems to enjoy having the young man around." She looked up. "I'm happy to have someone there to keep watch over him. I've been concerned about him being alone, especially at night." She paused and wagged a partially shelled peapod in the air. "But I guess I didn't have to worry after all. Do you know what Philippe told me this morning?"

Diamanté shook his head.

At that moment, Philippe entered carrying a huge crate of produce. Olivier followed. They seemed to be involved in an animated conversation. "*Oui*," Philippe was saying, "and he is said to wield a Napoleonic-era sabre when he goes into battle, too. It apparently belonged to his grandfather."

Olivier gasped. "*Ça alors!*"

Philippe nodded with authority.

"Who are you talking about?" Clotilde asked, intrigued.

"De Lattre."

"General Jean de Lattre de Tassigny," Olivier clarified, "Commander of the French army."

Philippe set down the crate and put his hands on his hips. "And you know what else?" he said, looking over at Diamanté. "He takes a personal chef with him everywhere he goes. A superb one, apparently." His head bobbed up and down enthusiastically. "The Americans are in great admiration of this."

"How do you know all that?" Diamanté asked.

"The customers. They talk." Philippe placed a finger against his earlobe, and a Cheshire-cat grin spread over his face. "And I listen." He cocked his head thoughtfully. "Do you think if I lied about my age, I could join him?"

Diamanté coughed, recalling his own experience in Marseilles when he had lied about his age to get the job in the metallurgical factory. "How old are you, anyway?" he asked.

Philippe straightened up. "I'll be sixteen next month."

"I wouldn't advise it," Diamanté said, not looking at him.

Philippe gave a quick shrug, then went to fetch another crate of produce.

"Do you think he was making all that business up about de Lattre?" Clotilde asked as she returned to her shelling.

Diamanté glanced at the amused look on Olivier's face. "If he was, he has quite an imagination." He chuckled. "Now, Clotilde, what were you going to tell me? Something Philippe told you this morning?"

"Ah, *oui*." She giggled. "He told me my father has a woman friend." She shook her head. "I didn't take it too seriously. Our neighbor lady looks in on him occasionally. I didn't think much of it. But Philippe insisted that he had seen them kissing."

Diamanté groaned and went back to work unpacking the produce. The image of old man Vergara embracing a woman was still dominating his thoughts when Clotilde interrupted him.

"By the way, *chéri*," she said, "I've arranged with Monseigneur Le Clerc to perform our *petite cérémonie* Sunday after the last mass. We'll be in the Chapel of Notre-Dame."

Diamanté stood to face her. "It's really going to happen?"

She smiled and nodded. "My father has promised he'll attend."

Diamanté shook his head in amazement. The old man was beginning to grow on him.

Chapter Sixty-Three

May 1944

Clotilde was seated at the counter in the restaurant kitchen snipping sprigs of herbs for drying. Suddenly she set down her garden clippers and held her head in her hands.

Diamanté stopped chopping vegetables and looked over at her, his knife poised in midair. "Are you not feeling well, *chérie?*" he asked.

"I'm just tired," she said, wiping beads of sweat from her forehead with the back of her hand. Her face was ashen. "I feel a little dizzy. That's all."

"You need to take care not to do too much now. Why don't you go upstairs and lie down? You can finish that later." He went to her and held out his hands. "Here, let me help you up."

"*Bof*! I'm not due for another two weeks. It's just the weight. I'll be fine." She allowed him to pull her from her chair and then wrapped her arms around him and kissed him. "I'm so *huge*," she lamented, laughing. "I'm starting to wonder if there's more than one baby."

Diamanté gulped. "Do you think that's possible?"

She laughed again and patted his cheek. "No, *chéri,* I don't think so."

He watched her shuffle heavily up the stairs, holding the railing with one hand and her back with the other. Once she had safely reached the top, he went back to his task.

An hour later, he heard her cry out his name. He dropped his knife and ran upstairs, two steps at a time.

She was lying on their bed having difficulty breathing.

"Go fetch Doctor Poulbot," she gasped. "The baby is coming."

"Shouldn't you go to the hospital?"

Her eyes widened. She pressed her hands across her belly and grimaced. "*Absolument non!*" she yelled. "Why would I do that? I'm a nurse." She took a deep breath. "I'm having this baby right here." The tone of her voice softened. *"S'il te plaît, chéri,* just hurry."

Panicked, Diamanté ran down the stairs and hollered to Olivier to watch the restaurant. Then he rushed out the door.

***

Diamanté tried to concentrate on the menu for the next day, but all he could think about was what was going on upstairs. He threw down his piece of chalk and sat down at the counter. "Do you think she's all right?"

Olivier finished sweeping the floor and came to join him. "She's strong, your Clotilde," he said.

Diamanté lit a cigarette. His hands trembled as he took a drag.

Olivier handed him a glass of cognac. "Here. Drink this. It will calm you." He chuckled. "You're a first-time father. To be nervous, *c'est normale.*"

Diamanté drank the entire glass of cognac in one gulp. "I should go tell her father."

Olivier shook his head and refilled Diamanté's glass, then he poured one for himself. "Stay here. You're in no shape to go anywhere. We'll send Philippe with the news when the time comes." He sat down on the stool opposite. "I was a new father once myself," he said, looking into his glass.

Diamanté raised his eyebrows.

"*Mais oui. Je t'assure.*" Olivier said, nodding. "Many years ago, but I remember it like it was yesterday." He took a swig of the cognac and set the glass down with a loud thud. "*Merde.* I went to sea right after the birth, and I never saw him again." A pained expression came over his face. He looked up and stared into Diamanté's eyes.

"What happened?"

"Dead of pneumonia, both of them." The rims of Olivier's eyes reddened. "I didn't know until…" He paused to take another drink, then he rose from the stool. "It was months later." He cleared his throat and picked up a knife. "I don't know if I could have saved them had I stayed, but I always wonder." He turned his back to Diamanté and pulled a crate of fresh produce close to the counter.

Diamanté sat in silence, listening to the rhythmic "thwack, thwack, thwack" of Olivier's sharp blade striking the vegetables on the wooden cutting board. Another hour went by.

Suddenly, an ear-piercing scream came from above.

Diamanté jumped from his stool and began to pace the floor.

Olivier quit chopping and put down his knife.

They waited. In seconds, there was a heart-wrenching "Waaaaaaaaaaaa!"

Olivier smiled. "Listen to that," he said, slapping Diamanté on the back. "*Félicitations*! You are a father."

Diamanté wiped tears from his eyes.

Minutes later, they heard a creak at the top of the stairs and the sound of heavy footsteps descending. The doctor appeared in the doorway, wiping sweat from his brow with a towel. He was a pudgy, balding man with heavy jowls and a red face. He wore an old black suit, his undone tie was draped around his neck, and his shirt was unbuttoned to reveal the cluster of white fuzzy hair on his chest. He put a hand on Diamanté's shoulder. "Your wife did well," he said.

"And the baby?"

Poulbot's blue eyes twinkled. "You have a fine son. Small, but robust." He turned to Olivier and eyed the bottle sitting on the counter. "Now, if you don't mind, *Monsieur*, I'd like a snifter, or two, of that cognac."

Diamanté bounded up the stairs. When he opened the door to their bedroom, Clotilde was sitting up in bed, smiling, with the baby nestled against her breast.

"Come meet Diamanté *fils*, *chéri*. He's handsome. Like you."

Chapter Sixty-Four

For the next several days, Diamanté watched Clotilde expertly manage the constant demands of their new baby boy. Nightly, unable to get any rest, he retreated to the storage room after the restaurant closed.

His sole company was his increasingly active transmission set. Messages came hourly from Algiers, sometimes more frequently. Because of Diamanté's numerous contacts in the Maquis, Dionysis was now the relay station to put members all over northern France on high alert. In Paris, Marcel and his *Francs-Tireurs et Partisans* reported that they were aggressively destroying lines of communication and transportation routes into and out of the city. In Normandy, Jacques, Guy, and Les Amis Clandestins monitored the whereabouts of enemy troops and passed on incidents where heavy bombing to the infrastructure would likely block the advance of Allied troops.

On a regular basis, Diamanté received test messages from Butch to make sure his station was still functioning. A note appended to one transmission informed him that Stu had flown home for a few days to get married.

Diamanté listened to his son's cries coming from their bedroom one night and thought about how all of them—Jacques, Stu, Marcel, Guy, himself—led dual lives now, one more or less normal, the other in the shadows. Suddenly, he found himself thinking about Elise. Where was *she?* On impulse, he sent Marcel a quick query. The cryptic reply came back: *Whereabouts unknown. Believed to have departed Paris.*

***

Diamanté and Philippe were in the kitchen late on the evening of the first day of June listening to a scratchy, static-filled broadcast on Radio Londres. Abruptly the news was interrupted by the opening bars of Beethoven's Fifth Symphony. *Dot-dot-dot-dash,* the first four notes corresponding to the Morse code letter *V* for victory, was the prearranged signal to put all the resistance groups throughout France on alert for a message.

Diamanté stopped what he was doing and rushed to turn up the volume.

The British announcer read the first stanza of "*Chanson d'automne*" by the French poet Paul Verlaine.

Les sanglots longs
Des Violons
De l'automne

As the message was being repeated, a wide-eyed Olivier raced through the archway. "Did you hear that?" he asked excitedly. "We were just listening in the bar." He repeated the stanza. "'The long sobs of the violins of autumn.' It's imminent."

Diamanté nodded. Operation Overlord, the invasion of France by the Allies, would happen soon.

Four days later, at 21h15 on June 5, Diamanté closed the restaurant early due to lack of customers.

Clotilde was seated in their small kitchen listening to the BBC, Diamanté *fils* sleeping peacefully in her arms.

"There's some bisque left. Are you hungry?" he asked.

She nodded.

Minutes passed. He was just placing warmed bowls of soup on the table when over the radio came the opening bars of Beethoven's Fifth—*dot-dot-dot-dash*. He hurried to turn up the volume, then sat down at the table opposite her to listen.

There was a slight pause, then came the message:

Blessent mon cœur

D'une langueur

Monotone.

"Wound my heart with a monotonous languor," he whispered excitedly as the last three lines of the Verlaine stanza were repeated. He took the baby from his wife and cradled the small, sleeping bundle in his arms.

Clotilde tasted a spoonful of the soup and looked up at him. "What is the significance of it?" she asked.

"It is meant to spur the Résistance into action. The Allies will arrive shortly."

She gasped. "France will be saved, then?"

He shrugged. "They are our only hope now."

He kissed his son's forehead. He had not anticipated the love he would feel for his namesake. He gulped and looked up at her. "You must understand something, Clotilde." He sighed heavily.

A pained expression came over her face. "What? What is it?"

"When the time comes, I am to join General Tassigny's Army B."

She put down her spoon, tears filling her eyes. "You will go to war?"

"Not immediately," he said, trying to assure her. He placed his hand gently over hers. "It will depend on the Allies."

Chapter Sixty-Five

BBC Broadcast, June 6, 1944: This is London. Allied naval forces began landing armies this morning on the northern coast of France.

In the following days, Diamanté, Clotilde, and Olivier listened constantly to the BBC. The flow of endless updates included a message to the people of Western Europe from General Dwight Eisenhower, supreme Allied commander of the operation, who called the initial assault by the Expeditionary Force a success. General de Gaulle, taking his turn, declared the invasion of Normandy a huge victory.

Then a month later, on July 14, Bastille Day, a transmission came from Bernard:

> *Top secret. Operational Priority. For Loup's eyes only. Begin quote. Proceeding with Operation Dragoon. Report immediately. Army B. More to follow. End quote. Top secret.*

Diamanté left the storage room. Trying to cover up his excitement, he entered the kitchen where Olivier was working at the counter. "Do you think you could manage the restaurant without me for a while?" he asked.

Part Five

Fortune favors the bold.
—Jean de Lattre de Tassigny, Marshal of France

Chapter Sixty-Six

The Dragoon Force, created to carry out the operation once called Anvil, was activated in Corsica on the first of August 1944. French and American forces, now consolidated into a single unit, were set to invade southern France.

By the sixteenth, Diamanté found himself aboard an amphibious landing craft in the Mediterranean Sea, wearing the uniform of a commando unit in General Jean de Lattre de Tassigny's Army B. Straight ahead lay the target assault beach between Saint-Tropez and Sainte Maxime.

Diamanté felt excited and ill at the same time. His stomach churned with the rolling of the flat-bottomed barge, and waves of nausea hit him. Was it seasickness or fear? He thought about Clotilde and his infant son. The morning of his departure he had stared at the pots and pans on the stove and nearly changed his mind. It had been the hardest decision of his life, leaving his family in Ajaccio, and he had watched them from the ship until they were merely tiny specks on the quay. The second decision, to quit his new restaurant, had also been difficult. It was Olivier who had convinced him finally by agreeing to stay behind and make sure nothing happened to jeopardize their investment. Now that they had promoted Philippe to sous-chef and hired two new waiters, Olivier would be able to carry on temporarily without him. He had assured Diamanté, too, that he and Clotilde's father would together make sure that his family was well looked after. Diamanté smiled to himself. Junior was now officially Olivier's godson.

He wiped the salt spray from his eyes. As the convoy slowly advanced and the golden reflections of the sun on the late-afternoon sea caused him to squint, he turned to look back at the men around him—shop owners, fishermen, bankers, farmers, lawyers—all Corsicans crowded together, kneeling, watching the fast-approaching coast, their eyes wide with anticipation, their normally suntanned faces drained of color. Despite the relatively calm waters, many of them retched. Some softly hummed the "La Marseillaise." Others crossed themselves and prayed. This wasn't the first time they had sacrificed their personal lives for their country. They had fought long and hard to free Corsica, and now the moment they had feverishly awaited at last had arrived. Diamanté himself had dreamed of this day when he was imprisoned in the Mauzac concentration camp. France was ahead. Her sons were coming to liberate her. Feeling his impatience growing, he clenched his jaw. It seemed to him to be taking an eternity to reach the shore.

The roar of approaching planes caused him to lift his eyes skyward. Within seconds, mushroom-shaped parachutes darkened the sky ahead.

As they neared the beach, Diamanté heard a swishing sound, and the motors began to accelerate. There followed a loud zing, and he realized it was a shell hitting the water nearby. He put his head down as more shells ricocheted off the metal sides of the landing craft, then tried to calm his nerves by thinking about his restaurant and what Olivier would be preparing for the *plat du jour*. He realized he hadn't eaten and felt suddenly hungry, imagining a steaming bowl of fish stew, a loaf of crusty bread, the sounds of his kitchen staff at work.

The boat shuddered. Was it hit? The man beside him said they were merely dropping anchor. They were still several meters away from the shore.

A loud explosion rocked another landing craft to the starboard side. It had struck an underwater mine and was listing badly. Hundreds of soldiers threw themselves into the sea holding their guns above their heads. Weighted down with heavy gear, some sank immediately beneath the water and didn't resurface.

The ramps of his landing craft were lowered. Diamanté swallowed hard, lifted his rifle above his head, and gave the signal to his men. They disembarked in a single file, struggling to keep upright in the waist-deep water. Ahead, in the smoke and machine-gun fire, bodies lay on the beach. The sound of coastal guns and flak batteries filled the air. Diamanté heard a round of German mortar fire and an explosion; the enemy's position had immediately been silenced by an American destroyer sitting in the water behind them. One after another, ships pulled the emptied landing craft away, and a tsunami of troops, vehicles, and armored tanks advanced onto the beach.

Finally he reached solid footing, dug in his heels, and started running. Ahead, more men fell. He knelt beside one who was screaming and writhing in pain. He rolled the man over. He had received a direct hit in the abdomen. Diamanté gagged at the stench of the spilling intestines and blood. Within seconds, the man's eyes went lifeless. Diamanté gently moved his fingers over the eyelids and closed them.

More gunfire; bullets whizzed past his ears. Allied bombers roared overhead. Anti-aircraft fire filled the air. Detonating bombs and grenades shook the ground. Dead men lay all around him on the sand.

All of a sudden, from behind, a hand grabbed the back of his collar and lifted him to his feet like a rag doll.

"There's no helping him now. Get out of here," the voice yelled into his ear. He could have sworn it sounded like Ferdinand's. The hair on the back of his neck stood up, and he shivered as he felt a sudden gust of wind. He swung around, but there was no one there. Dazed and confused, he looked around him. Where was his unit?

Those who had made it to the beach were running to seek cover in a nearby wooded area. He rejoined his men. The pines and thicket had caught fire. They advanced, stepping carefully amid the flames and in the thunder of bursting shells and the explosion of munition dumps. When they came to the edge of a clearing, Diamanté halted, then put up his hand and motioned to the others to stop. He heard Ferdinand's voice once again. "*Attends*," it warned. They crouched and waited, listening. Diamanté scanned the periphery for any signs of movement.

Another corps of the French army came up from behind them. Instead of stopping, they ran past. The first ones to enter the clearing encountered a minefield. Instantly several men, including their leader, were blown up. From the other side of the glade came a solid burst of enemy gunfire. It was a trap.

Diamanté stood and motioned to the men behind him to run in the opposite direction. By the time they reached a deserted farmhouse several kilometers away, all of them were exhausted. As darkness approached, they strung up barbed wire and hung tin cans around the perimeter, then hunkered down as best they could to wait until morning.

All night, they listened to the sound of sniper fire.

The next day, they joined a large force of soldiers moving westward in the direction of Toulon and Marseilles.

Chapter Sixty-Seven

Marseilles
25 August 1944

The Germans were firmly entrenched on the hill; the broad expanse of the port lay below, also under enemy control.

Diamanté led the early-morning attack on the basilica. He knew well the narrow streets leading up to Notre Dame de la Garde, but no matter what approach he took, his unit was met with a barrage of shells and the terrifying jets of flamethrowers. Around every corner, they stepped carefully, fearful of land mines. Sniper fire from the roofs impeded their advance.

They were crouching in an alley to evaluate their position when a man wearing civilian clothing and carrying a hunting rifle approached from the shadows.

Diamanté raised his Sten.

The man stopped. "Maquis," he said. Behind him stood a half dozen others. *An odd assortment of weapons*, Diamanté thought. Some carried pistols, others knives. One had an axe hoisted over his shoulder. They all wore berets bearing the cross of Lorraine.

Diamanté studied their leader's face. "Delouche?" he said finally. Despite the beard, he recognized the foreman. Delouche from metallurgy who had shown him how to tap the blast furnace. Delouche who was a member of the PCF. It wasn't surprising that he was fighting for Marseilles.

The foreman fixed his eyes on Diamanté, then smiled and held out his hand. "*Salut,* Loupré. I didn't recognize you at first." He turned and mumbled something to the men behind him. They nodded.

Diamanté shook Delouche's hand. "My unit is trying to get through to the basilica," he explained.

"We can help you," Delouche said, nodding. His eyes sparkled with excitement, and he winked at Diamanté. "We have a way that is unknown to the Germans."

Delouche guided them through a twisted maze of cellars and back alleys. Finally, they reached a long hallway that ran the length of the building and led to a staircase.

They arrived at the top and stepped out into the street across from the basilica. Within thirty seconds, they came under heavy fire. German army blockhouses covered the exterior of the church. Crouching behind a pile of rubble, the men watched as two Sherman tanks belonging to the French army slowly approached the front steps of the sanctuary.

The first tank, hit full force by the enemy, was almost immediately enveloped in a cloud of thick smoke. Behind it, the second tank hit a mine, and the resulting explosion tore off its track. As it slowed to a standstill, it continued its bombardment of the church's heavy wooden entry door.

While acrid black smoke billowed from the first Sherman, Diamanté saw the commander of the disabled tank trying to pull himself out of the wreck. His face was bloodied, and one arm appeared to be immobile, but he carried the tricolor. Diamanté hurried to help him. Under heavy machine-gun fire, the two stumbled to the church railings and began unfurling the flag. Delouche ran to help them.

With the arrival of a section of Algerian riflemen, the French army was finally able to take the hill and enter the church. Inside, they encountered the monseigneur who came forward from his hiding place in the crypt and greeted them. Statues had been shattered, pews smashed. The impacts of bullets dotted the walls. A small fire burned where the prayer candle rack had been kicked over. An unmanned machine gun sat next to an open window. A dead body lay next to it. Spent shells littered the floor.

The promontory seized, the three hoisted the French flag atop the bell tower and moved on to the Canebière.

In the vicinity of the St. Charles train station, streets were strewn with debris and dotted with the burned-out skeletons of vehicles. Tramway cables hung above the grim thoroughfare like dead vines. Avalanches of shells fell blindly here and there, riddling the roofs, shattering windows. Explosions could be heard as entire houses collapsed.

Local citizens, poorly armed as they were, swarmed into the streets to help.

Attacks and counter-attacks went on without respite in the torrid heat of the Mediterranean summer. Acrid white dust from crumbled walls and buildings filled the air. Boulevard after boulevard was liberated. Together with the *Marseillais*, Army B. was succeeding in gaining control of the city.

***

Jean de Lattre de Tassigny arrived three days later, and the official surrender of Marseilles was issued. Diamanté walked a few steps behind the general in the victory parade on the terre-plein of the Vieux Port. On either side, the joyful crowd pushed forward, shouting and singing "La Marseillaise." It was the twenty-eighth of August. Twelve days had passed since the leading elements of the French army had begun the landing, and nine had been spent in incessant fighting. The cities of Toulon and Marseilles were emancipated.

They buried their dead in the hills above the city where once Diamanté and Maurice had hunted rabbits.

When the solemn task was done, Diamanté sat down, exhausted, on a boulder. His hand shook as he lit a cigarette. He stared at the port below. All the quays were dislocated, torn up by mines. Sheds had collapsed; railway and electrical installations had been destroyed. The cranes had been sabotaged, and over a hundred shipwrecks obstructed the harbor. The old neighborhood where he and Ferdinand had lived was an indescribable chaos of twisted ironwork, shattered concrete, and entangled cables. What remained of the metallurgical factory was visible in the distance, recognizable only by the bombed-out walls of the old brick buildings and the still-standing iron gate.

Chapter Sixty-Eight

Letter from Diamanté to Clotilde
Christmas Eve 1944

You cannot know, mon amour, *what man can do against man. It has been five months. I am tired to the core. My boots are covered with human brains and entrails.*

This war is vile, and yet, I fear I have not seen the worst of it. The enemy is violently aggressive. We have had little rest since Marseilles.

Still, we have made it all the way to Alsace. I have seen inexpressible joy on the faces of the villagers as we have moved northward liberating village after village. The tricolor waves again over the town halls from Lyon all the way to the Rhine.

But the prospect of a formidable winter lies ahead. Autumn came early and cheerlessly. The brilliant sunshine of the Mediterranean almost instantly gave way to uninterrupted rain and cold in October. Floods carried away temporary bridges and drowned everything in mud. Now the roads are covered with glazed ice. It is so bitterly cold that we have broken into several abandoned farmhouses and taken blankets in order to fight the frostbite threatening our toes.

It was in the farmhouse we raided just last evening that I found some stationery and a pencil. I could think of nothing else all day but what I wanted to write to you. Immediately after the midnight mass, I set to it.

We are warm enough, under blankets amid the haystacks in an old deserted stone barn. We have wine to drink, and the Americans have provided us with chocolate.

The forces of the Maquis from all parts of France have joined Army B. (now called the First French Army). They are a fearless group. Most are younger than I am, fiercely independent, used to living in secret. Their armament and supplies are clearly inadequate, and many believe, arrogantly, that they alone are qualified to give France its new army, made over in the image of the Maquis, of course. That attitude has created some tension, as you can well imagine. Nonetheless, they have signed on for the duration of the war, as I am sorry to have to tell you so have I, by a decree that was issued in September requiring all volunteers to do so.

That said, I can think of nothing but you and home.

Diamanté stopped writing and stared at the candle on the floor in front of him. His twenty-first birthday would be in a week; his son was already seven months old. He swallowed the last of his wine and lit a cigarette. He would be lucky if he arrived home to celebrate his son's first birthday. He pinched the bridge of his nose and forced back tears. He was lonesome for the first time in his life.

In kilometers, ma chérie, *we are a long way apart, but in spirit and mind, I am always with you and Diamanté fils. I hope I will be able to see your faces and kiss you, again and again and again, soon.*

Diamanté could hear the faint sound of sniper fire in the distance.

He stopped writing and listened, his heart beating fast.

Almost immediately, he heard the soulful sound of a harmonica coming from the far corner of the barn. The men around him lifted their heads as a boy, no more than sixteen, cupped his hands around his mouthpiece and began playing "O Holy Night."

Diamanté lit another cigarette and drew the blanket around his neck and shoulders. He was cold and his hands were shaking, but he had to finish his letter. Think about the restaurant, he told himself. How often had he conjured up happier times to calm his nerves?

Thank Olivier and express my gratitude for his being there for you. Tell him to be sure to order enough supplies for the Easter celebration so that we won't run out. I think we should roast two boars, too, don't you? If I am lucky enough to be home by then, I will again make nougats for all our guests.

Let Philippe know also that I have yet to see de Lattre's supposed "superb" chef! (I am beginning to believe that is a myth.)

Your father, I hope, is staying healthy.

The harmonicist continued playing yuletide hymns. Some of the men hummed along with it; others wept.

Diamanté finished his letter.

> Bonne nuit, mon amour, et joyeux Noël. *Remember that you are always in my heart. D.*

At daybreak they were awakened by the sound of approaching panzers. Machine-gun fire followed cannon explosions.

Diamanté stuffed the letter into his helmet and grabbed his rifle.

The men around him scrambled to pull on their boots.

Someone yelled to get out.

Outside a fierce wind blew. The sky, low and gray, was lit with flashes of gunfire. A meter of new snow had fallen overnight.

Hearing an explosion behind him, Diamanté glanced back at the barn. An enemy projectile had blasted a hole in the wall next to where the harmonicist had been.

He looked through the smoke for the young man, but he was nowhere in sight.

The cannonade continued.

Diamanté couldn't force himself to move forward. He returned to the barn to find the boy lying next to the door, his arm flung out at an awkward angle. His mouth organ rested in the palm of his hand.

"*Merde alors.*" Diamanté knelt down. Just days before, he had witnessed de Lattre himself decorating this youthful member of the French Forces of the Interior with the Croix de Guerre. He put his ear close to the body. Hearing a slight groan, he slipped the harmonica into his pocket, gathered the boy into his arms, and ran.

Chapter Sixty-Nine

Vosges Mountains, Alsace
January 1945

"Takka takka." The automatic machine-gun fire coming from the German bunker rained down on the small unit of the First French Army.

Diamanté moved out alone in the morning darkness. It was bitterly cold. They were pinned down and exposed by a pocket of enemy soldiers. Bullets zipped around him as he trudged carefully through foot-deep snow. When he was close enough, he pulled the pin from his grenade and tossed it. There was a flash, followed almost immediately by a loud bang. He rushed the bunker and peered inside. The grenade had done its work. Six Nazi soldiers lay dead; there were no survivors.

Diamanté spat. *Bastards*.

Just then, another round of machine-gun fire echoed through the barren forest. He swung around. It was coming from the next bunker. A barrage of bullets was directed at him with terrifying intensity. He felt a powerful blow to his side and fell gasping to the ground, the air knocked out of his lungs.

Merde. Putain de Merde.

He lay motionless in the snow until he was able to breathe again. He felt an excruciating pain in his shoulder when he tried to move. His left arm was bleeding profusely.

"Brata-tat-ata-tat-tat." A bullet slammed into his right leg.

If I'm going to die, he thought, *I'm taking those Boche bastards with me.*

He crawled in the direction of the second bunker, leaving a trail of deep-red blood in the white snow behind him. When he was close enough, he flung himself down to wait behind a tall bush covered in a mantle of white.

Bullets whizzed all around him. He took out another grenade, readied it, and threw it into the trench.

All was eerily quiet, except for the ringing in his ears. Heavy snow fell. He shook his head. He had seen the flash, but the impact of the grenade had muffled his hearing. He looked around for his rifle. *Merde*. It lay where he had dropped it after he'd been hit. It was out of reach. Good thing he had his Walther. He removed the pistol from the holster inside his jacket and released the safety with his thumb. Then he edged cautiously forward.

In the bunker, the single, dug-in machine gunner was dead. Of the four others, only one had survived. Dazed and bleeding, the German looked up at him and raised his rifle.

Diamanté aimed his pistol and pulled the trigger.

The Nazi's head snapped backward, and he collapsed to the ground, his body jerking.

A searing pain made its way up Diamanté's side and across his back. His left arm and hand racked with uncontrollable spasms. Darkness crowded around the edges of his vision, and a strange lightheadedness overpowered him. He closed his eyes and felt himself slipping to the ground.

***

When he awoke, he didn't know where he was. He was inside a building, in a bed, and he felt warm. He tried to focus his eyes on the ceiling. Gradually the memory of the battle came back to him. The snow and the naked trees. The dead Germans in the trench. The motorized medical unit that had carried him away. He lifted his head a little to glance around the room. There were rows of beds on either side, all of them occupied by soldiers wrapped in blankets and bandages. Some moaned; others slept. A nauseating odor filled the air. Human waste mixed with rubbing alcohol. Feeling sick to his stomach, he turned his head to the edge of the bed and retched. Spasms of excruciating pain racked his body. Dry heaves. He couldn't remember when he had last eaten.

The face of a young woman appeared in his blurred vision.

"Clotilde?" he mumbled.

The field nurse smiled and felt his forehead. "*Non*. My name is Suzanne. But I wish I were your Clotilde," she said in perfect French but with a slight American accent. "You've been mumbling about her in your sleep. She's a lucky woman."

"Where am I?" he asked in a raspy voice.

"St-Dié. The Fifty-First Evacuation Hospital. We're housed in an old Cavalry barracks. Good thing, too, given the weather outside. The buildings are heated."

"Thirsty," he said, barely able to talk.

The nurse held a glass of water with a straw to his mouth, and he sipped. "Easy now. Not too much at first." She placed the glass on the table next to his helmet.

"You were fortunate," she said. "The bullet missed your heart." She checked his bandages and positioned the pillow under his head.

He tried to see the lower part of his body. His right leg was bandaged. What about his manhood?

She smiled. "You lost a lot of blood, but there was no fracture to the leg. The wound will heal in time."

Diamanté groped the table with his uninjured arm. He couldn't lose the Walther. It was all he had left to remind him of Ferdinand. "Where's my pistol?"

"Weapons aren't allowed in here," she said. "I'm sure you'll get it back when you're well enough to return to the front."

He winced in pain. "My helmet," he said. "There's something…"

The nurse handed it to him, and he carefully removed the letter he had addressed to Clotilde on Christmas Eve. "Can you post this for me? I've been carrying it around for a month now."

The nurse took it from him and studied the address. "Your Clotilde is in Corsica?" She smiled. "My grandmother lives there. Near Bastia. I spent summers with her when I was growing up. I've been able to get mail to her only occasionally since the war started, but she's written back so I know she received them." She placed the envelope into the pocket of her olive drab wool shirt and pulled the blanket over him. "You need to get some rest now. I'll see about some food. You must be hungry." She leaned over him and patted his cheek. "I'm sorry we can't give you anything for the pain. We're short on supplies, and only the worst off get something."

He nodded.

When she had gone, Diamanté settled his head back into the pillow and closed his eyes. Nothing would deter him now. Not even these injuries. He wasn't afraid to die. *Rhin et Danube.* That was the motto of the First French Army. They were at the Rhine. As soon as he was able, he would rejoin the front and go all the way to the Danube.

Then he would go home.

Chapter Seventy

8 May 1945

The ship's quartermaster handed Diamanté a message marked *URGENT* as he prepared to disembark in Bastia. It was from Olivier.

"Speloncato."

Despite the joy of being back in Corsica, the single word was alarming. Why had Olivier sent it with no explanation? Did it mean he should go directly to his mother's native village instead of home to Ajaccio as he had planned? There had been no news of Clotilde and the baby since he had left nine months ago. So many fears played out in his head. So many longings. In the end, the decision seemed obvious. Speloncato was not far from Bastia. Hopefully the trains were running again. He would still have to find a way to travel the last ten kilometers up the mountain. He spat as he limped along the quay. It was obvious he wasn't going to be able to walk it. Damned leg. He disliked having to use a cane.

***

The mountaintop village was bathed in yellow sunshine as the horse-drawn wagon slowly climbed the steep ascent. Low stone walls covered with creeping thyme lined the sides of the road, and the scent of the maquis was strong. A steady clanging of church bells resonated from across the massif.

When they pulled into the village square, Diamanté descended from the wagon and thanked the farmer who had kindly offered him a ride from the train station. The man saluted him. "*Non, monsieur*, it is I who thank you. You and all your comrades. *Vive la France!*"

The horse made a blowing sound and pawed its hoof as if it were anxious to get going. Then the wagon lurched and moved forward.

Diamanté removed his beret and waved. As he listened to the fading clip-clop of the horse's hooves on the cobbles, he ran his fingers through his long hair and rubbed his bewhiskered chin. He had not told the old man he was returning from the war, but he had guessed it anyway. *I must look like hell*, he thought with the sudden realization that he had been so anxious to catch the first ship out of Marseilles he had not considered his appearance.

He replaced his beret and turned around.

Joyous laughter came from across the square where a crowd was gathered on the terrace of the local café listening to a small band playing "La Marseillaise." Couples sat under umbrellas at the outdoor tables kissing, cheering, and drinking Champagne. Next door, a single headline flashed from the newspapers in front of the kiosk: *VICTOIRE!* Germany had capitulated. The war was finished.

A group of children formed a circle around Diamanté, holding hands and dancing; a young woman about his age came forward to present him with a bouquet of flowers. The café's proprietor handed him a glass of Champagne and shook his hand.

It was good to be back in Corsica. He wondered where his mother could be. Surely she would be here in this crowd celebrating, too. He searched for her familiar face, but he didn't find it.

Her house, shaded by a single pine tree, stood on the edge of the village overlooking the vast valley below.

Diamanté put his hand on the door handle and hesitated, remembering the last time he had entered this house. He had had to tell his mother that he had brought Ferdinand's body home for burial. He pushed open the heavy front door and entered. Inside it was cool and serene. He set his beret and the bouquet of flowers on the table in the foyer and propped his cane against the wall.

When he entered the front room, he saw two women sitting next to each other on a sofa. Their backs were to him, and they were talking in hushed voices.

Neither was his mother. He cleared his throat as he approached. They turned around in unison, and he recognized both of them instantly.

"Clotilde? Elise?"

His wife put her hands to her mouth, then she rose and ran to him. "*Chéri!*" She flung her arms around him and kissed him.

He pulled her to him and buried his chin in her neck.

They clung to each other while minutes passed.

The only sound in the room was the regular tick... tock...tick...tock of the old pendulum clock in the corner.

Elise had risen from her seat and was watching them. "*Bonjour, Lobo*," she said finally. Her eyes were red from crying.

He pulled away from Clotilde and went over to embrace her. "What are you doing here, Elise?" he asked. "How did you manage to get here?"

"When Ferdinand didn't return to Paris after the liberation of Corsica, I feared the worst. I heard nothing for months. It was torture not knowing. *Oh là*. Paris was like hell to me. I was scared all the time and hungry. I couldn't stand it any longer." Tears flooded her eyes. "*Enfin*, I left in the middle of the night. It was difficult traveling, but I eventually made it to the coast, and a fisherman took me from Marseilles to Calvi. From there, I found my way to Speloncato where I discovered my husband..." she wiped her cheeks with the heel of her hand, "in the cemetery."

Diamanté put his hands on her bony shoulders and looked into her eyes. "Ferdinand was very brave," he said, his voice cracking.

"You were with him then? At the end, I mean? Tesa said you were."

He nodded. "Ferdinand was a hero; he saved all our lives."

Speaking of his mother, where was she?

He went over and peeked through the archway into the kitchen. "Is my mother here? And the children? I didn't see them in the village square celebrating."

Elise fixed her eyes on him. "We didn't know the whereabouts of the children's parents," she said, "so they were sent to an orphanage after—" She paused and glanced nervously in Clotilde's direction.

Diamanté turned to his wife and saw the look on her face. "Has...has something happened to my mother? Is she all right?" He'd had a foreboding feeling ever since he arrived in Bastia that something was wrong.

Clotilde went to him and took his hands in hers. "She's gone, *chéri*."

"Gone where?"

"She died, Diamanté. Your mother passed away three weeks ago."

He stood staring at her, his pulse racing, trying to comprehend what she had just said. "Three weeks ago?" It would have been while he was still at the front. "But how? Why?" he asked finally. "She wasn't that old."

"Your mother was very ill when I arrived here," Elise said. "*Oh là*. I thought she was going to get better, but her health deteriorated quickly." She sighed. "The village doctor said she had a cancer of the stomach. She couldn't keep any food down. She basically starved to death."

"When I wrote to her after you left Ajaccio," Clotilde added, "Elise had just arrived. We corresponded regularly, but I couldn't travel easily with the baby, so I waited." She looked at Elise. "Too long, as it turned out. I never met Tesa."

"She was very happy about having a grandson," Elise said to her. "She understood. She didn't want you to risk bringing him here."

Diamanté glanced from one woman to the other. It was obvious they had formed a bond.

A soft whimper came from the next room.

Clotilde smiled and let go of his hands. "Your son has awakened," she said. "I'll go get him."

Diamanté felt a catch in his throat. He swallowed. "He won't know me, will he?"

"Give him time, *chéri*." She left the room.

Diamanté and Elise stood awkwardly facing one another. Finally, Elise said, "You seem much older, *Lobo*. I didn't recognize you at first."

He stared at her. She was so thin that her blouse hung loosely from her shoulders, and dark circles rimmed her bright blue eyes. She, too, seemed much older. He had once thought she would be his wife one day, but she had chosen Ferdinand. He cleared his throat. "You are as beautiful as always, Elise."

She smiled and nervously smoothed the front of her skirt with her hands, then looked up at him. "I…we, Ferdinand and I, thought you were dead. Your wife told me you were in a concentration camp and how ill you were when she first saw you in the hospital in Toulouse."

"Clotilde saved my life," he said. "She helped me escape."

Elise nodded. "She is a wonderful person. I'm happy for you, *Lobo*."

"What will you do now?"

She shrugged. "*Bof*. I'll probably stay here a little while longer." She crossed her arms and stared out the window. "I like it here. Someday, maybe I'll return to Paris. I hope my apartment building will still be there."

Clotilde returned carrying a sleepy little boy with fair hair and chubby cheeks. He was rubbing his eyes. She kissed the little one's cheek and said, "Your papa has arrived, *petit*, just in time to celebrate your birthday."

Diamanté thought he was the most handsome child he had ever seen. Overjoyed, he took a step forward and reached out to touch him.

Diamanté *fils* took one look at his father and burst out crying.

"*Excusez-moi*," Elise said, and she hurried into the kitchen, brushing more tears from her cheeks.

"*Chut chut, mon petit*." Clotilde comforted the little one and rocked him gently. Finally, the boy settled down, put his thumb in his mouth, and nestled his head shyly against her neck. She smiled at Diamanté and winked. "It's the beard. You need a shave, *chéri*."

He felt his chin and chuckled. "I seem to recall you are very good at shaving."

She laughed. "Indeed I am," she said, adding in her most seductive voice, "I think you will need a bath, too."

He stared into her eyes. Overcome with longing, he approached again and cautiously put his arms around them.

The boy clung to his mother but remained quiet.

Clotilde nestled her head between the two, a cheek next to each of theirs, and wept.

"Why are you crying?" Diamanté whispered.

"I'm just so very happy you are home," she said. "When I learned that you were wounded…"

He drew back a little. "How did you know that?"

"Your letter came. Along with a note from your nurse explaining where you were. She tried to reassure me, as we nurses do, but I..." She looked into his eyes. "I feared the worst."

Diamanté *fils* squirmed. She lowered him to the floor and held his chubby little fists with her fingers. The barefooted one-year-old took a tentative, wobbly step on tiptoe, then another.

"It was just before Easter," she continued, "the last week of March actually, when Olivier found out you had been released from the hospital. By that time, he had moved the transmission set into the kitchen so he could keep up to date on everything that was happening at the front while he prepared for the big holiday meal."

Diamanté rubbed his neck. "I'm sorry I missed it. I can't wait to return to the restaurant." *And get back to my life,* he thought.

She smiled. "I swear Olivier never slept, he was so excited about the war coming to an end and your being home again. When we left for Speloncato, he said he would try to get word to you where to find us."

That explains the message, Diamanté thought. *Somehow he must have discovered I had boarded the ship to Bastia.*

Clotilde's eyes widened. "You were in Germany, then?"

He nodded. The memories of the massive piles of rubble, the smell of smoke, and the stench of rotting bodies lying everywhere, the hollow eyes of those who had lived and survived the horror, all of it flooded over him at once, and he suddenly felt faint. He collapsed onto the sofa, put his face in his hands, and closed his eyes. "I just want to forget, *mon amour.*"

"You will, *mon cher*," she said. "We will help you, your son and I."

***

The next day, Diamanté and Elise went together to the cemetery. They passed through the iron gate that led to the ancient churchyard and wandered through the maze of raised tombs, many crowned with white crosses.

The Loupré family crypt was in an obscure corner of the graveyard under the shade of a giant chestnut tree. Diamanté knelt and ran his fingers over the names etched into the stone: his father, Jean-Pierre; his mother, Tesa; and brother, Ferdinand.

Elise placed a bouquet of flowers at the base. Then she touched Ferdinand's name and closed her eyes. Finally, she blessed herself. Tears ran down her cheeks as she fumbled in her pocket, and her hands shook as she pulled out a piece of folded paper and handed it to him. "Tesa left this for you," she said. "She had so wanted to see you again before she died, but she knew her time was short."

He took it from her.

She bent over and planted a quick kiss on his smooth, newly shaven cheek. Then she hurried through the side door into the church, leaving him alone.

Diamanté stared at the paper. He lifted it to his nose and sniffed. It smelled of his mother's lavender perfume.

His father's death had forever changed his mother's life. He was glad now that he had saved her from further abuse by his stepfather. Maybe the last few years had been easier for her, in spite of the war and her illness. He placed his forehead against the cool stone, remembering her reaction when she learned that her eldest son Ferdinand was dead. She had clutched her stomach, vomited. Had the cancer already invaded her body then?

He hadn't told her that he had suspected André of killing Ferdinand. He wouldn't ever know for certain.

André. He spat. *Salaud moche. L'enculé.* The question of his whereabouts still remained. The more he thought about it, the more convinced he had become that his half brother had collaborated with the enemy. He had personal evidence: the setup at Guy's farm, for example, and his subsequent imprisonment. And what about that strange message André had sent on Easter Sunday a year ago before he had departed from Ajaccio on the *Casabianca*?

The war with Germany was over, but the other war, the vendetta with the Narbons, was not. Diamanté knew that if André were still alive, if he had survived the war, he would come for him eventually. Corsican vendettas could take decades to carry out. He would forever have to remain on alert.

He glanced over his shoulder then unfolded the paper and began to read.

EPILOGUE

Diamanté took his family back to Ajaccio where he resumed management of his beloved restaurant, The Blue Anchor. Clotilde and he had no more children, and they both doted on their handsome son, Diamanté *fils,* as he grew up in their apartment above the restaurant.

In 1946, Diamanté was recruited by Interpol Paris. One of his first assignments as an intelligence agent was to spy on his half brother, André Narbon. In the months after the war, there had been many assassinations in Europe—collaborators and political figures who had carried out Nazi orders. In Corsica, an upsurge in vendetta-style feuds took place. André, thought to be a suspected terrorist and assassin, continued to elude Interpol for years.

As the Cold War conflict intensified, Diamanté became more active in top-secret covert operations for French intelligence in Europe while at the same time running the restaurant in Ajaccio with the help of Olivier.

Neither Diamanté nor André returned to northern Corsica. Thus, for the time being, the vendetta between the Narbons and the Louprés remained quiet.

ACKNOWLEDGMENTS

Special thanks to Peter Berkos, Lillian Balinfante Herzberg, Mark Carlson, and Terry Ambrose of the Rancho Bernardo Writers Group in San Diego, California. Your tough critique, diplomatic suggestions, sound advice, and steadfast support made this story better. A special thank you also to Jewell Hill and Kathy Weyer, who so graciously read the manuscript and provided extensive comments. Finally, *merci beaucoup* to my brother, Chuck, for his help with the World War II research, to my daughter, Kirsten, for her artistic eye, and to my husband, Denny, whose love and encouragement I truly value.

ABOUT THE AUTHOR

Mj Roë is a self-proclaimed lifelong Francophile, who lives in Southern California. She has worked in France as a business and marketing executive and previously taught French and creative writing.

Roë's first two novels—*The Seven Turns of the Snail's Shell* and *The Blue Amulet*—won awards at the Paris Book Festival and the Los Angeles Book Festival.

Printed in Great Britain
by Amazon